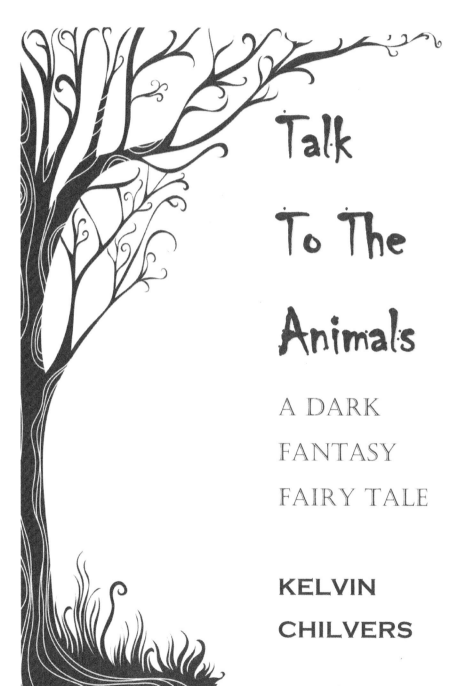

Talk To The Animals

A DARK FANTASY FAIRY TALE

KELVIN CHILVERS

TALK TO THE ANIMALS

Publication of this book is by: AMAZON KDP

Available in soft cover and eBook.

ISBN: 9798379050078

TALK TO THE ANIMALS

I wish to thank family, friends, and all beautiful souls who are following my author's journey. Your support is inspirational and a source of encouragement.

I reserve a special thanks to Katie Kavanagh whose selfless, spiritual nature was inspirational in having me focus and for my dreams to become reality.

As with my collection of crystals, their energy as a source of comfort and creativity, as with my alignment to the universe, guardian angel and spirit guide, I continue this beautiful journey I have forged with unwavering passion.

LOVE AND LIGHT!

TALK TO THE ANIMALS

Previous publications by author: KELVIN CHILVERS

HOLDING ON TO HOPE

ANGEL WARS TRILOGY:

DREAMING ANGELS: Volume One

FIRST ANGEL THE PREQUEL: Volume Two

LEGACY OF ANGELS: Volume Three

CHAPTER 1

Imelda was aware she was making keening sounds as she kept running and pumping her legs so hard, they threatened to meet with her stomach.

Not that she could recall who or from what she was fleeing. With terror stalking her, an intangible entity crawled around her thoughts, throwing each one in disarray.

Fear of the unknown gambolled on her heels, motivating her to quicken her pace, so that she felt her lungs would burst. Even as her heart beat a deafening crescendo, that which reverberated in her ears, her stomach began to cramp, her legs growing leaden.

She slowed, and near exhaustion served to exacerbate her fears.

Of the unknown horror she believed, was stalking her.

She was attuned to a Summer sun's oppressive warmth on her face, her bare arms and legs, as soiled trainers continued to plough a path across a field of ripening corn.

Ahead lay a vast woodland, and Imelda saw it as her salvation.

TALK TO THE ANIMALS

She could hide amongst the trees and vegetation; and wait.

For how long? She had no idea.

She was running from something bad; despicably so, not that she could comprehend the reasons as they had deserted her.

Why else would she be fleeing; afraid and with tears burning runnels down her cheeks?

And she was sad, terribly so; like she was leaving behind something she had grown to love.

Why would she flee from something she loved?

And her mind quipped; *you're not running from love. You are fleeing something quite loathsome. Something dark. That, which threatens your fragile mind.*

Imelda felt elation as she met with the fringes of the beckoning woodland, and instantly wondered if she had made the right choice.

There was no man-worn path to navigate, and the statuesque trees and dense shrub became her enemy, as they sought to hinder progress.

It's okay; she berated herself. As the more cover she had, there was less chance she would be seen or found.

Despite making sporadic keening, wretched sounds borne of panic and terror she had become accustomed to, like it was a language she'd devised for herself to express an emotional state of mind, she was certain it had not always been this way.

She recalled all those times she'd laughed and frolicked, gave of her love and had it reciprocated. That love had been misplaced by an unspeakable entity. She felt its oppressive and tangible closeness, almost as if she was carrying the burden on her shoulders.

Imelda sensed her panic ballooning, as she felt her long trailing red hair being snagged by inquisitive twigs and bramble spines. It reminded her of having her hair pulled when she was a child.

And there had been recent occasions when she'd experienced her hair pulled.

It gave the nasty person doing the tugging, control over her. And there were times, she recalled, when she fought back to salvage some pride from a fearful situation, and as a result, suffered humiliation and pain.

There were often-times, when Imelda had no self-esteem left to her, as it had been systematically dismantled; a process deigned to leave her feeling hollow and worthless. Insignificant.

A shadow of her former self.

Imelda imagined her eyes had grown improbably wide, as the trees and vegetation sought to repel her advance and secure salvation for herself.

And it was getting darker; gloomier, the further she travelled and clawed a way through into the thicket.

This alien world she'd entered was her only option as she saw it. It appeared hostile, on the surface; or was it, she had become used to viewing all within her miserable world with distrust?

CHAPTER 2

The thick and stifling press of trees began to thin-out, and dense swaths of the sun's rays cut vertical paths to the mulch.

Imelda was forced to close her eyes against the glare, to slow her flight and steady her breathing.

She was tired and needed to rest, to restore the energy she'd spent fleeing whatever she believed was chasing her.

A small glade beckoned, where an area of lush grass gleamed as emeralds in the bright Summery haze. She chose a slight depression at the base of a gnarly oak tree, where exposed roots hugged her slight frame and kept her cosily protected for a time.

Imelda took a moment to appraise herself; at first, scooping back her thick red tresses to waterfall down her back. She was wearing a thin cotton summery dress, having an array of colourful daisies, and punctuated by a random sequence of printed sunflowers.

She was imagining, it was a favourite form of attire, especially on warm days such as this one. It hugged her thin frame like a second skin, was buttoned all the way to her cleavage, and having two thin straps clinging resolutely to her shoulders.

She let her head rest against the rough bark of the tree's formidable trunk and closed her eyes, feeling a lambent warmth seep down inside her dress and tease her flesh.

She came awake with a sudden start, confusion having her look around and wonder how she had come to be sitting in a woodland glade, of all places.

Was she lost? Had she been allowed to leave her home unescorted?

The questions came thick and fast.

She remembered then; she had been fleeing an unspeakable terror. Not that she could remember, and it had her wondering why her mind was suppressing the reasons from her.

The questions kept tumbling around her fragile mind, without cohesion, and she became frustrated and anguished.

Imelda froze as a fox appeared, silently and stealthily, pushing its pointed black snout from around the succulent leaves of a nearby hardy shrub. It sniffed the air and was perhaps perceiving Imelda's scent.

Instead of ducking away, as Imelda would have expected, the vixen quite brazenly stepped into the open, gave a little shake of its body, and stared at the human stranger in her midst. The fox became transfixed, and like Imelda, was not sure whether to stay or run.

'Hi!' said Imelda. 'You're a beautiful fox. I hope you are friendly. I'm not a threat. Just someone who needed to rest-up.'

TALK TO THE ANIMALS

'Don't see many of your kind around these parts,' the vixen answered, and Imelda was momentarily speechless.

'Why,' she finally responded, while trying not to make any sudden movements, 'You're a fox who can talk.'

'Naturally,' said the vixen, and casually sniffing the air again. *'As you are the reason I can talk.'*

'But this is wonderful, and so unexpected!' Imelda exclaimed, her excitement lifting her spirits out of the doldrums. 'I hope that we can be friends.'

'You look like you need a friend,' the fox intimated. *'Sorry, I can't stay long, as I have little ones to feed.'*

And with that, the fox turned and went back the way she had come.

Imelda puffed out her cheeks and pondered the confrontation she'd had. *With a fox!* Her mind clamoured. It could have been so quite different; she surmised, knowing the fox could have attacked her in the belief she was a threat.

Imelda chuckled, and no longer feeling fearful; of the woodland, its creatures, or the nightmare she believed was chasing her.

CHAPTER 3

Imelda was unable to contain her excitement, as she turned and looked up at the tree.

'I had a conversation with a fox,' she beamed up into the canopy of branches and leaves overhead. 'How bizarre is that?'

'It appears so,' growled the tree, almost as if being disturbed from slumber after hundreds of years displeased it.

'Oh my; a tree who can talk.'

'Naturally, I can talk, as it is your wish.'

'My wish?' she asked the tree, and scuttling into a confrontational position, so that she was better able to appraise the speaking giant, in much the same way the fox had approached her. 'I do not understand,' she added. 'Is there some form of magic within the woods? For a fox to converse, and now a tree. It's not natural; you know.'

'Define, what is natural and what is not?'

'Oh, I don't know,' she pouted, and stretched, and felt all her joints cracking. She lay back and became fully kissed by the gloomy shroud descending on the glade.

11

TALK TO THE ANIMALS

'Have you always been able to talk?' she asked sleepily.

'Only in recent times,' the tree replied, and a light breeze coursed along its sturdy branches and ruffled its leaves.

'You're singing,' said Imelda, aware she was smiling and couldn't stop herself. Neither could she recall a moment as joyous, as her past was an indistinct memory.

'I suppose I am,' the tree remarked, and rustled its leaves a little more vigorously.

'Beautiful,' Imelda mumbled, and closed her eyes again. 'You have a lovely voice, Mister Tree.'

'It is, what you make it and wish for. Creating something beautiful, is simply a reflection, of that which is beautiful inside you.'

'Will you watch over me, while I sleep?' she asked, already dozing.

The tree did not respond on this occasion.

When Imelda eventually clawed her way out of repose and disturbing nightmares, it was to find the glade cloaked in darkness. A shimmering mantle of stars reflected a pinkish hue from around an almost full moon.

Imelda was again fearful, to feel alone in an alien world, cloaked in an irrepressible darkness, and knowing she had been having terrible dreams. Not that she was able to recall even a snippet.

TALK TO THE ANIMALS

In her thin dress which didn't even reach her knees, she shook with cold and fear.

She was not alone; she chided herself. She had Mister Tree watching over her.

She crawled further into the deep depression at the base of her guardian friend and snuggled up to its protruding roots. They seemed to touch and hug places, only a lover would know to give comfort.

A gentle lover: she mused.

Not a cruel, demanding master.

TALK TO THE ANIMALS

CHAPTER 4

Imelda came alert to scrabbling, rustling sounds nearby, and as her eyes became accustomed to all the dark, foreboding shadows around her, saw something which had her freeze and cling frantically to the sturdy tree root she was hugging.

A full-grown badger waddled into plain sight, seemed to pause, and sniff the air. It seemed to notice the unnatural intruder to the woods, itself freezing into a position with the intent to flee or approach.

Are you friendly, Mister Badger?' Imelda asked, her voice soft so as not to startle the animal, despite the words trembling off her tongue.

'I might ask the same question,' the badger replied. 'Don't see many of your kind in the woods.'

The bulky animal continued to draw her scent from the air and seemed content to stay and engage the human.

'Are you lost?' the badger enquired.

'I suppose, yes; I am lost,' Imelda pondered. 'I have no idea where I am to go, or for that matter, where I have come from.'

TALK TO THE ANIMALS

'Then, you are hopelessly lost, child,' and the badger went to amble away on a private quest of its own.

'Wait, please,' Imelda pleaded.

'What is it? What do you want? I am rather busy. Things to do; always, there is something for me to do.'

'I hoped, we could be friends,' said Imelda. 'These woods are strange, and quite magical. I have spoken already, with a fox and Mister Tree here. Now, I am in the presence of a badger who speaks to me.'

'I speak through you, my dear. You are the one creating magic. The woods? They are just trees and shrubs, with the usual inhabitants to be found in any woodland. There's a stream, an area of rocks where no vegetation grows, and there is a road. That is a dangerous place for us animals, a long dark stretch where mechanical beasts roaring up and down, having no consideration of the wildlife wishing to cross to get to the other side.'

'I do understand,' said Imelda thoughtfully. 'I wonder though, as you are another to say that you speak through me. I fail to understand what you mean by your remark.'

'My dear child, I am simply a product of your subconscious, and will answer any question you might pose, as you seek to understand the meaning of your life.'

'If, as you say, I speak through my subconscious; how would I know there is an area of rocks and a stream?' she enquired and smiled triumphantly.

'Is it not a possibility, you may have visited the woods at another time? Obviously, you don't remember, as there is so

16

much you have repressed from your mind. As to why you ran away, and from what or whom. And now you find yourself in the magical woods.'

'Okay, but how is it, you didn't mention the cave where there are rocks?' she tested the badger.

'Don't know about a cave in the rocks. Have no idea what a cave looks like. There you go; it's your memory, not mine.'

'Just saying. There probably isn't a cave, anyway. I just find, the idea of a cave, romantic; if you must know.'

'There probably is a cave. Now, child, I must be away from here. I must forage for food to take back to the little ones waiting patiently in the set. Let me just say; it has been an interesting interlude speaking with you. Now, tootle-pip, got things to do.'

And with that aside, the badger waddled away to continue its journey through the undergrowth, where its muffled movements soon faded.

Imelda sighed and smiled.

All will be okay; she told herself, not that her words sounded convincing in her head.

Tomorrow is another day; she added.

She fought to remain upbeat and would not allow her mind to dwell on negative issues, with regards to the next day, and the one after.

CHAPTER 5

A sharp, throaty sound startled her and had her craning her head to see higher. And it was there she espied the tawny owl gripping a branch with its bright talons, swivelling its rotund head, and letting loose another greeting; *t-wit, t-woo.*

'So, it appears, I am to greet a wise owl this night. Can you speak?'

'What would you have me say?' the owl called down, while maintaining a vigil partially hidden by a spray of leaves.

'Oh my, how wonderful,' said Imelda, and was surprised she no longer felt the cold. 'I suppose, you are able to see so much more from your elevated position high-up in the tree.'

'I am a species of bird, young lady. I have wings; I fly, and I can swoop on my prey from above.'

'All this talk of food, has me feeling quite peckish, And thirsty. Odd, to think, I can't remember my last meal or drink.'

'If you were to remember, it would explain why you fled into the woods, and have not returned to where it is you fled from.'

TALK TO THE ANIMALS

'I have no intention of returning home. No, no, that would be foolish. I have made mistakes; who hasn't? Not that it makes any difference. How can I return to a place I have no memory of?'

'Good point. A truly valid point. You might remember; in time.'

'Supposing, I don't want to?' Imelda posed and feeling the terrors returning to constrict her chest and cause breathing to be difficult.

'Then, welcome to your new home,' said the owl, and suddenly called out to have her cry answered by another of her kind. *'That will be my other half, keeping tabs on me. I swear, he doesn't trust me.'*

'I understand; about issues of trust and who you can give it freely to, and of those you cannot trust.'

'Of course, you do, as I am a wise owl and it grieves me to say, you have ventured along some very difficult paths in a short time, and it's obvious to one such as I; you have put your trust in the wrong people.'

'I suppose.'

Imelda felt saddened and hoped to instil the joy she'd felt for a time, by putting on a fake smile.

'Are you still there?' she asked, for those tears to have sprung to her eyes, blurred a view of the branch the owl was perched on.

'Have to go,' the owl blurted. *'I've just seen our next meal.'*

19

TALK TO THE ANIMALS

And with a crack of her wings, the owl swooped down and seemed to effortlessly glide around the shrubs at the edge of the glade, its talons snatching-up something from the grass, and then the owl was gone.

Imelda heard its triumphant call; just the once, and all around became eerily silent once again.

CHAPTER 6

Imelda awoke to another gloriously fine day, the unencumbered sun spilling its warmth over her, encouraging her to smile, despite having so much on her mind.

She felt it was important she remain positive. Mister Tree had told her as much when she said her farewells.

'Come visit again,' the tree called gruffly after her. *'I'm not going anywhere.'*

Imelda entered the thickest press of vegetation, not relying on bearings, as she had no idea where she was, or where her journey would take her.

She had no watch about her person, so time didn't seem to matter too much; especially, as she'd left one life and entered a new one.

She presumed she'd trudged around suffocating shrub and trees for upward of an hour, and more; not really knowing where she was headed.

Her stomach began to gripe with hunger pangs, and her throat was parched. It was a feeling which made her feel giddy and weak, the light-headed sensation causing all that she was seeing to swim in and out of focus.

She came to a stream, where a memory surfaced and flickered, and was gone.

Somehow, she'd known it had existed. Had not fox, or badger, spoken of a stream?

Something else teased a path into her memories. Imelda knew the water in the stream was quite fresh and was fed by a greater source further ahead. And there was an area of rocks close by, that which nestled quaintly at the heart of the woods. She supposed there existed a cave, of sorts.

Knowing this had Imelda feeling a surge of elation, having found the swift-flowing gulley of water, as if a life-sustaining miracle had been served to her.

She knelt in the mulch at the edge of the stream and scooped handfuls of water to her parched lips.

TALK TO THE ANIMALS

It was the best feeling, ever, and as she sipped the cool refreshing water, Imelda believed the source had magical properties, as in an instant, the fog around her thoughts lifted and she felt energised.

Rising, she looked all around, and surmising it was safe to do so, unbuttoned her dress all the way and fed it off her ridiculously thin frame. One day without sustenance, was not a cause for her condition.

In a previous life, that which she'd endured before this one, she must have eaten sparingly, or not at all.

It was another memory lost to her.

Feeding her panties down her legs conservatively, she stepped naked into the narrow stream, and thrilled to the pummelling flow of crisp cold water around her ankles.

Giggling, Imelda proceeded to anoint her skin with the clear water she scooped up with her palms and let it runnel over her skin. She rubbed herself gently at first and then more vigorously, as if she needed to erase a particular memory which made her feel dirty and ashamed.

Her gaze flitted apprehensively side to side, believing the woods had eyes, and whosoever hid themselves in the undergrowth, was watching her.

When she was satisfied she'd finished her ablutions, she next washed her dress and panties, laying them out to dry where a patch of sun licked an area lichen around the base of a hardy shrub. She sat alongside her clothing and could only think about foraging for food. As the woodland animals did.

TALK TO THE ANIMALS

Not that she could ever stoop to eating insects and grubs.

She recalled another time, when someone had tutored her in distinguishing various species of fungi; of which was edible, and those to be avoided.

Vacating her position, Imelda went in search of a meal. She seemed to instinctively know where to look and what to look for.

Despite having had a feeling for a time the woodland environment had been watching her bathing in the stream, Imelda was surprisingly confident and relaxed she had the freedom to move around and be naked.

She returned to where her clothes were drying, grasping a cluster of succulent mushrooms. She recognised the varieties she'd plucked from the mulch as chanterelle, shitake, white beech mushroom and another referred to as chicken of the woods.

Her tutorial on determining edible fungi from the poisonous varieties had been thorough and it was odd she should have retained the knowledge yet couldn't remember why she had fled in a panic and ended-up in the woods.

She was trying to remember who had taught her as she again sat herself down and studied the earthy selection she'd picked.

Taking the time, she washed the mushrooms in the stream to remove all the silt from around the base and roots, and patiently peeled away the outer flesh from the caps and stalks.

TALK TO THE ANIMALS

She munched on one at a time, savouring her first gastronomic meal as if it was manna from heaven.

Once she had devoured the last and smiling beatifically, Imelda lay back again, with her feet draping the water of the gentle flowing stream.

Her gaze drifted to the sky and she had to shield her eyes from the glare with one hand. The other toyed with loose chippings of bark and leaves.

She was unable to settle as she would have liked, because she needed to do her toilet. The idea horrified her to begin with, until it dawned on her, there was no one standing over her to watch.

Imelda wanted to know where the notion of someone looming over her while she did her toilet had surfaced from.

Was it a belief; this had been a humiliating experience she was forced to endure in her previous life, the one her mind had favourably blocked?

It was another thought to horrify her.

When she returned, she washed herself clean, and was further appalled the act of abluting her private parts should open doors on her memories. The door to her mind was open a fraction; certainly not to the extent where she was plunged into a nightmare.

She lay down again and sought to steady her breathing and even quieten the crescendo of each erratic heartbeat.

The weight of a hand draping a breast felt familiar and quickly dismissed the thought, as at no time could she recall ever being touched with exquisite tenderness or caressed lovingly as she was mindlessly doing to herself. She supposed there might have been occasions of an intimacy which had made her smile.

The consequences of her actions had her weeping, and she once again felt miserable and desperately alone.

She wanted to sleep, and never to wake up.

It was a spurious thought, and quite shocking; but she wouldn't mind if she was to die.

CHAPTER 7

When she eventually had the wherewithal to continue her journey, she followed the stream, instinctively knowing where it would lead her.

She wished she had a plan.

An understanding of the situation she found herself in, would be an advantage.

She had neither.

Only fathomless time, and an opportunity to live beyond an experience she had fled from.

She didn't suppose a wicked witch lived within the woods, as with so many fairy tales she'd read as a child. Not that she was ready to concede she had plunged herself into a fantasy fairy tale of her own devising.

Wickedness existed in the real world, and she didn't doubt for a moment, the woodland she'd escaped into had its own dark secrets yet to be revealed.

Removing her trainers, she waded up the stream against a persistent flow. The water seemed to be chuckling. Its frivolous voice had Imelda chuckling.

TALK TO THE ANIMALS

Up ahead, where the trees and vegetation appeared to lean away in quite spectacular fashion, Imelda saw the first signs of the rocky mound she once again remembered from another time in her life.

Stepping out of the water, her gaze travelled over a wide, deep expanse of rock; an ancient monument which had stood the test of time.

From her position, she saw the cave set back from a shallow ledge, and it was to there she began to scale the precarious edifice.

Off to one side, the gentle and calming waterfall to feed the stream, gurgled happily against the rocks. It was not exceedingly high, as she recalled, and there lay a rockpool in a deep depression beyond a wide flattened edifice, fed by a natural inlet beneath its surface.

Imelda carefully thread a path along the rising and dipping ledge and approached the entrance to the cave, where the granite had sheared away in areas and boulders having collapsed together. Laser beams of sunlight stabbed the murky interior through numerous small gaps.

She instantly covered her mouth with a hand as a fearful stench met her arrival. Slipping on her trainers she crossed a short distance to the farthest point and saw the reason for the terrible smell. An animal had obviously used the cave as a toilet. There was also a few rotten carcases scattered around; the bones of a rabbit, a rat, and even a squirrel, she noticed.

'Well, this won't do!' she exclaimed aloud, and set about making the shelter homely.

TALK TO THE ANIMALS

It would take time, gathering displaced bark and leaves as cleaning and removal tools, but she did so with single-minded determination.

Eventually, she had all the disgusting, unsightly deposits removed, and used vegetation and water to scrub areas where the stench lingered.

It would suffice; she told herself.

Pleased with her efforts, Imelda realised she had a plan formulated in her mind. The hollow in the rocks was to be her home.

Before setting out to gather food to sustain her another night, Imelda scaled the rock until she arrived at the smallish rock pool, becoming completely enamoured by the bubbles erupting on the surface from where it was fed further down, and where it overflowed a shallow lip to create the small waterfall. The sound of tumbling water was musical and soporific to her ears.

She stripped out if her clothes and immersed herself in the pool, clinging to the flat ledge as she was unable to feel the bottom. Hoisting herself up she sat astride where the ledge formed a narrow promontory. She quickly became accustomed to the cold lapping her lower legs, in contrast to the fire on her skin.

She was happily giggling, and then it occurred to her; whatever creature used the shelter might return at some point, and it might not take kindly to her intrusion.

She would make a fire and keep it fed. Animals were wary of fire.

TALK TO THE ANIMALS

Imelda had another thought; in that she'd been tutored on how to prepare a campfire, even without the means to light one.

Something someone had said, *'having been a boy scout in his youth, he could start a fire with two pieces of wood, skin an animal, and other things besides'*

Not, that she could recall who had told her, or had shown her how to make a fire in the open without matches or a lighter.

Bathing in the rockpool felt sensually delicious as Imelda slipped from the sturdy promontory and sank deep beneath the surface. She saw the way her long red hair fanned around her shoulders and moved with hypnotic grace, like the colourful fins of a giant fish.

She kicked with her heels and dragged herself back onto the slab.

Beneath a waning sun, she realised she was gazing down on her nudity.

She sensed there were occasions when being naked repulsed her, as there were other times she loved the idea of being carefree and shedding her clothes. She saw it as a tease. Her body, she'd come to understand, gave her power.

She didn't think she was beautiful, or even pretty. Others, apparently, thought she was.

Not wishing to venture along that path, as she feared it would open a door to memories she was unwilling to confront, she quickly leapt to her feet and put on her dress over wet skin. The thin cotton stamped itself to her frame and seemed to constrict her breathing.

TALK TO THE ANIMALS

Food and fire! she chided herself. She would seek a means to harness water so that she could drink and gather enough mushrooms to create a meagre feast.

There had to be something else edible.

If only she could remember more of all she had been taught.

CHAPTER 8

Having successfully created a fire in a wide, shallow depression in a central area of the improvised shelter, using dry kindling, and grass, and by rolling a thin piece of wood vigorously between the palms of her hands, the wispy trails of smoke and the glittery tendrils of the first flames, had her chuckling triumphantly.

She used a thin, flat wedge of stone, having a few eroded holes in it as an improvised griddle.

The flames began to roar and the spiralling columns of smoke had her choking for a time.

She had a campfire; and it was a good and positive start.

Her meal that evening was of a medley of sauteed wild mushrooms and a variety of plant shoots, which cooked and sizzled in their natural juices.

Careful not to burn her fingers with her eagerness to eat, she used two thin twigs stripped of their flesh as chopsticks, and they sufficed.

The meal was splendid; she congratulated herself within her mind.

TALK TO THE ANIMALS

It was n ow dark outside and having removed the cooking grate, allowed the fire to breathe and gain momentum. She kept it fed with wood she'd collected and stored in a respectable pile. She didn't think it would last the night, but she hoped it might deter any inquisitive and dangerous animals, supposing dangerous animals existed in the woods.

She was not forgetting the one beast, who had used the shelter for a time. She hoped it had moved on.

The pungent smoke removed traces of the faeces she'd removed earlier, and the majority escaped via the fissures in the walls and ceiling. Some of the smoke rolled languorously along the uneven roof and dispersed at the entrance to the shelter.

Imelda was about to settle on the hard floor, making a mental note to fashion a bed of sorts come the following day.

If she somehow survived the night.

As next, she was confronted by a great beast, which almost blotted-out a view of the sky and the trees beyond.

Firelight flickered in the yellow feral eyes observing her.

The beast had paused, was as surprised to see the human, as Imelda was to confront the large dog.

The dog bared its teeth and snarled a warning, as it trusted nothing and no one, from having been neglected and beaten by its previous owner.

Imelda recognised the breed as a German Shepherd and didn't look particularly healthy. Its thick coat was matted and patchy, its body beneath the fur appearing scrawny.

TALK TO THE ANIMALS

Imelda identified herself within the creature she was facing.

The dog continue to growl a warning, its shaggy body trembling, legs quivering.

'Oh, shush, I mean you no harm,' Imelda said to the dog, as if it was not their first meeting, or recognised the threat as being quite weak. She was cautious, without necessarily being afraid, believing the fire between them was her talisman.

The beast growled another warning, and Imelda refused to react or show any fear, knowing it was necessary not to make any sudden movements.

'You look like you could do with a good meal,' she continued, as if it was completely natural. 'Cat got your tongue?'

The analogy had her tittering.

She reached across to add more wood and dry grass to the fire, a burst of flame showering sparks between her and the dog.

The animal leapt back, barked once, and growled some more.

'This is my home now,' Imelda responded defiantly. 'You're welcome to stay and join me, but only if you behave, and quit being so argumentative.'

'Don't want to share,' the dog grumbled, and with that aside, turned away and fled.

'Oh, well,' said Imelda quietly to herself. 'Can't say I didn't try.'

TALK TO THE ANIMALS

Even though she believed the dog was gone and meant to leave her alone, she kept the fire roaring. She was unable to relax, and sleep was out of the question, so that she was left only with her thoughts for entertainment.

One had her pondering; as she wondered if she'd travelled far, and whether the place she'd fled from was close or far away.

It was conceivable; someone might come searching for her.

What then; if she was found and taken back, to wherever it was she felt the need to escape from.?

Imelda didn't want to entertain noisome, negative thoughts ruining the experience of utter freedom she was feeling. On the contrary, she didn't want to be found, or have to return. She only wanted to be happy.

She leaned back against a flat area of the wall and closed her eyes. Imelda dwelt on events since she'd arrived at the woods.

She had talked to animals, an owl, and even a tree; and it seemed, they were all willing to have a conversation with her.

It had to be something quite magical; she was thinking.

She realised she was smiling, with the warmth of the fire caressing her bare legs and kissing her face, neck, and shoulders.

It was a nice feeling.

More importantly, she felt safe and secure, her confrontation with the large mangey beast, already forgotten.

CHAPTER 9

She supposed she might have dozed, and movement beyond the shelter had dragged her from her reverie and a pleasant dream. It thrilled her to be having a nice dream, and once again believing there was magic afoot in the woods she'd chosen as her home.

Her joints complained as she leaned forward to inspect the remnants of her fire. There remained a few glowing embers and placing some dry grass on them had flames quickly burst to life. She followed with a cluster of slender twigs and something more substantial to get the fire burning fiercely in no time at all.

A menacing silhouette filled the entrance and she instantly recognised the feral eyes, and then came a warning growl.

'Oh, dog, stop with all the spiteful growling and make your mind up.'

She supposed the animal had been hoping she might have vacated its former home and was probably deeply disappointed she'd chosen to stay and kept the nasty fire burning.

TALK TO THE ANIMALS

Imelda realised the dog had dragged something quite substantial and dropped it, even as it stood possessively over the furry heap.

Imelda was intrigued, however, and dared to rise and approach, receiving a warning snarl and then a snap of the dog's powerful jaws.

Inside, she was quaking, yet was determined not to show fear. She hesitated only to remove a short flaming branch from the embers and held it in front of her.

The dog went to grab-up the partial carcase of a small muntjac deer and failed, as it reluctantly retreated from the glowing torch the human waved side to side.

Imelda stared at the sad offering and was disgusted, even as she eagerly assessed its potential.

Another memory surfaced of a time she had been on a camping trip; she supposed and was gone in a flash. Because she wanted it gone.

The carcase was of the hind end of the deer and not the head, otherwise she might have cried. She suspected the dog had come across the small deer on the road nearby, and not killed the animal itself.

Screwing up her nose and pursing her lips together, she dragged the carcase nearer to the fire, ignoring the entrails and blood smearing the floor.

She placed the pierced flat plate across the fire to heat and using a sharp wedge of granite she'd found earlier, began reluctantly to hack, and slice away select portions of the flesh from the inside.

TALK TO THE ANIMALS

It was an unpleasant task which had her feeling nauseous. She persevered though, and when she was done, threw herself back against the wall and blew out her cheeks. Her fingers were caked in congealing blood and she had no choice but to use her dress to rid her skin and nails of the worst.

The slender fillets sizzled, and Imelda had to admit, it was an enticing aroma and had her drooling.

Even the dog seemed captivated and deigned to enter, while keeping a respectful distance.

'I will feed us both a wholesome meal this night, and together we will grow healthy, big and strong.'

She giggled, the moment she caught the dog grinning and salivating. He was panting with expectation, and no longer trying to intimidate the human.

Imelda felt she had won a small victory.

Not wishing the succulent strips of meat to overcook, she grabbed up the larger portion and tossed it to the eager dog before it burned her fingers. She blew on them anyway.

Another, smaller strip, she lifted off the grate with the wedge of granite, allowed it to cool, before summoning the courage to nibble on it.

The dog had greedily devoured his morsel and huffed and shimmied, to let her know he wanted more.

'It's good, yes? You want more?'

She launched a couple of thick chunks in the dog's direction and finished her own.

TALK TO THE ANIMALS

Imelda was amazed at how good the venison tasted, and without hesitating, scurried across to the smelly carcase and sliced away a few lean steaks.

A while later, both Imelda and her companion were sufficiently satiated.

The dog watched her warily from the side as she dragged the remains outside and hoofed it over the lip of the narrow ledge. She'd expected the dog to become overzealous and try to reclaim its prize before she had an opportunity to dispose of it. Instead, he was content to laze, with its muzzle resting on its front paws.

Imelda turned back, picked up a large section of bark which was concave in shape, and disappeared outside. A bright cheery moon lit her way to the pool. She washed the residue of blood off her hands and arms, scooped water into the makeshift vessel and carefully returned with it to the shelter.

She only spilled a small amount, and what she'd gathered, she placed near the dog's snout so that he had something to drink.

Imelda shuffled across to the far wall, removed her dress, and became lulled by the sound of lapping.

She smiled in the gloom and became tired quickly.

She felt certain the dog posed no threat while she slept and with the fire almost spent. She, however, kept with her the sharp wedge of rock, as a precaution.

She lay down on her side, knees drawn up, and became mesmerised by the individual sounds from the fire beneath the grate, and the occasional animal and bird cries from nocturnal woodland inhabitants.

Imelda supposed she was in for a restless night; considering the hard rough floor, she lay on. She'd already made up her mind to remedy this come the next day and try to fashion a cot from whatever she could find strewn around the woodland floor.

When next she opened her eyes, a softening gloom illuminated the set of eyes watching her. Fortunately for Imelda, the dog appeared content and of a better disposition, having had a substantial feast she'd prepared.

'We need to establish a couple of rules,' she spoke softly. 'There's to be no pooping or weeing in the shelter from now on. Other than that, I am pleased to have made your acquaintance. You're not so fierce, not really. You're actually, unbelievably cute.'

The dog huffed and grumbled.

'Thank you,' she heard the dog answer, *'For the food, and thinking I'm cute.'*

Imelda smiled and rubbed her arms vigorously where she had them crossed over her breasts for warmth and modesty. She thought about reviving the fire she'd created and found she could not get past her inertia.

It had been a good day; she quietly informed her mind. *The best!*

CHAPTER 10

When she came awake, it was to be greeted by daylight flooding into the shelter, where it burned her eyes and had her lightly protesting.

Her companion was gone, and she was thankful the dog had not crept up on her while she slept and savaged her.

With considerable effort, Imelda slipped on her dress yet left it unbuttoned. It was only natural, she supposed, she needed to do her toilet. It was a thought to spur a chuckle, as she'd come to realise dog had not fouled the shelter in the night.

Imelda staggered outside and paused to stare out over the huge expanse of woodland. All appeared quiet, except for nature's symphonic serenade. The birds were very chatty and liked to sing.

There were a few static cotton wool clouds, not that she sensed an arrival of inclement weather. Despite the stiffness in her joints, she found herself smiling unapologetically.

She went to an area of cover in the woods to do her toilet. Following which, she washed in the stream and swilled her mouth out with the refreshing chill water, which seemed to invigorate her immensely.

TALK TO THE ANIMALS

Not wishing to venture too far, Imelda set about creating a few home essentials.

She gathered-up groups of long twigs, and plucked the larger leaves she discovered in abundance, carrying them back to the shelter. It took several trips, not that Imelda saw it as a chore. She had a plan, and she found the freedom of the woods was therapeutic.

With a two separate piles of spindly wood and succulent leaves, Imelda removed her dress and naked, and began to intertwine the longer flexible twigs to create a sturdy frame and template for cohesion.

Next, she placed several large leaves and smaller ones as padding for the framework she'd manufactured. Following which, she lay more wood and leaves until the cot was some distance off the hard unyielding floor.

Imelda was pleased with the results of her strenuous and patient efforts, and there came the moment of truth, as she crawled onto the bed and lay back. It groaned and crackled as it assumed a durable mould to accept her lissom frame.

Stretching out, Imelda gave a gleeful cry.

It was perfect; and already she had solved one issue, and that was to not have to sleep on a hard floor.

She couldn't quite believe she'd made the bed herself.

After a short time, relaxing, Imelda once again returned to the stream and to wash and cool herself down.

More ideas pooled inside her head, and then she was collecting a variety of leaves, where she sat and patiently removed the central veins from each. Twisting and braiding a few strands together created a durable twine. Using a pointed sliver of rock she'd acquired, Imelda began to thread the twine through the hole she pierced in one leaf, and diligently continued with others she had gathered.

It was time-consuming, as she'd expected it to be, but she had time and in abundance.

By the middle of the afternoon, she used the partial blanket as a carrier for more leaves and returned to the shelter.

There was still no sign of dog, and noticed the deer carcase she'd dispensed with, had disappeared from the base of the rock promontory.

The next task she set herself, was to venture into the woods and collect mushrooms and roots, in preparation of her next meal. Returning with more than she had expected to find, Imelda set about starting a fire.

Once it was done and burning fiercely, she took herself off to the rockpool, wanting only to bathe and wash her hair, before settling for the encroaching evening.

A few of the more succulent leaves produced a creamy unguent when squeezed and hoped it would serve as a shampoo and conditioner for her hair.

Where she had acquired knowledge of self-sufficiency and sustainability, remained an enigma. That knowledge was to serve her adequately, in the present time.

The salve applied to her hair seemed to work, and after she slipped onto the shallow flat ledge and relaxed, letting the waning sun bask her skin in a subtle warmth.

CHAPTER 11

Having eaten another satisfying combo of sauteed fungi and roots and feeling refreshed from her time at the pool; by the light of a vibrant fire, Imelda sat cross-legged on her crib and wiled away her time in the early evening hours continuing to weave her own blend of magic, on the blanket she was fashioning from the leaves she'd gathered.

She was tugged from her reverie at sound of panting and paws padding along the ledge to the shelter.

The returning dog stopped and froze at the entrance and dropped his prize of a pheasant.

'You're still here?' he grumbled.

'And for once, you're not snarling and growling, and baring your teeth.'

'Thought you might have left.'

'I have no intention of leaving. As it is, I am making this our home, if you choose to stay. As you can see, I have been busy.'

'I can tell.'

'What have you there?'

TALK TO THE ANIMALS

Imelda leaned around the gambolling, flickering tongues of flame for a closer look.

'I could prepare and cook that for you,' she said eagerly. 'I've eaten, but |I don't mind. It will take a while, as the big bird needs plucking and then cutting up. I found another piece of bark and thought it might serve as a bowl. There's water in it; supposing you're thirsty.'

'I'm hungry,' said the dog, *'and you're still here.'*

'As I said, I'm not going anywhere, so I suggest you get used to it.'

Imelda audaciously approached, the dog snatching up its prize and dropping it quickly when confronted by the loquacious human, whose dress flapped side to side when she moved, and with her flaming hair resembling the broken bird lying forlorn on the ledge.

He took a step back, and not once did he take his eyes off her, as she stooped to steal his meal. He neither growled, or barked; or bit, as he quickly came to realise the human did not pose a threat.

The dog, in his former life, had not known kindness, or laughter, or have someone speak to him in a musical lilt; and not in the harsh threatening tones he was accustomed to.

The dog seemed to have become mesmerised and caught within a spell he could not break from. Or indeed, it was more to do with the fact, he was not inclined to break free from the spell cast on him.

TALK TO THE ANIMALS

He watched from afar, as the human plucked away feathers from the fat body of the pheasant and lay them in a tidy heap.

Imelda had already formulated a plan in her mind, to do something fanciful with the colourful feathers, having it extend from creating a crib to lie on and an almost finished blanket.

She cut into the breast of the bird and was surprised; the blood and gamey scent did not have her running out and retching.

As with everything she did, she was single-mindedly attentive to the task she'd set herself.

She only hesitated when all began to swim in and out of focus. Following an eerie minute or so, her mind cleared and she continued preparing good-sized strips of meat to put on the hot plate.

With the meat sizzling and sweetening the air, Imelda apologised, as she needed to wash her blood-smeared hands with the water she'd collected.

She noticed, the dog seemed content and was laying down, observing her every movement. Every so often, he inched further inside the shelter, settling during these spells; but the appetising aroma of cooking meat was becoming too much of an enticement.

Imelda squatted on the edge of her cot and turned the meat with two slender twigs she'd stripped of their flesh and could use them as chopsticks.

She saw that dog had approached and was lying just the other side of the fire, no longer afraid.

TALK TO THE ANIMALS

Imelda used the sticks to flick a few morsels of cooked pheasant to her pitifully thankful companion.

'Bloody lovely, and the best grub I've had in a long time,' the dog admitted, and was even more thankful when Imelda kept tossing meat his way.

Imelda savoured just the one piece, and dutifully acknowledged, just how juicy and tasty it was.

The fact she had already eaten meant she had no wish to over-indulge. To her way of thinking, the dog deserved the greater spoils. He was the one found it and brought the bird back to the shelter, probably as he'd found it on the side of the road. As with the muntjac deer carcase.

If she fed him a few hearty meals, the dog would benefit from getting some extra meat on his bones, and for his patchy fur to grow evenly.

When all the bird had been devoured by the dog, mostly, Imelda pushed away the hot plate and fed more wood to the fire.

She lay back; not necessarily feeling unwell, only, in that the walls and ceiling began to spin. When she closed her eyes, vibrant colours exploded behind her lids, like the rapid unfurling of Spring blossoms.

She laughed, for no reason. Except, to her way of thinking; her meaningless life had become meaningful.

She squirmed around the cot to gain satisfaction from her industrious craft. It was surprisingly comfortable; she was thinking. Not hard, cold, and rough, as with the floor to the shelter.

TALK TO THE ANIMALS

Her flesh began to burn and she fanned herself exuberantly by flapping her dress. Not only did she feel afire, as her heart was beating a deafening crescendo, and seemed to move up from her chest to her ears.

She laughed some more and delighted in the gyrating whorls of colour behind her kids, and the way her skin tingled deliciously.

The feeling was almost reminiscent of something she'd experienced at another time; and as quickly dismissed the thought as irrelevant, as she had no wish to be reminded of a past existence.

This was the now! Her mind cried fervently. *I mean to live the now, and not the past!*

As she spiralled along a tunnel into sleep, she entertained a thought: *bad mushroom!*

Her sudden peal of laughter tapered away to a deep sigh, and then a light raspy snore, with a hand settled on a breast, the other down between her thighs.

CHAPTER 12

Imelda crawled back along the tunnel towards consciousness, and believed she was in the grip of panic.

Someone was touching her!

The thought was given substance as a tongue flicked and sucked her fingers.

She gasped aloud and hurried out the tunnel within her mind when she felt the rough tongue briskly slap her belly.

She sat up sharply and was staring into the forgiving eyes, of not a monster molesting her, but those of her companion who had stretched out on the ground beside her and was perhaps trying to say thank you. There was also scent of bird on her fingers, she surmised.

'Sorry, dog,' she blustered. 'I thought; no, silly me.'

She slowly raised a hand to scrabble the thick ruff of fur at the back of his neck, and as he seemed to like it, persevered by scratching behind his ears.

He gave a pitiful and servile whine of acknowledgement, which had her smiling joyously.

TALK TO THE ANIMALS

Imelda risked losing her pert nose, as she dropped a kiss to his narrow forehead and another along his snout. The dog kissed her in return, by slapping a long warm wet tongue along her arms.

Imelda lay back, as she was still feeling disoriented from having eaten some rogue mushrooms.

She slept some more, helped in some ways, to feel a great warm weight press around her flank. Her mind briefly wondered if it was the arm of a drunkard falling across her stomach and held a breath for interminable seconds.

It was only dog, and his presence comforted her, so that she was able to fully relax, and sleep.

She was startled awake the moment she felt her flesh being clawed, believing a dark angel had descended and meant to impale her with one of its talons.

Where colour frolicked in her mind, a sinuous silhouette metamorphosed, having no substance or definition she could relate to, yet appeared monstrous, dark, and insidious.

She came fully awake, only to find it was dog against her, and with a huge sigh of relief, hugged him fiercely and lay back, lazily stroking his hind quarters. He responded with another of his little trademark whines of capitulation and slapping his tongue against her chest.

In a world, where miracles were not commonplace, she had acquired a friend; her mind acknowledged. He was neither a faceless monster nor a demon. He was 'dog,' and she had won his heart, as he had won hers.

TALK TO THE ANIMALS

Reeling from the hallucinogenic effects having eaten suspect mushrooms, Imelda allowed her mind to wander in the realms of a fantasy world, of her own devising.

She could talk to animals, birds, and the trees; and they in turn, answered her call. It was magical; she would tell herself. Perhaps, she surmised; she was the one gifted with magical properties, so it made sense her wishes would come true.

The outside cruel attributes of a world she'd left behind, were almost a blur and dispensed with. Not that she fully understood, why she would think the world beyond the woods was a cruel place.

She gave some thought to the new life she'd acquired for herself and saw herself as a princess. It was a thought to make her smile. It only evaporated, when her mind believed as in any fairy tale, there had to exist a wicked witch, or its equivalent, who would want to see her suffer.

If that was true, then it was fair to assume, a handsome prince was on a quest to save her.

If only; her mind quipped, and her smile became even more generous in the gloom of the shelter.

Would she, however, recognise her knight in shining armour if he revealed himself to her? What if the wicked witch had sent someone who paraded a black heart behind the guise of goodness, to have her ensnared?

She had no reason to trust anyone; and it had her wondering why she would think such a thing.

She could trust dog, and there was the badger, the fox, the owl, and the tree she'd already met in the woodland.

TALK TO THE ANIMALS

It was important, she ascertained, to apply her trust sparingly. There were undoubtedly creatures, unlike those she had met, who might not be as friendly. They, too, might exist as wards of evil.

Yet, would she know in her heart, the difference?

Imelda drifted into sleep once again, and her dreams were joyous and at times; very weird, she would say.

CHAPTER 13

The morning of the next day beckoned, and it was to find dog had vacated her side and had done so without disturbing her.

Her head thumped an unpleasant dirge, and her focus was absent. She was lethargic in all her movements and when she went to rise off the crib, she could only stagger in small ungainly steps.

She slipped her dainty feet into her soiled trainers; *and oh, how she wished they were glass slippers.*

She gave a chuckle and thread a precarious path to the entrance.

It was overcast, yet the clouds were soft white pillows against sporadic patches of blue. The sun peeked at her, briefly, and ducked behind a scudding cloud as if to play a childhood game of hide and seek.

Her itinerary stretched as far as doing her toilet and taking a relaxing dip in the pool. She had no desire to venture too far from the shelter, as she was feeling far too delicate and suspect, so planned to while away time making some clothing from leaves and twine and finishing the coverlet for her cot.

Having completed her ablutions and feeling decidedly much better than she did to begin with, Imelda went about gathering suitable hardy perennial leaves and twine to create a fashion statement and accessories.

She carried everything she needed back to the shelter and used the cot for comfort. When her eyes began to strain and her fingers became sore, she took a catnap. She took several over late morning and early afternoon.

The moment eventually arrived for her to test her creative flair. Removing her dress, she fed a makeshift bikini top over her breasts and tied it away round back and looped another strong cord over her head to splay her neck and shoulders.

Another section, she'd fashioned as a small skirt, which she could lengthen at leisure, if she so desired.

She was thrilled with the results and went to the stream, so that she could see herself reflected in the water.

'Sexy,' was all she could say, with pride and delight. 'This girl has hidden talents; oh yes!'

She liked, how the overlapping rows of leaves caressed and hugged her skin, accentuating all her curves. The result was profoundly provocative, sensual, and it saddened her a little; in that there was no prince to see her dressed so wantonly. Another thought flitted in a part of her mind; in that there was also no nasty person to see her dressed sexily and would try to take advantage of the situation.

Imelda supposed, given the late hour, she should be considering her next meal; even as the idea of mushrooms and roots repulsed her. Not that she was afraid of being poisoned. It was the hallucinogenic effects which troubled her, as it left her feeling like she'd lost control. At the same time, leaving her feeling quite vulnerable.

TALK TO THE ANIMALS

And it was not a feeling to savour.

In the night, she had dog for protection, and it concerned her dog would not return.

She hoped he might, and accept the shelter as their home, and not just his.

It was early evening, with a cheery fire snapping at the air, when the first rumblings of thunder startled her. She had wondered if there was to be a storm, as the air was quite humid.

The smoke from the fire seemed to take longer to disperse, and it had her coughing and gagging often.

A little forlorn, she spent moments appraising her attire, and questioning her motives for making the undergarments skimpy. It shouldn't matter if she was wearing clothes or parading herself naked. There was no one around to spy on her, or forcing their will on her, to intimidate her and make her commit to things she didn't want to.

She became distinctly wary of the dark thoughts insinuating a path into her mind.

She came alert to a familiar panting and snuffling sounds. Dog appeared, and on this occasion, was awkwardly dragging a full-grown muntjac deer into the entrance, its teeth embedded in the neck to assist in managing such a difficult feat. He had to have dragged the deer all the way from the road, and even to scale the rocky outcrop and shimmy along the narrow ledge.

Imelda leapt up and greeted her companion with irrepressible joy, her enthusiasm momentarily startling dog. He forgot himself for a moment and snarled.

TALK TO THE ANIMALS

She shushed him, kissed his head, and helped drag the carcase into the shelter.

'I just knew I could rely on you to bring us food,' she said happily, while setting about preparing the venison into good-sized steaks for dog, and dainty palatable morsels for herself. 'We have enough food to keep us fed for two, maybe three days. Bless you, dog.'

He responded with another huff and observed the human taking up a tool to hack into the carcase he'd found.

'Just for the record,' Dog grumbled, *'I'm sharing the spoils because I like you. You're friendly, and pretty and you smell nice. Not forgetting; your kindness towards me.'*

'Thank you, Dog.'

Imelda straightened-up and wrinkled her nose against the unpleasant coppery odour where she'd slit open the abdomen.

'Hey!' she called to Dog, 'What do you think of my new get-up? All my own creation; I'll have you know.'

'Very nice,' Dog muttered as he lay down, waiting for the human to continue preparing a feast, as he was ravenous following his exertions getting the food to the shelter from the road. *'And sexy. I would just like to add; you look like a princess.'*

'Why, again, thank you. I have a confession to make; I am a princess.'

'You are? I thought as much. Does it mean; I am your prince?'

TALK TO THE ANIMALS

Imelda guffawed, and not wanting to hurt Dog's feelings, quickly gave a response. 'Oh, Dog, I wish. Perhaps, if I was to wish hard enough, my dreams may just come true.'

'I think you've been eating those naughty little mushrooms again, if you believe that.'

'As a matter of fact, I have done no such thing. I'm just being fanciful, and hopeful. And if I start acting a little weird, it's because my period is close. A time of the month I despise. And so that you know; before all the unpleasantness occurs, my body gets all these unnatural feelings. Those, I cannot always control.'

'What's a period?'

Imelda was instantly exasperated by the question playing around her mind. 'Oh, you're a boy; what would you know?'

'I'm actually a dog.'

'Yes, of course, I do know that.'

'But you wish I was a young man? A real prince?'

Imelda stayed quietly thoughtful as she single-mindedly cut and sawed and hacked into the suppurating flesh.

'Despite the fact, you're only a dog,' she said, 'I appreciate you thinking I'm sexy.'

'You're welcome.'

The meal later that evening surpassed even Imelda's expectations. Following which, she washed herself with water she'd collected earlier and settled down to give affectionate cuddles to the dog, who had become a wonderful companion and friend; she was thinking.

The thunder had abated before it had even amassed a head of steam, even as the rain battered the woodland and rocks and funnelled into the shelter through numerous gaps. It was a natural source of refreshment and saved her going out in difficult conditions to wash and to drink.

She used the bark vessels lined with leaves to collect the water, and dog was eternally grateful he was able to quench his thirst.

As the rain eased, the rhythmic plip-plopping and occasional steady trickle was melodic and soothing. It wasn't long, before Imelda drifted into sleep.

Dog remained alongside her; smelly and warm, and wonderfully comforting. He too, was quickly into slumber, and snoring loudly.

The princess of the woods was content, and safe. And she was not alone to face the rigours of a cruel world.

CHAPTER 14

On the morning of the next day, with a fierce sun blazing down on a vast canopy of saturated vegetation, Imelda made up her mind to galvanise herself and investigate a wider expanse of the woods.

A dense and sensuous mist emanated off the carpet of mulch and shrub where the early morning heat stamped its authority on the wet ground.

Imelda was surprised and thankful, dog should have stayed throughout the night, and let him know she was pleased and enjoyed his company. As she spoke of her plans to explore their domain, she invited Dog to accompany her.

Dog was acting petulant and non-committal and said he would think about it; as he knew the woods already, since he spent his days exploring them anyway.

Wearing her latest two-piece raiment and affixing the leafy blanket around her as a cloak, Imelda was ready for an adventure.

She was to take with her the largest of the bark vessels she'd acquired, supposing there was something edible or of interest to collect on her journey.

TALK TO THE ANIMALS

Dog was still loitering and seemed interested in all she was doing, and obviously quite liked the occasional petting she gave him, so she supposed he meant to accompany her, whether he was to admit it or not.

As they vacated the shelter, with Dog hugging her heels as they navigated the narrow ledge, Imelda believed she'd had an epiphany.

'I think, Dog, this day is going to be one of magic and mystery. And should I meet with the Wicked Witch of the woods; I just know you will defend me.'

'And who might that be; this wicked witch you speak of?' she believed he'd answered. *'I've been around these parts for as long as I can remember, and don't get to see many folks. Not like you, anyway.'*

'That's because I'm different.'

They made it safely to the woodland floor.

'What makes you different, is that you're a princess.'

'I'm not a real princess, silly. It's only, that I wish to feel like one.'

She turned to Dog and crouched down, fearlessly rubbing his muzzle, and petting his nose.

'Now, Dog, there are rules in place. I mean to engage with animals and birds on our journey, and you are not to frighten them, okay? And heaven forbid, you should attack any of them.'

'Can't promise I won't, as I'm a dog, and it's only natural.'

TALK TO THE ANIMALS

'At least try to behave. We have enough venison for two days, so I'm asking you to restrain yourself from adding to the pile. If we are to make the woods are home, we must learn to have a good relationship with all the wonderful creatures who live here. So please, try to be nice and on your best behaviour.'

'Can't make any promises. As I said, I'm a dog. Hunting is an instinct, and I've had to survive using my instincts and cunning for as long as I can remember.'

'Dogs don't have short-term memories; do they? What did you do yesterday?'

'Don't remember.'

'I was right.'

'I know enough to follow my scent, and return to the shelter, with food for the two of us.'

'Yes, you did that, my handsome young man.'

'And I get to snuggle up to you; my friend.'

'And yes; I like that we have become friends, and you like to cuddle up to me. I don't have as many bad dreams when you're around to watch over and protect me.'

'I can do that.'

She kissed his narrow snout and chuckled when he sneezed in response.

Their journey began; neither taken in earnest, or at a snail's pace.

TALK TO THE ANIMALS

Imelda would be governed by the positioning of the sun in the sky, on when to return. Something else she'd learned at another time.

She didn't suppose they would become lost, not with Dog's instincts and keen sense of smell to guide them. He was her own personal compass, and the thought had her tittering.

It was not only about Dog and his attributes, as Imelda had her own magical powers with which she'd been blessed.

Or so she believed.

They followed the stream for a time and Dog happily trudged through the swift current to cool his paws.

Imelda let him know she intended leaving the trail they were following, as she felt compelled to explore other areas, where the vegetation became suffocating and the trees seemed to hug one another with obvious intimacy.

It was almost as if she knew where they were headed, as if the faded memory was again resurfacing, for whatever purpose it chose for her. As Imelda was of the belief, there existed unnatural forces to guide her on her quest.

After only a short travail they came across a smallish glade and a narrow river, where the banks were shallow and not steep.

Dog frolicked and gambolled in the open space as Imelda became momentarily locked in position on the periphery.

The sunny vista looked like an area which might, on occasion, be frequented by families on a picnic, of courting couples wishing privacy away from prying eyes, or anglers who liked to while away their time away from the natural stresses of the real world.

The area stirred memories within her, as it was a place she'd come to recognise, having visited the glade at a time lost to her.

It made sense; she told herself, she might have visited on a camping trip at some time, where she would have been taught the basic principles of making fire, and how to sustain oneself in the wilds.

She was unable to define whether her recollection was evoking happy memories, or not. It was the glade's remoteness and ultimate privacy she found disconcerting. It was somewhere, so far removed from habitation, one could cry for help and not be heard.

Whatever memories threatened to creep to the surface, were thwarted by the impenetrable wall she'd erected around the thoughts in her mind.

No matter, she deduced, it was perceived as a beautiful and idyllic paradise. Not that it was a place which invited her to stay. It would have been nice to lay for a while at the water's edge and feel the sun dancing on her skin, yet she chose to leave, and called Dog to heel.

It took a while, but the unnerving despondency she had felt for a time, slowly dissipated.

CHAPTER 15

She was humming to herself as she thread a path through the wet cloying shrub, feeling like Little Red Riding Hood; she was thinking, except she was in a cloak of green and was camouflaged against the vegetation. And she didn't have a hood. And something which made her titter, was knowing the fabled young girl would not have been dressed in a skimpy top which barely covered her modesty, or the thong at her waist which was far too provocative for a fairy tale.

Why the thought would suddenly spring to mind, she couldn't be sure. Yet a police helicopter hovering overhead might not see a person but could be drawn to the flaming trails of her red hair. It would only occur, should the authorities be out looking for her.

Dog suddenly barged past her and she almost lost her footing. He was barking frantically and when Imelda approached the spot where her companion was bounding up and down and trembling, while snapping its jaws like a crazed beast, she saw the reason and became cautious and quite still.

Dog had picked up the scent of an adder, hidden in a shallow depression and where a large leaf had been used for cover, and it had now been disturbed from its slumber and was quite agitated,

TALK TO THE ANIMALS

'Oh my, but you're a frightful creature,' Imelda blurted, and realised her heart was beating faster and louder, as she clutched her chest to quell her trembling, 'And quite dangerous, I imagine. I don't mean to disturb you, Mister Adder, or to startle you. We were just heading, to no place special.'

'I suggest you move along to this 'no place special, in particular', ' the raspy snake answered, and it was a clear warning.

Imelda tried to shush Dog and bring him to heel, but he was having none of it.

'Move along! Move along! I don't wish to sink my fangs into you or the beast. But I will! I will!'

'We are leaving, and please, don't follow.'

Imelda ducked to the side and clawed a frantic passage away from the angry reptile. She called to Dog and heard him bounding after her.

Breathless, she eventually stopped in her flight, dropped to her knees, and threw her arms around Dog, showering his snout with kisses.

'Brave warrior, you saved me from that nasty snake.'

'Not all who reside in the woods are friendly,' he uttered, while enjoying the praise heaped on him, and the lavish attention.

'Do you suppose, the Wicked Witch of the woods introduced herself in the guise of a snake, as a warning?'

'Supposing there is a wicked witch hereabouts.'

TALK TO THE ANIMALS

'I believe there is, as there is much wickedness in the world, my wonderful hero.'

'Then I suppose there must be, and we should be always on our guard. Stands to reason, I suppose, as I ran away from wickedness. You're not wicked; you're kind, and loving, and quite beautiful.'

'Why, thank you, Dog. Now, I suggest we keep going, and keep our eyes peeled,' she insisted. 'Let us hope we can find a suitable place to rest.'

'Somewhere out in the open, would be nice.'

After quite some time, and a difficult sojourn it turned out to be, as the press of dense undergrowth was at times, quite cumbersome. They eventually came to an area of gently undulating hillocks and grassy knolls, and sight of the verdant green splendour, took Imelda's breath away. It was an area of mystical beauty and seemed quite magical and out of place in the woods.

Imelda removed her cloak and went to investigate numerous rabbit burrows dotted around supposing a colony of the cute furry animals had claimed this part of the woods as their home.

She lay down and gazed to the sky, closing her eyes against the glare as Dog went off to investigate.

She heard him yipping excitably and hoped he wasn't chasing the rabbits. He was nowhere to be seen even though she could hear him over the brow of one hillock. She settled down again and had the lambent warmth of the sun caress her skin. It was a sensation which ultimately thrilled her.

TALK TO THE ANIMALS

She even considered it to be romantic, in that she was able to imagine her prince laying with her. Even with her eyes closed, she would know her prince was greedily devouring her with his own eyes and wanting to touch, to caress, even to kiss her.

Oddly, she sensed she was being observed, and did not think it was her prince on this occasion.

'Has he gone, princess? Has the beast left?'

Imelda opened her eyes and smiled at sight of the small rabbit hopping and skipping in small circles only a short distance from her outstretched limbs.

'I'm nervous around large savage beasts,' remarked the rabbit and stopping what he was doing to listen and observe the gently undulating hillocks all around.

'Dog isn't really savage,' Imelda answered and slowly turning onto her front. 'He is boisterous admittedly, but that is because he is happy. As far as I know, he doesn't go out of his way to attack animals who are living, only brings home roadkill.'

'he is a beast, and all that barking and snarling is going to frighten the little ones. Dear me, dear me, when once it was so peaceful and quite safe. Now, you have come along and it's not the same.'

'I'm sorry little rabbit. Would it help you and the little ones if we were to leave?'

'Yes, oh yes, please. I don't mean to be rude, but I fear for the children, you see. You are welcome to visit anytime, princess, so long as you come without the beast.'

TALK TO THE ANIMALS

The rabbit hopped some distance away as Imelda scrambled to her feet and reached for her cloak and bowl.

'I hope the children are okay. I will bid you farewell, Mister Rabbit. So sorry for the intrusion.'

Imelda called out to Dog and went in search of him.

CHAPTER 16

They called it a day when Imelda observed the sun dipping away to afternoon, and both she and Dog seemed to know instinctively the route they should take.

The journey home was heralded with birdsong in the branches of the trees, and Imelda was heartened most of those trees wished them both a warm welcome and safe passage. She was tempted to loiter and engage each in conversation, yet her body was complaining and had the beginnings of stomach cramps.

Imelda knew what to expect and her monthlies could be exceedingly difficult and uncomfortable to endure. Not having the luxury of pads and tampons served to make her increasingly distraught. She already felt dirty, and worse was to come.

It came as a relief when they eventually stepped out from a dense forest of trees into the clearing leading to their shelter.

Dog bounded ahead of her, his tail wagging furiously, and Imelda supposed he was hungry. She was famished. Lighting a fire with a stick and dry kindling always took time, as with the cooking of meat.

Soon though, she had everything prepared and couldn't wait to complete her chores so that she had time to relax.

TALK TO THE ANIMALS

Relaxation came as dusk cast a mantle of gloom beyond the shelter.

Having done all that she needed to do and with dog content and staying to keep her company, Imelda lay out on her crib and pulled the leafy blanket over her. She did so, not because she felt a chill, but from necessity as she didn't want Dog as a witness to her escalating discomfort or to notice her dirtiness.

She could not help herself smiling, despite her cramps, as she was immensely proud of her loyal and faithful companion. He seemed to sense her growing anxiety and snuggled close to give comfort to his princess.

'Have you been munching those mushrooms, those you should avoid?' he enquired.

'No,' she answered quickly in her defence, 'And there is no point me explaining why I am feeling down and ailing. You wouldn't understand. Only girls understand.'

''Sorry, I'm not a girl or even a handsome prince,' the Dog chuntered and resting his muzzle and blowing around her delicious fan of red hair. 'I take it then, if your prince was here, he wouldn't understand your problem either, because he wouldn't be a girl?'

'I don't suppose he would,' she answered dreamily while lazily massaging her stomach. 'But like you Dog, I just know my Prince would watch over me and offer comfort in my hours of need. He would neither tease or taunt, or ever make me feel bad.'

'How long does it last, this nasty discomfort you are in?'

'A few days usually. But, oh dear me, I have no pads or tampons. I never gave it a thought when I fled and ended up here.

TALK TO THE ANIMALS

All I know is that I had to get away, but from where, I have no idea. Do you suppose, I fell and banged my head? It's called amnesia, you know.'

The Dog seemed to chuckle at the strange word she used. He chuckled a lot. It was more to do with having a full belly and being content, Imelda supposed.

The evening wore on and Imelda became increasingly restless, even as Dog slept soundly at her side.

'I will make you a crib, just like this one,' she whispered as she leaned forward and fed kindling to the embers of a dying fire. 'As it is, as much as I love you, you hog too much of the bed young man.'

Even with his eyes closed Dog answered. 'If your prince was here, would he be offered a separate cot, or would you have him up close?'

'Well, I don't have a prince. If only.'

'This prince may not be all that you imagine he might be. Do you think, he will be as attentive and kind? And loving? We both know, it is rare to find these attributes in a human. What do they know of faithfulness, loyalty, and genuine compassion?'

'I am all of those,' she answered, and as she lay back let an arm drape her furry companion.'

'Then, you must find a reflection of yourself,' Dog added. 'Good luck with that.'

Imelda grew pensive and became mesmerised by the capering images on the walls and ceiling as tongues of flame grew out of the fire.

TALK TO THE ANIMALS

Her imagination allowed her to create a story from these, where she was able to define figures and creatures in the moving pictures.

She saw herself, or at least a parody of herself and was confronted by another who was taller. They could have been dancing, on an incredibly special occasion conducted at court in a castle far away. Other images portrayed an excitable crowd of observers, and they might have been giving rapturous applause to their prince and princess.

Imelda's gaze drifted to the outer fringes of the scenes her mind had concocted and back again, believing in her heart, the crowd were celebrating an engagement. She even believed there was music playing and a chorus of robust approval. The music she heard playing in her head was on medieval pipes and string instruments, was melodic and neither contemporary nor discordant.

A draft sought passage into the shelter through glaring chinks in the rock and had the flames of the fire distorting the images, so that Imelda believed the characters had vacated the great hall to another room.

She felt her chest constricting as the taller image seemed to dwarf the other, so that she imagined herself being pushed down. She became fearful, in that she was not the one instigating events to unfold, was in fact being cajoled into complying and not given a choice.

Could her prince be so cold, calculating, and unforgiving?

Her eyes became drawn to an area of the stone wall which remained untouched by the greedy firelight. As with a

73

dark form without features who existed to exert its will. Imelda saw the amorphous shadow as the Wicked Witch and her prince had fallen under her spell.

She knew this to be true as her prince had renounced his love, and with darkness tainting his heart and soul, he had become cruel and demanding. He called her dirty, worse; he drooled and said she was his whore.

His form began to grow out of all proportion and became a monstrous incarnation of all that was evil in the world. The Wicked Witch capered and was gleeful.

Imelda closed her eyes and buried her face against Dog's thick fur. His steady rhythmic breathing and light, almost inaudible sighs slowly soothed her.

The portentous imagery was gone from her fevered mind and she was quickly asleep.

If she dreamy, she did not recall any of them on awakening the next morning. It was once again overcast with the potential of more rain. It might even have reflected the mood she was in and in the way she felt physically.

It was to be expected; she told herself. Just have to get on with it and keep busy. And furthermore, she needed to cease with dwelling on negative issues.

It could be worse! Her mind clamoured.

It was a thought to have her smiling.

Finally.

CHAPTER 17

Dog had taken himself off on one of his regular jaunts while Imelda busied herself abluting and washing her dress and panties. She followed this by gathering essentials she required to craft a second cot for her companion.

She had only just completed her final trip to the woods and back when the first drops of rain began to fall. With a leaden sky it was conceivable, the rain would persist throughout the day into the night.

Imelda was able to quieten her thoughts and concentrate on the laborious task she had given herself. She only stopped to drink the rainwater teeming through the overhead gaps and to wash herself regularly.

Her period began in earnest and it was not only the griping cramps she had to contend with, but she also bled heavily. She just wanted the next few days to pass quickly.

Dog had yet to return from wherever he had taken himself by the time she had finished the spare cot.

It was while preparing a fire for the last meal of venison Imelda would swear she heard a baby crying over the relentless roar of rain falling. The thought of a stranded child in the woods and caught in a storm horrified her and she went to investigate the source.

The persistent rain made it difficult to see and hazardous on the ledge. Her gaze drifted across the tableau of trees around her and at their base, not that visibility was good. She almost gave up and returned to the shelter when a plaintive cry, much nearer this time, had her peering along the face and summit of the rocky outcrop.

She had her answer in the form of a cat with sodden black fur, trying unsuccessfully to wedge itself into a small crevice out of the rain. Imelda eased herself along the ledge until she reached the frightened, bedraggled cat.

'Well, you're not exactly a native woodland animal,' she said in soft tones. 'Are you lost?'

It occurred to her; the cat was black and had to wonder if it was one of the Wicked Witch's acolytes sent to spy on her. Anything was possible, she surmised.

'I'm not lost. Are you lost?' the cat asked and gave a hiss of annoyance, and a warning for Imelda to keep to a respectful distance.

'Why are you here?' Imelda asked. 'You're lucky Dog is not around as I daresay he might not be friendly around cats. They rarely are.'

'I've seen the mutt around from time to time. I'm not scared of him, so that you know. If he comes near me or looks at me funny, I'll scratch his eyes out and bite his nose.'

'You will do no such thing.'

TALK TO THE ANIMALS

'Oh, but it's okay for that lumbering beast to have a pop at me, right? Look at me, I'm smaller and cuter, and out here in the wilderness us girls have got to look out for each other.'

'I am quite capable of looking after myself,' said Imelda defensively. I would invite you into our home where its warm and cosy, but I must consider Dog's feelings and how he might react if he was to find a strange cat with me.'

'Who are you calling strange?'

'I meant no offence with the remark. I'm only saying. Perhaps you should head on back to wherever your home is.'

'Why do you suppose I have a home to go to? Like the mutt, I might be a stray who has fallen on hard times and looking for some charity, a little kindness and companionship.'

'And you could be in league with the Wicked Witch of the woods.'

'I could. Does she exist then? Can't say I've met a witch here in the woods.'

'I suggest, you do what you think is best. I'm going back inside to get dry. Fact is, I'm not feeling one hundred percent and need to lie down. You take care, little cat.'

Despite the heavy rain it was quite humid and the shelter was unpleasantly smoky. The water teeming through the gaps prevented smoke escaping that way and was billowing along the length of the ceiling and pouring out the entrance. Once inside Imelda removed her two-piece ensemble and lay down.

She became drawn to the mewl of the adventurous and quite stubborn cat, who had jumped down and entered the shelter. Imelda rolled onto her side and saw the way the cat was eyeing the portions of venison she had set aside for a last meal. It sat nonchalantly a short distance in from the entrance, out of the rain, and proceeded to wash itself.

Imelda became fascinated with the cat's determined and meticulous cleaning program.

'As I said outside, should Dog find you in his home I imagine there will be frightful scenes of uproar,' she called to the new arrival. 'Quite the kerfuffle, I daresay. The reason I'm warning you in advance is that Dog has little reason to trust anybody or anything. He trusts me, however.'

Imelda sat up and crouched by the fire where she fed two slender scraps to the hot plate which she had placed over the depression and the flames.

'The least I can do is put some food in your belly, moggy cat, and then I suggest you take your leave. I'm not in any mood to have to wade in and stop a squabble. I don't like arguments and fighting is a definite no-no. Here in the woods, I want the animals, birds, and trees to just get along and be happy. Not too much to ask, I would think.'

As Imelda turned the strips over she was aware the cat had approached. She was either growling or it was her stomach grumbling, Imelda could not be sure.

Lifting up the meat with her chopsticks she blew on them and placed both on the ground alongside the second cot.

The cat was extremely interested by the heady aroma and was enticed to approach. She gazed at the cooked meat and salivated, before snatching-up a morsel and tossing it in the air. She began battering it with a front paw.

TALK TO THE ANIMALS

'Still hot!' she complained.

'Take your time, but not too long,' said Imelda, smiling and wishing she could feel in better spirits.

She lay down again on her side as it afforded her a view of the sleek and glossy black cat gorging on the meal she had prepared. The cat was making little throaty growling noises and Imelda was delighted.

'Wow!' she exclaimed. 'You were hungry, young lady.'

The cat ignored her comment as she finished the last pf the strips of meat.

Imelda felt her eyelids grow heavy even as her body ached and her head began to sound a familiar discordant timpani. She pursed her lips and gritted her teeth knowing she had no choice but to endure the discomfort with determination and fortitude.

In a few days she would be back to her normal self.

TALK TO THE ANIMALS

CHAPTER 18

When she eventually opened her eyes and clawed her way back from a deliciously sweet and evocative dream she noticed the fire was sputtering and there was more ash than kindling. It was late evening judging by the level of fading light and still raining, but not as heavy as earlier.

She wanted to recall the content of her dream but had only a few fragments to ponder. She recollected her prince was involved, not that she remembered if he possessed features she might recognise. She was unable to retrieve a clear picture in her mind and it frustrated her. She knew, that in her dream, he had made her laugh and liked that he was attentive. Very attentive.

Her prince had been brazenly tactile and had possessed a hunger and need which kindled desire in Imelda as she lazily massaged her stomach. Her prince had been patient and tender and all was a prelude to more.

He had kissed her and had imagined his hands on her waist, moving surreptitiously to her breasts. Where this could have led she will never know, as it was the moment she came awake.

TALK TO THE ANIMALS

Panic flared as she attempted to rub confusion and sleep from her eyes as a heavy weight was against her and constricting her movements.

Easing the coverlet lower she was able to sit up caught between a protest and a scream, only to find Miss Cat had made a comfortable nook between her legs.

'You decided to stay then?' Imelda asked the dark form heaped into the depression her parted thighs made, and at the same time was wondering why Dog had not returned.

The cat yawned, fluttered her eyes, and languidly stretched all four limbs and grumbled a response. 'Yes, so it appears, as your kindness has made me very welcome and at home and found a nice comfortable bed between your thighs.'

'Have you seen Dog this evening?'

'No and I'm not sorry. I hope the stupid mutt has become roadkill. Now that would be karma, don't you think?'

'Don't say that and don't even think it!'

Imelda angrily gave the cat a shove and crawled to the side to place more kindling and grass on the embers. Feeling pangs of guilt suddenly she reached across to stroke the newcomer and was surprised not to receive a bite or a scratch. The cat was another who liked attention and wrapped herself into a tight ball and purred shamelessly.

It had Imelda smiling, and thinking, if there was to be a confrontation they would have to sort out their differences between them. She would only serve as mediator should an argument get out of control and one or the other stood to get hurt.

TALK TO THE ANIMALS

She had no money for vet bills, nor transport, and had no idea where the nearest veterinary practice was.

It was only when she slotted her hands beneath Cat and lifted her up and place her on the opposite side of the cot and against the wall did she receive a little warning nip. In response Imelda quietly chastised the cat and let her know she was moved so that she could prepare the fire better and ablute herself.

Cat said nothing to the contrary and curled herself into another ball. She did however continue her grumbling as if to let Imelda know, being moved from the comfortable warm niche she had made was an inconvenience to her.

It took no time to have the fire burning fiercely with huge tongues of flame licking towards the ceiling before settling. Imelda staggered to where rainwater still teemed through one of the holes in the ceiling and washed herself thoroughly.

The coolness had her feeling refreshed and of a better disposition and as she feeling quite peckish, took a few thin strips of the prepared venison onto the improvised grate she placed over the fire. She had every intention to wait for Dog to reappear and as he had not, left a good portion of meat wrapped in leaves to one side.

Cat's interest was stirred instantly and she unravelled herself and moved to the edge of the second cot, content to watch proceedings and in the hope she would not be excluded.

Cat hoped her feistiness of earlier had not discouraged the young girl from including her in a meal.

'Do you have some for me?' she asked and gave Imelda a look which could easily have translated as a smile.

TALK TO THE ANIMALS

'Naturally,' said Imelda. 'Do you think me a tease and would leave you out? Looks like it's just the two of us.'

'Suits me. I'm sure the mutt is fine and is most likely sheltering from the rain. He'll be okay, and not as I said before, lying dead in the road.'

Imelda said nothing, as she had been thinking the same.

'Why the mutt wants to be out in this weather, beats me,' said Cat. 'Not that I want him to come in here and pick a fight.'

'For your information, Dog not only provides for us, but he is also my eyes and ears and will tell me if there are unwelcome visitors to the woods.'

'In what way, unwelcome?'

'I mean, there are horrible people outside these woods who take that which is not freely given. If they find me here alone, they might attack me and yes, take what is not freely given. Oh shush, I don't know what I'm saying.'

'Don't worry yourself, princess. With the mutt out of the way, I'm here to protect you.'

'Thank you, but it's not the same. No one is afraid of a cat, even a grumpy one.'

'If you say so.'

'I'm very worried, if you must know as yesterday, Dog did not leave my side even for a minute. Well, except to do his toilet. He's getting good at not cocking his leg or pooping near the shelter.'

TALK TO THE ANIMALS

'That was yesterday. Now the mutt's deserted you and here you are, defending him when you're feeling vulnerable. Some friend he's turned out to be. Some bedtime companion. And now where's your protection, if not me?'

'Whatever.'

'You're only acting this way because of the dreams you had. Of your prince. The way he made you feel.'

'Oh, shut up, what do you know?'

To take her mind off her thoughts Imelda lay the tender strips of meat out on the ground and moved to the cot she had prepared for Dog. She was a little disgruntled he had not been around to witness her hard work and try it out for comfort.

The cat tucked into her meal and raised its head up suddenly to watch her with curiosity glinting in her eyes.

'Are you not hungry?' the cat enquired and thinking there might be more to savour.

'Not anymore,' Imelda answered morosely and lay back whilst attuned to the plip-plopping of water striking the floor. She was also listening out for sounds beyond the shelter.

Dog eventually returned in the early hours, a sorry bedraggled sight and Imelda was unable to contain her excitement and relief.

'Don't ask,' Dog bemoaned. 'I've traipsed the road for miles looking for roadkill and have nothing to show for my efforts. Nada.'

'That's okay,' Imelda responded. 'I'll cook you a fine meal with the rest of the venison.'

TALK TO THE ANIMALS

She spoke to him in between lavishing kisses to his forehead and snout.

Dog stiffened and shook his fur, Imelda squealing as she was showered with spray. It was the moment Dog saw the interloper dragging its head out of the coverlet.

'I made you a bed,' said Imelda and not realising what was to come.

Until, that is, she saw the ferocity in Dog's eyes and in the way he tensed and his muscles bunched.

'What and who is that?' Dog snarled

'Ah,' Imelda acknowledged, and was surprised she should have forgotten about the new arrival. She prepared herself for the quarrel to come without truly knowing how to manage the situation should it get out of control. 'This is Cat. Say hi to Cat. And cat, this is Dog.'

Cat arched its back and flexed its claws, hissing a warning for the beast not to approach. Dog retaliated with a flourish of barking as the cat's tail whipped side to side.

'Now, now,' Imelda cried, 'I want you both to just get along. Okay? Do you think you can do that for me? Yes? I won't have any bickering or squabbling; do you hear me?'

Dog's interest in the unwanted and unexpected guest soon waned as attention was on his mistress who was placing slabs of venison on the grate. Keeping one eye respectfully on the cat he watched the human fastidiously turning the meat so as to cook it evenly.

The cat's growling was an annoyance and Dog flicked his head and stared daggers at her. Cat tried to settle and appear nonchalant and every so often fired a warning hiss and growl at the big mutt.

Imelda ignored the exchange and hoped they might just get along. She was surprised, as Cat was the one who seemed most agitated. She bravely moved to the edge of the cot and attempted to comfort the little 'furball.' Cat continued to vent her displeasure as Imelda shuffled to the fire and using her improvised chopsticks, tossed a generous portion of venison towards Dog and lifted and blew on a smaller piece for Cat.

'Now guys, what's it going to be? I need to know if you will just bury your differences and get along. Otherwise, I have no option but to ask one of you to leave.'

'You're going to choose the mutt over me,' grumbled Cat and licking her whiskers.

'Dog was here first. And as I have already explained, he is my best friend in all the world. He is both provider and my protector.'

'I get it! I get it! But if the brute so much as sniffs my butt, I'm going to have him. I will1.'

'Oh, quit with your negative vibes. This is going to be our happy place. Stay and be nice or leave. That is your choice to make. Prove to me you are not a spy sent by the Wicked Witch.'

CHAPTER 19

Imelda opened her eyes as a knifing pain sliced across her abdomen, had her raising her knees and moaning. The pains eventually subsided and came to realise Dog was stretched along his cot, huffing into her hair as he slept. She thankfully had not disturbed him with her sudden movements and complaining.

Cat was curled up between her hip and the wall and seemed content. She was purring and another whose sleep had not been disturbed. Knowing they were both with her had Imelda smiling. They appeared to have settled their differences and there was every likelihood they might just get along.

Needing to be comforted in the absence of a prince, she turned her back to Cat and snuggled-up to her canine companion, draping an arm and one leg over him. It had him quietly grumbling to have been woken from a peaceful slumber but was immediately content to have his flank and stomach tenderly caressed. Better was to follow as the human petted his head and scrabbled fingers behind his ears.

'Just peachy,' he muttered against her ear.

'What did you just say?'

'Nothing. Ignore me.'

TALK TO THE ANIMALS

Imelda settled and strived to think why Dog's remark should have evoked a reaction and spark a memory in her subconscious, that which she had successfully suppressed for a time. It was not an affectation to inspire feelings of warmth, she surmise. On the contrary, a dark mist seemed to swirl around her thoughts.

She had no wish to sleep at that juncture, so as not to invite unpleasant dreams, especially as she was feeling out of sorts and vulnerable. Laying her cheek to Dog's furry collar she peered out across a vista of tree tops all of which were illuminated by the moon and stars, now that the rain had abated and cloud had dispersed.

Was this the life she wanted for herself? Her mind quipped.

She nodded as if to answer herself.

Life wasn't perfect, she reminded herself and elaborated in a way which would have her smile. *In any magical kingdom, I would not have to worry about periods. I could flounce around in long dresses with a tiara clipped to my hair. My handsome, attentive prince would keep me entertained and take me on adventures, and just know his kisses would take my breath away. At night I would sleep in a sumptuous four-poster bed with my prince alongside me. He would notice the desire in my eyes and witness his naked need in his own. I can imagine the way he would lean in and I close my eyes and hold my breath, in anticipation of the moment.*

The moment?

TALK TO THE ANIMALS

Her mind gave a scream and she sat up and wished she hadn't moved with such force as the walls in front began to shift in and out of focus.

She wondered if it was a result of her not eating anything. Or, as to whether the Wicked Witch of the woods was, at that moment watching her and had access to her thoughts as she stirred a bubbling cauldron of magical broth. Imelda supposed the Wicked Witch had cast a spell so that she would become disoriented.

If the Wicked Witch had access to the corridors within her mind could she be seeking those memories Imelda had subverted? And would she expose them, given an opportunity to do so?

Imelda stepped over dog and went outside to breath in the sultry night air and dank vegetation, and to feel the subtle caress of a light breeze on her naked flesh.

She carefully traced a path to the rock pool where it seemed to glow beneath the silvery light of an almost full moon mysteriously and magically.

Ignoring the cold clench on her skin, Imelda slipped carefully into the water using the jutting platform for support as she slowly kicked her legs.

As she reclined with dampness chilling and stippling her flesh, a sound cut across the tranquillity, that of a displaced stone falling. She strained to see beyond her position, to determine if an intruder was thereabouts. She wanted to believe Dog had followed her scent, yet there was no sign of him in the vicinity.

Imelda realised she had been holding her breath as she studied all the nooks and crannies and deepest shadows whilst being alert to any suspicious movements. All around was eerily quiet once again, except for the persistent babbling of the small waterfall at her back.

A large bird took flight and squawked. It had Imelda wondering if the bird had been disturbed from a peaceful slumber. She let her breath out slowly and scooped-up water in the palm of one hand to drizzle over her chest and stomach.

Her heart beat loud and erratically. She was trembling even as she ascertained this was not a product of fear. If it had been the Wicked Witch of the woods she had to wonder why she had not taken the opportunity to engage with her having realised the princess was defenceless and vulnerable without her canine companion at her side.

She gave a gasp at sight of the big dark shadow creeping towards her and when moonlight gave substance to the creepy silhouette, Imelda was smiling and ever so thankful.

'When I saw you had vacated the shelter, I thought it prudent of me to come looking for you,' Dog muttered, grinning and panting, before squatting on his haunches beside her. He gave her cheek a lick before swiping his tongue down her upper arm.

'That is so sweet, Dog,' said Imelda and grabbing his head to kiss him. 'Thank you, for being so thoughtful and concerned. As you can see, I'm okay, and let me just say I was incredibly careful navigating the ledge to get here.'

'Now I'm here, I suppose it's only polite and good-mannered to wait until you have finished whatever you're doing. If I'm honest, I didn't feel wonderfully comfortable being left in close proximity to that moggy friend of yours. She has a very nasty disposition I can tell you. Took another swipe at me she did. I was only trying to sniff her. It's what us dogs do, you know. The scent of an animal or human tells us dogs a lot, as to whether they can be trusted for one thing.'

'Dear me, I hope you didn't hurt her.'

'Ha, she's not worth my time,' Dog answered with an indignant huff. 'Suppose now I have to find food for three hungry mouths.'

'I will help. We go to the road together and hope there is something worth salvaging, if it's not too squishy or has been lying around for days, festering, and riddled with maggots. Yuk!'

'I think I would know as I'm out there hunting our next meal constantly. For your information, it's not exactly a busy road. There have been occasions when I have gone days without food in my belly. It gets difficult to stay motivated when you're hungry and desperate. I know what it's like to go without and it's not much fun I can tell you.'

'It will change. I was thinking; if I make a rod and use twine, I could do some fishing in the river. It won't be the first time.'

With that thought surfacing Imelda went quiet and was then raising herself up.

'Come on pooch, let's get back to the shelter and snuggle-up.'

CHAPTER 20

Imelda awoke to a new day with Dog glaring into her eyes from his outstretched position beside her, looking more than a little disgruntled, and even a little shocked. Imelda instantly understood why Dog should be feeling uncomfortable as, looking down, she saw and felt Cat vibrating like a tractor's engine between them.

'What the...!' Dog exclaimed in low tones and was abruptly cut-off from finishing his protest.

'Don't say it,' Imelda chided him and could not help herself smiling. 'It's not considered polite etiquette to blaspheme.'

'Really? It's fucking okay from where I come from,' Dog slavered, tensing, as he was unwilling to move and disturb the spiteful beast nestled between him and the girl.

'Dear me, but I never knew you had a rough edge to your character.'

'Jesus, lady, I'm a dog lest you forget, and my mortal enemy who is the obnoxious creature tucked into my belly is invading my personal space. Like it's the most natural thing in the world.'

TALK TO THE ANIMALS

'It's magical.'

'It's offensive, as I can feel her touching me. And look, see, her claws are out and plucking my fur.'

'Shall I move cat to a safe distance, if it will make you feel better?'

Dog seemed to pause, ponder, and postulate before giving a response.

'Actually,' he admitted, *'It's quite nice. Comforting.'*

'Yes it is.'

'Doesn't mean we're friends though.'

'Listen to you, you big softy. You have such a big and beautiful heart, Dog.'

'Not where these infernal creatures are concerned.'

'We all need a little friendly companionship in our lives,' she answered him and kissing his muzzle. 'Kindness goes a long way, and actually makes life wonderful and joyous, giving and receiving.'

'Yes, well, if you say so. Not that I like anything or anyone taking liberties with my kind nature.'

'Naturally.'

She sat up slowly and carefully so as not to disturb Cat.

'Today, we are to go hunting,' Imelda said to Dog. 'Look on the bright side, it has stopped raining and the sun is trying to smile. This is going to be a good day. We are going to remain positive, no matter. I think, I will wear my dress today. And it is only fair I should warn you in advance, that it might be necessary for me to take regular toilet breaks.'

'This monthly business, I don't doubt.'

'Yes.'

'It's okay. I'm a dog and we are always cocking our leg to pee.'

'That's enough, Dog.'

'We do it because we're leaving our scent, as a warning to other animals. Not only that, but it also helps me to find my way home. To you.'

Imelda almost gave in to sobbing with Dog's remark and blamed her emotional state on the time of the month.

She began the morning by removing the inedible carcase of the muntjac deer and eased it over the lip of the ledge. She then departed to do her ablutions and to wash herself. In the process of washing herself down in the stream Imelda believed she caught the sound of crunching mulch and sensed the airy movement of a shrub being brushed against.

She had to wonder if Dog had followed her even though he had not made an appearance. Looking around herself she saw nothing to alarm her, despite all the bird chatter heralding a new and exciting day. It was important she stayed positive, realising it was natural to perceive noise and movements, as this was a woodland coming alive to another day.

Even as she rolled water down her skin she remained alert. Rubbing herself gently and ever so slowly, Imelda gasped and held her breath as the sensual slide of her fingers, initiated sensations she saw as unwelcome in her present condition. It did not help that she nurtured a feeling someone was watching her.

She chided herself for entertaining the thought as no one was stalking her. It was all in her mind.

She hoped, it was all in her mind.

As she made ready to return to the shelter another thought popped into her head to evoke feelings of uncertainty. She thought it conceivable, anyone spying on her, could be her nemesis the Wicked Witch of the woods.

It made sense, as a witch could assimilate any form it chose to and if the witch was hereabouts she could be scheming and finding ways to inveigle herself into Imelda's confidence.

She turned to the trees and undergrowth and smiled, letting defiance prove to anyone, she was not afraid. A chill clenching her skin and having butterflies erupt within her stomach told a different story.

She hurried back to the shelter and was both surprised and gladdened Dog was stretched along his cot with one big paw draping his so-called enemy, the Cat. Chuckling to herself Imelda slipped on her dress and fastened it at the front. Not wishing to spoil her panties she fed the leafy thong around her slim waist instead.

'Are you coming?' she called to dog the moment she had fed her trainers onto her dainty feet. She noticed the way Dog's ears had perked-up and then he was rolling over clumsily. Cat grumbled without hissing or lashing out as Dog bounded over to his mistress.

'That cat is so lazy,' said Dog.

TALK TO THE ANIMALS

Imelda smiled with affection.

'Are you ready for a big adventure?' she enquired. 'Let's go bag ourselves some game for our next banquet.'

Imelda led the way with Dog scampering dangerously on her heels.

CHAPTER 21

The damp clinging to the vegetation soon had Imelda's flimsy cotton dress clinging to her slight body like a second taut, unforgiving skin. Dog did not seem to mind getting wet and Imelda supposed he was used to it.

They trudged and parried their way through dank shrub for almost a mile and eventually they came to where a bleak narrow road cut a swath through the woodland.

Dog gave an exuberant bark as if to herald their arrival, of an area he had traversed many times. His narrow snout was already to the ground seeking a possible scent which might lead to their next meal.

Imelda walked behind at a leisurely pace and remaining wary of approaching vehicles or cyclists in both directions. She was reluctant for anyone to see her as the enemy could be searching for her at that time. Not that she wished to dwell on any ramifications as to why she would believe someone was searching for her. For that matter, why she should have fled to the woods as if her life depended on it.

Imelda and Dog progressed along the road for miles, it would seem, and neither had luck finding fresh roadkill to take back with them. There were two occasions she became alert to an engine in the distance and called to Dog to find cover until the vehicle had passed their position and was out of sight. Neither car stopped or turned around and Imelda was satisfied they had hidden without causing suspicion.

They eventually left the fringes of the woodland behind them and followed the path of a river and open pasture beyond it. At sight of the gently meandering river Imelda was thinking about her idea to make a fishing rod. She only slowed when she espied a parked people carrier further along. It was jutting away from a gap in the hedge with its tail end at a precarious angle.

Her heart beat a little faster and she almost turned around. Curiosity won over as she approached the car with caution. It had not been one of the vehicles to have passed them earlier and on closer inspection, saw no signs it had occupants within, which did not necessarily mean they were not too far away.

She stepped closer even as Dog approached the vehicle fearlessly. He stopped and cocked a leg against the outside rear wheel. Imelda was peering along the river banks and saw no sign of anyone in the vicinity.

She tried the doors and all were locked. It occurred to her the car may have broken down and the driver had abandoned it to get assistance. Maybe they could not get a signal on their phone, that is, if they had a phone about their person.

What gained Imelda's interest was sceing two large canvas bags ladened with all manner of groceries in the rear well, stacked so high the pull-down tail board did not completely cover them.

Imelda envisioned several possibilities and before making her mind up, once again checked the road in both directions, the river banks, and the pasture. Approaching the tailgate, she took a deep breath and launched a kick at the wide tinted window. It took several attempts with Dog bounding and barking and getting himself stirred to giddy heights of excitement.

The window only cracked without shattering, even as Imelda noticed the seal was damaged along one side. Gripping the glass, she levered it away and the entire pane became dislodged and slumped away at an angle.

Dog had stopped jumping around and barking and was regarding his mistress with a wry grin.

'What are you doing?' he queried.

'What is it you think I'm doing?' she answered.

'You're stealing someone's shopping, is what you're doing.'

'Yes, and these are desperate times sometimes requiring desperate measures. Wow, just look at all these goodies. Tonight, we can feast as it is right a princess and her prince should.'

'If you say so.'

'For once, I am the provider.'

Having taken the bags out she grabbed the handles for a better purchase and hefted them up and without loitering began to carry them back the way they had come. They had not even reached the trees and her arms began to scream with pain. It did not deter her and refused to rest until they had reached cover.

TALK TO THE ANIMALS

Dog was content to bound alongside her, his salivating tongue lolling off to one side as an expression of excitement and anticipation.

They reached the secure blanket of trees and shrubs without another vehicle passing and Imelda found a depression amongst the exposed roots of a sycamore tree to release the bags and settle for a rest.

'Wow!' exclaimed Dog. 'You're full of surprises princess. Never thought you had it in you to pull off a stunt like that.'

'Yes, well needs must, Dog. I must rest awhile so let's have a gander in the bags, shall we?'

She began tugging items out of the first bag and placed them around her with eyes widening with delight.

'This is like divine providence, Dog. It must be the magic of the woods. We were guided to that abandoned car and meant to find all these treasures.

'If you say so.'

'I do.'

'Look; we have steak, sausages, bacon, bread. There's milk and two cartons of cream. Toilet roll! Dear Lord, there is even chocolate and biscuits.'

She put the items back and started on the second bag. It revealed fruit juice, bags of sweets and then she gave a haughty chuckle.

'Did I not say it was divine providence which took us to that abandoned car? There are cans of dog food and biscuits and there is even two bones. And cat treats; oh my! What do you have to say for yourself now, Dog?'

Her eyes lit up even more as she stared open-mouthed at two boxes of tampons hidden beneath a packet of wet wipes.

'Oh, my Lord!' she screamed aloud and without hesitating, she prised open the lid on one box, slipped a tampon out of its sleeve and was on her knees inserting it. 'Fucking unbelievable!'

'You swore.'

'Yes. I must have picked that up from you, Dog. Come on, let's make tracks and get home. I hope you know the way.'

She scooped-up the provisions and placed them in the bag, not leaving anything as they prepared to resume their journey.

Imelda was of the conclusion the trek to the shelter was twice as far as when they left and seemed to take forever. She had to take frequent rest-stops to free her hands and for the aching and trembling in her limbs to abate.

CHAPTER 22

Cat was nowhere to be seen on their return and Imelda sorting the perishables by the use by and best before dates, with Dog alongside her, panting and whining with anticipation.

She unwrapped and tossed him a bone and for herself, munched on a few squares of milk chocolate. She sipped from a carton of orange juice to slake her thirst and believed she might die and go to heaven. She then lay on her side to rest while watching Dog gnawing the bone with obvious glee and contentment.

'I still cannot believe you broke into that car,' he mumbled and without looking up from the prize he was greedily devouring.

'Give it a rest,' she responded. 'Did I not provide for us on this occasion?'

'Who are you trying to convince? You're feeling ashamed and a little guilty, I can tell.'

'Yes, but in desperate situations, desperate measures are sometimes required.'

'If you say so.'

TALK TO THE ANIMALS

'I won't be made to feel bad.'

Imelda pouted and stamped her feet in frustration as it appeared she was the one posing the questions and answering herself. She became annoyed with herself and with Dog, and huffily removed her dress and leafy thong before stretching out on her cot.

'I have tampons,' she muttered defensively. 'You cannot imagine how it makes me feel.'

This was an occasion Dog did not answer.

'I'm not going to feel bad because I stole those things.'

She gazed off to the side as Dog finished the last of the bone and noisily smacked his lips.

'Was that good?' Imelda asked.

'The best,' came the response for which she had hoped.

She patted the cot next to her for Dog to join her and was overwhelmed he should oblige her by strolling over and laying down on his belly. He appeared to be studying her.

'What?' she wanted to know. 'Why are you looking at me in that way.'

'I know what you're thinking,' was the answer even as it seemed to form within her own mind. 'You are imagining this moment with your prince alongside you.'

'Why, yes, you are right. I would love my prince to be here.'

'To make you feel better?'

TALK TO THE ANIMALS

'It's complicated. Yes, I would have my prince be attentive and tell me I am not a bad person and that my heart is in the right place. Damn it, I want so much more from my prince.'

'Like what?'

'There are some things you should not ask.'

'Oh, dear me, you're feeling horny.'

'Bloody Hell, Dog, are any of my thoughts to remain private?'

There came a moment's silence and Dog expelled a huff, before rolling to the side with his back to her.

Imelda snuggled up to him, anyway, draping an arm across and down his flank.

'I don't mean to be a pain,' she apologised.

'I suppose, you're going to tell me your behaviour and pattern of thought is a hormonal imbalance, and in that you have no control over these urges?'

'Exactly, Dog. Wow, you are incredibly intuitive and know me so well.'

'Probably, as I am you.'

'What do you mean?'

'Nothing.'

'You think I'm made, don't you.'

'You're not crazy. You can't help feeling the way you do. It's natural. It will pass in time, as you know.'

TALK TO THE ANIMALS

Imelda buried her face against the fur on Dog's back, content for him to console her in the absence of her prince.

She admonished herself for feeling out of sorts when she should be delighted to have found their next meal and snacks and even tampons and toilet tissue. She supposed she had some time on her hands before she needed to prepare everything. She wondered if it was better to sleep for a short time despite the rock pool calling to her. Then she was thinking, it might be nice to wander down to the stream and to bathe before she needed to prepare a fire.

She and her companions could expect a royal feast this evening, should Cat decide to return. If she decided to stay away, it would be her loss, she was thinking. She had Dog. Dog was all she needed.

At least, she was not pining for her prince. Imelda managed a smile as Dog responding with a little whine as she caressed his fur.

Whatever was left behind in another world at another time, something she believed which had been so terrible it had made her flee to the woods, she was embarking on a new era and could forge new and happier memories.

'Dog? Are you sleeping?'

There came no reply, even as she sensed his breathing had grown deeper and his hind legs twitched when she stroked them.

'Do you think me beautiful?' she purred against one stiffening ear, and sensed Dog was feigning sleep. 'Do you like my hair? It's natural, you know.'

TALK TO THE ANIMALS

Not getting the response she had hoped for Imelda blew out her cheeks and wriggled her rump into the depression she had made in the mattress of interwoven leaves.

'Do you think my breasts too small?'

She traced the contours of her bosom with tremulous digits.

'I like them,' she said and hissed quietly, 'As I know my prince will love them.'

Having not received an answer from Dog, she supposed he was sleeping. She closed her eyes and invited slumber to eradicate the flow of erotic thoughts and have her fervour dissipate.

CHAPTER 23

Cat returned and there came a stand-off, almost as if they had both forgotten how well they had gotten on together the previous day and night.

Imelda left both to squabble and settle their differences without intervening. She knelt by the fire and hot plate she had prepared in advance and lost in her own thoughts, dreamily turned the sausage, bacon, and strips of steak to cook each evenly.

The appetising aromas soon gained the interest of the brattish Dog and Cat as they sat side by side watching her.

'Best of friends now, huh?' she quipped around a triumphant smile. 'Maybe, I should make you both wait and teach you a lesson.'

Imelda scooped the cooked morsels into a bark panier she often used to collect mushrooms and roots, letting the food cool as she put extra portions onto the hotplate.

Imelda, Dog and Cat enjoyed a hearty feast together. For dessert, there was cream for Cat, biscuits for Dog and Imelda snaffled more of the chocolate.

TALK TO THE ANIMALS

Imelda was thinking, all was sublimely wonderful in her small castle. With the animal's content and wishing only to slumber, Imelda went to the rockpool and bathed.

Despite a clear sky, a full moon, and a vast canopy of stars to herald her arrival, it was a seasonably warm night.

She had taken with her a few succulent leaves which she squeezed and used their secretion on her hair.

When she was done she eased herself up onto the platform and lay back with her feet splashing and treading water.

A melee of sound of sporadic animal chatter punctuated the tranquillity of a barmy evening. Despite her discomfort, which came and went, she was desperate to remain upbeat and made her mind up she would go on a tour of her realm the next day.

She wanted to meet with other animals and to converse with the trees. She desired to have the magical woodland embrace her and have her believe she truly belonged.

She came out of her reverie the moment she sensed someone was again watching her from the shadows not touched by moonlight. She sat up and cast her gaze over the area around her position wanting desperately to see into the gloom.

Had Dog been beside her his keen sense of smell and acute hearing along with his uncanny intuition, would let her know there was someone out there.

Imelda was unafraid and even refused to cover her modesty, which was a surprise to her considering it was only a few days since she fled to the woods from something unknown and quite terrible she surmised.

TALK TO THE ANIMALS

It was her solemn belief she acquired her courage from the magic woven into the woods. If it was the Wicked Witch come to observe her Imelda was okay with it. She would fight magic with magic if it came to it.

The Witch would know she possessed a strength and power she had possibly not expected her to have. Imelda had kicked in a car window, in broad daylight, and stolen the food abandoned within. She had struggled and suffered great pain to get her purchases to the shelter. She had done it though, with mettle and determination and a keen sense of self-preservation.

Not even the Wicked Witch could take that from her, even if she was to cast her spells.   Imelda swept her legs around in lazy circles and delighted in the splashy, squelchy sounds her motions created.

She looked up from the agitated surface of water as, the continuing feeling she was being observed, intensified. It was a feeling to excite her. A memory quietly surfaced to the fore of her mind and instead of forbidding its passage on this occasion, she encouraged its intrusion.

She recalled other occasions, of another life, when she had felt eyes ogling her from afar. There had also been occasions when she encouraged attention and knew that she could be quite the tease if she put her mind to it. She was a young woman and liked others to desire her, and believed it was natural to want attention directed at her.

Imelda seemed to know instinctively how easy it was to use her feminine wiles to get the response she hoped for. It was a thought to inflict shock and she almost reluctantly conceded and would have returned to the shelter. To Dog and safety.

TALK TO THE ANIMALS

Curiosity and bedevilment won over and she chose to stay and even to confront her ghosts, should it become necessary. The magical power of the woods flowed in her veins.

She leaned back again, closing her eyes and quieting the rapid beat of her heart, as the sultry night air enveloped her slight frame and kissed her flesh.

She summoned the magic and willed whoever it was hiding in the shadows, to reveal themselves.

Imelda became frustrated and almost called-out and decided on another tack as she had no wish to alert Dog unless necessary.

She sat up again and tried a cajoling approach instead.

'What are you afraid of?' she asked the eerie shadows in the foreground. 'Do you see me as a threat? Look around, for I am alone and without anyone to protect me.'

There came no sound which would support the presence of an unseen entity.

'Coward,' she rasped and was further surprised she should be feeling unexpectedly aroused to be instigating a confrontation. 'So, instead of showing yourself, you prefer to skulk in the shadows?'

She kicked the water to create an arcing spray in a display of rising frustrations and petulance.

'It is plain to see, you are no match for someone like me,' she goaded the quiet. 'Cast your silly spells and see where they get you, or do you fear the possibility my magic is greater?'

TALK TO THE ANIMALS

Imelda rose and stepped off the platform with the intention of leaving. She hesitated, with hands on hips and legs akimbo, her fan of rangy damp hair glowing a patinated bronze in the moonlight. Her gaze swept with intensity over the broad expanse of jutting boulders and the numerous shadows and nooks.

Instead of returning to the shelter she chose to clamber down onto the woodland floor and enter an area of trees which were not heavily overgrown, in the hope she could lure the witch to follow.

She further she went her eyes could no longer penetrate the gloom and had to feel her way carefully. After several cautious minutes she arrived at the chuckling brook. If someone was to follow she would undoubtedly hear them approaching. As it was, the night creatures had fallen silent.

Deep within her mind, frustration and angst simmered, as with a cauldron coming to the boil. She wanted desperately to have all the magical powers she believed she possessed to guide and prepare her. Getting on hands and knees she foraged around until she saw what she had hoped to find.

Fingers caressed a small cluster of mushrooms having small insignificant caps and slender stalks, recognising them as those to induce hallucinations. She believed they were an integral source of her powers as before; they had heightened her senses and expanded her mind to receive knowledge she would not ordinarily comprehend without them.

As with the genie of the lamp, Imelda hoped her wishes would be granted.

TALK TO THE ANIMALS

With the magic flowing in her veins, she could face anything. Even the Wicked Witch should she force an engagement.

Plucking away a few stalks she fed them to her eager mouth and chewed on them, her nose wrinkling as they tasted bitter and rancid and quite earthy.

In no time at all she experienced the first starburst to ignite in her mind. It had her chuckling and was unable to stop herself. Then she was dancing incircles and waving her arms around. Going to the stream she waded in to where the water lapped across her calves.

She gave a gasp to feel her eyes bulging almost out of their sockets and for her limbs to have the consistency of rubber. She stumbled and fell, using her hands to prevent a nose-dive into the water.

The entire concept of her clumsiness and the sporadic fireworks going off in her head had her cackling quite dementedly.

Like a witch, she was thinking.

Still laughing she rolled and fell back with her rump slapping the surface and gave a yelp of surprise when she felt loose stones pummel and scrape her skin. Everything around her seemed to ooze and change form and had her wondering if the trees had come to life. Especially as they seemed to lean in to better observe the young girl with the fiery red hair, only to recede again.

Imelda crawled across to a sturdy tree trunk and kneeling, giggled uncontrollably as she swept the residue of water from her skin. It was another sensation to stir memories and give substance to 'naughty' thoughts,

She leaned against the tree and closed her eyes and thrilled to the plethora of interwoven colours behind her lids. She gave a gasp as finger tips drawing lazy circles across her stomach thrilled her almost to delirium.

She once again called to the Wicked Witch from within her mind and invited a confrontation.

CHAPTER 24

She experienced bodily contractions and emitted a sharp keening sound as she grabbed the mulch and dispersed it.

Opening her eyes had her vision swim in and out of focus. She gave a start when the tree she was leaning against appeared to creak and sigh. Looking up she was witness to its branches becoming fluid and sinewy, as with tentacles. She even believed they meant to ensnare and embrace her.

She needed to battle the poison's influence and relentlessly slapped her thighs to regain feeling and substance. With the tree looming over her she almost screamed and reacted by slapping her face several times.

'Is that all you've got?' she clamoured, as she wondered if the Wicked Witch had turned the woodland against her. 'Give it your best shot, bitch! I'm not afraid of you!'

The tremors to have taken control of her limbs slowly subsided when the urge to throw herself to the side and vomit came over her. She gave a despairing moan and dry-heaved a couple of times as pain flared in her chest.

Imelda felt herself slumping to the carpet of mulch, all her strength having seeped away. Panic flared the moment she felt pressure between her shoulder blades. Her back and the nape of her neck was being kneaded, yet not in an unpleasant way. A hand, and it was indeed a hand, moved lower and weaved an intricate pattern on her lower back and flanks.

It had her relaxing as any fear was magically removed. Lank trails of her hair obscured a view of the person at her side, if indeed her saviour was real and not imaginary. She was made to moan as the hand pushed around her buttocks, giving pleasure and not pain.

'Are you the Wicked Witch of the Woods?' she muttered, believing a spell had been cast to sap her strength.

The hand continued to stimulate her as it rubbed the backs of her thighs with purposeful fluidity.

There was no answer from the shadowy entity. There were no sudden movements to have her wonder if the person was a threat.

She again tried to lift her head to gain a view and the moment the hand returned to the back of her neck; Imelda felt the first stirrings of concern. She collapsed onto the bed of dry and brittle leaves as all substance oozed from her arms.

She was still conscious when she felt herself being pulled unceremoniously onto her side, expecting the worst, only to have a person's arm slip across her back the other beneath her legs. She was lifted almost as if she weighed no more than a feather.

There came definition to her saviour's profile as she wrapped her arms around his neck and was carried away from the gurgling brook. As her eyelids intermittently fluttered the constant tiny explosions of colour were dispelled. She had focus for a time and there came confusion. Imelda was of the opinion she recognised the person carrying her, not that she understood how it was possible.

She was a witness to a young man who was perhaps around the same age. He had a coronet of tight blond curls and effeminate features. Pretty, she was thinking, over ruggedly handsome.

She was hoping the magic of the woods had granted her wish, to have her prince appear to her in the flesh. The young man was gazing along the precarious path through the undergrowth and not on her.

She sighed to think she was safe and secure, having her prince with her, as it meant she did not have to face the sorcery the Wicked Witch meant to inflict on her.

When moonlight kissed his face the dark around his eyes faded to a pale blue.

Imelda snuggled her chin into the crook of his neck, surprised she should feel comfortable in her nakedness. Her prince was bare-chested and she delighted in the feel of his skin, tracing lines across his smooth chest and around firm nipples.

He casually glanced at her and had her wondering if he meant to stop and kiss her. She studied his mouth, the fullness of his lips and in the way they were parted slightly to reveal teeth so white, they gleamed where the lunar light touched his face.

She considered the way he held her, her hip rubbing his belly, the way in which one hand was pressed against a breast, not that she meant to admonish him for an indiscretion. Her prince had arrived to rescue her from the clutches of the Wicked Witch. He had placated her as the poison in her veins made her ill.

TALK TO THE ANIMALS

'I feel like I know you,' she murmured, just as her focus fragmented once again.

The bouncy, jerky movements as her saviour forged a path through the thicket had her feeling nauseous again. She inhaled sharply as the press of vegetation dissipated and tried to understand how the young man knew where to take her, for she was again back at the shelter, her home.

Something did not sit right with the situation and confusion served to fuel her anxiety. The important thing was in that she was safe.

She was lowered to her feet at the base of the incline she was expected to scale to reach the ledge. She wobbled unsteadily and hugged the lower section of the edifice for support. She giggled, as the rock she clutched became metamorphic. It had her squirming. Her prince had his hands on her hips to prevent her stumbling.

'I'll help you to climb up,' came a soft voice worming a passage into her head. 'I won't let you fall.'

His hands gripped her more firmly and as she was reluctant or incapable of movement, one dropped to a thigh and raised her foot to the sloping edifice to get a purchase.

Imelda leaned forward and clawed her way up as hands moved to support her buttocks. She was unsure if the contact thrilled or appalled her. It take time and effort and eventually she made it safely to the ledge. The gaping maw of the shelter was only a short distance from her precarious position, even as Imelda saw it as a daunting feat to get to it without losing balance and falling away from the edge.

TALK TO THE ANIMALS

Her gallant rescuer suggestively pinned her to the rock wall and with hands on her waist, helped guide her to take small steps until they reached the opening. Imelda was relieved and could only think of her bed to lie on. Her mind and body seemed saturated with emotional responses caused by the flow of poison in her veins.

Her prince still held her at the waist as Dog leapt off his cot to greet her and the stranger. Not that Dog acted as if he was greeting a stranger. He did not bark or snarl and bare his teeth. He seemed to be smiling and with his tail wagging frantically.

He sniffed her scent before satisfying himself the stranger was not a threat.

'Good dog,' Imelda giggled and liking the possessive way she was being held. 'This is my knight in shining armour, Dog. Did I not tell you, he would come looking for me?'

Having lost all substance in her limbs she would have dropped onto the cot had the young man not supported her. She was further surprised the ball of fur who was Cat had not perked up to see what the commotion was. Her indifference was as confounding as Dog's behaviour.

Imelda closed her eyes for a moment and purred with contentment the moment she felt the coverlet being drawn over her to settle at her chin.

'Thank you,' she mumbled. 'I couldn't have made it back without you.'

'You should be wary of what you eat,' a voice answered. The young man had spoken his first words and Imelda was delighted.

TALK TO THE ANIMALS

Dog was sniffing her ear and then scrunched down to settle against her.

Directing conversation at her saviour and not to dog she enquired as to whether he was hungry or thirsty. Her heavy eyelids struggled to open and even then, all before her was a blur with colour at the fringes of her vision.

'Strange,' she said in soft tones, 'It feels as if we have met already. How can that be possible though? Unless, you appeared in my dreams. That has to be it. I made a wish and the magic of the woods has made it come true.'

'If you are okay now, I should leave,' the young man answered, his voice coming to her from the far reaches of a deep tunnel.

'No! Please, where will you go?'

'I sleep under the trees.'

'Really? You live in these woods?'

He did not answer, as if he was suddenly reluctant to admit why he was there and living amongst the trees.

She patted a vacant space on the crib beside her.

'Dog can shift over to make room. It's comfortable. I made these myself.'

'Probably full of bugs.'

'No different to sleeping under the stars.'

He went quiet again as he caught her studying his face. She was seeing his golden halo, despite his features swimming in and out of focus.

'Stay,' and her whispering tone suggested she was wheedling.

She went to raise a hand as if she meant to trace a smile. She couldn't find him and wondered if she was imagining his presence. All became unbearably real when she felt a weight easing down alongside her, fingers touching her cheek and removing wayward strands of hair from her face.

'Do you have a name?' she enquired softly, sleepily.

'I'm surprised you don't remember,' a husky voice answered.

'Why do you say that?'

He was again reluctant to answer.

Imelda sensed her prince studying her in the shadow and gloom. He was resting his weight on an elbow. Finger tips lingered against her neck. She felt his sultry warmth, his close proximity. Imelda held a breath as feelings evoked from this stirred forgotten memories.

'Do you consider me beautiful?' she asked.

'You know you are beautiful,' came a whispered reply in a voice which had lost its youthful timbre.

Imelda raised a hand and let it float aimlessly until her own fingertips connected with a frown around a generous mouth.

'What are you thinking?' she asked. 'I hope you are not going to change into a monster and take advantage. Did the Wicked Witch send you?'

TALK TO THE ANIMALS

'I would not, under any circumstances, take advantage. And no, I do not consider myself a monster.'

Even though her vision was better and she had clarity, much of his form and facial features were as a silhouette.

'Why do you sleep in the woods? Don't you have a home to call your own?'

'Like you, I ran away. Why don't you get some sleep? I'll watch over you.'

'You will stay? Please.'

He lay down and straightened his limbs with Dog grumbling and climbing off the cot to get some privacy.

Imelda closed her eyes, leaving her arm to drape his bare torso. In her befuddled state of mind, she allowed finger tips to caress his smooth chest and dared to tease her fingers lower.

Well, you're wearing shorts, that's something,' she mumbled against his bicep. 'Do you have other possessions?'

'I didn't think it was important at the time to put together a wardrobe once I made up my mind to leave the orphanage.'

He sighed and sucked down a breath to feel her fingertips beneath the waist band of his shorts, even though Imelda had drifted into sleep. Her breathing was raspy yet steady, the stale warmth gliding over his skin.

He smiled in the darkness as he was feeling fortuitous to have found Imelda and to be alongside the remarkable and beautiful young woman he was obsessed with. He was aware there existed darker elements to her persona and had been a frequent witness to those moments. Unlike Imelda, Aidan had not pulled a comfortable shroud across his memories.

He closed his eyes, thinking; this is nice. *Better than I could have hoped for. Imelda! Imelda!* And he played her name repetitively in his head. Sleep finally stole his thoughts and he was to sleep with a broad smile on his face.

CHAPTER 25

Dawn was breaking when Imelda spiralled out of a deep and disturbing slumber, not that she was able to recall the content of her dreams. She knew, they had been ominously dark and left her close to panic and breathing raggedly.

Her head pounded a discordant timpani.

She was unable to recall her dreams however, she remembered her prince materialising in the woods, at a time of despair. He had lifted and carried her to the shelter as she was no weight. She could have been a feather or a leaf.

Desperation had her whipping her head to the side and it was then she saw him in the flesh, an amorphous shape in the muted early morning light.

He'd stayed and was lying beside her, his naked, slender back tapering away where loose cargo pants hugged his hips. Dog was on the other side and was another sleeping peacefully, with her prince's arm draping Dog's neck.

Imelda rolled onto her side so that she could drink in the sight of him. Despite the gloom, shadow could not erase the weal's and welts criss-crossing his torso where livid lines disappeared beneath the waistband of his shorts.

TALK TO THE ANIMALS

She felt sure they were residual marks from numerous beatings and she was horrified to think her prince had been made to suffer.

A deluge of impure thought streaked her mind and tightened her chest.

She was naked!

He had seen her naked!

Dear God!

What impressed her was in the manner he had conducted himself at all times. At no time had he imposed his will when she was at her most vulnerable. He had carried her home and stayed to watch over her in the night. It meant, he had been concerned. He cared for her.

He was the one she had been fantasising about and spoke of with fondness to the animals, birds, and the trees of the woods.

He bore the scars of his own tormented existence.

She dared to reach across the short space separating them and trace tremulous digits along the pattern of raised and indented weal's traversing his back, all the way down to where his tan ended and the white of his buttocks were a glaring contrast. The horrid scars continued out of sight into his shorts and she was appalled.

Imelda inhaled and held a breath when she felt him react and tense under her tender scrutiny. He was awake.

Indecision had her remove her hand and she dared not move.

TALK TO THE ANIMALS

Last night had been different; her mind relayed to her. She was under the influence of mind-expanding mushrooms and for a time, was not immersed in reality when her prince appeared to her.

Now, was reality, and she wasn't sure how to react.

'Thank you,' and her words seeped out on a steady, slow exhalation of breath.

'You're welcome,' came his answer, even though he was disinclined to make any sudden movements.

'I must apologise, as I was unwell when you came to my rescue. I'm okay now. Well, better than I was.'

'You were as high as a kite.'

His retort came, not as a condemnation, more like an observation.

'I must ask, but have you been watching me from time to time?'

He did not reply immediately as Imelda was thinking on the two occasions she'd bathed at the tiny rock pool and believed she had not been alone on the atoll.

As he was reluctant to give an answer Imelda saw it as proof of his guilt.

'Why didn't you introduce yourself on those occasions?' she queried.

'I wasn't sure how you'd react, if I'm honest.'

It was him! Her mind exclaimed, and not the Wicked Witch of the Woods she secretly feared was stalking her.

TALK TO THE ANIMALS

'I didn't want you freaking out,' he remarked, and she was witness to the tension seeping from his posture. 'You had no clothes on.'

'I was naked last night. You carried me home and put me to bed. I'm naked now, and you're here beside me.'

'I stayed to make sure you didn't go staggering outside and lose balance on the ledge or be sick again.'

'Yes, gross. Sorry. And again, thank you.'

There came a moment when the silence was like a heavy shroud.

'How did you get those marks on your back?' she enquired.

He gave a haughty chuckle as if to say, it was no big deal. 'We all wear them. Receiving regular beatings was their way of controlling us.'

'You said, we. Who are you referring to? Who was it exerting control?'

'Fuck! You really don't remember anything, or do you choose not too?'

Imelda was unable to answer as her mind was clamouring to reveal events she had suppressed since arriving at the woods. She didn't want to remember and held the deluge at bay.

Pouting, she said, 'I don't bear scars as you do.'

As there was another moment of hesitancy she again traced the garish lines on his back, as if to remind her they were real.

127

TALK TO THE ANIMALS

'I have seen your scars,' he answered, tensing again with her tender and sensual touch.

Imelda was speechless and did not want to believe him. She stiffened perceptibly the moment he shifted position, turned and was facing her. She froze, saw the way his eyes affixed on her face before sliding down the length of her body, as she had expected he might.

Men couldn't help themselves; she told herself.

He took his time looking along her nakedness and Imelda quickly ascertained she didn't mind him staring. He wasn't exactly ogling her with a lascivious expression. Instead, he was perusing a canvas, as with a work of art, and was giving the subject consideration and his admiration. For that reason, she did not try to cover her modesty.

She surprised herself, in the way she leaned away, so that the soft light at the entrance to the shelter found a way to highlight her gentle curves and softness. She flicked her hair back coquettishly and rested her weight on an arm. She blatantly cast her gaze to his chest and embraced the moment as one to forge a new memory.

'Do you not remember anything?' he quietly persisted. 'As to why you ran away from the orphanage?'

'I don't remember having a life before I came here,' she answered him ruefully. 'I don't recall the orphanage you mentioned. I don't want to remember if you must know. I live here. This is my home.'

'The day you ran away, I left soon after and came to look for you. I'm surprised the cops haven't been called. I have no idea why it surprises me, as the ones who run the orphanage are not likely to invite the law or social services in case they delve deeper into the running of the home and uncover their sordid, squalid secrets.'

'Lucky for me, I have no idea what you're talking about or who you are referring to,' she countered.

He suddenly smiled and even in the gloom she saw the beauty in his smile. His face was beautiful, she conceded. She loved his thick blond curls. Having him alongside her seemed natural and she felt an affinity with him. Everything about him under her scrutiny let her know it was familiar, as if she knew him. Had known him, before this moment. He was speaking truthfully, not that she was comfortable with his narrative of a life he had fled from.

As she had.

He was no longer perusing her nudity was, at the same time, studying her face.

He continued to smile. She let a hand hug his hip.

'You broke into the car abandoned on the road,' he said, as a statement and not as an accusation. 'I noticed the bags of goodies. You got there ahead of me. I would have done the same.'

'Needs must,' she answered him. 'It must be awful, you sleeping rough on the ground, amongst the trees and shrubs.'

'This is cosy. You have made it cosy. It doesn't surprise me if you must know. I have always known you to be independent, smart, a survivor. I imagine you could put your mind to anything to get by.'

TALK TO THE ANIMALS

Again, he was describing a life he believed she had led before arriving at the magical woods and making a home in the shelter. It had her feeling uncomfortable and disoriented.

In respect of the way he looked at her she let the hand trail away from his hip and allowed fingers to outline his ever-present smile.

'Do you want to kiss me?' and her question surprised and dumbfounded her, not knowing where the idea or inclination came from.

'I would like it if I was the only one. You were different to all the other girls. Courageous but just a little bit crazy. Nothing seemed to faze you. You were someone who did whatever came to mind. A reason you often crossed the boundaries and flouted their laws, not that you cared if your behaviour was to invite recrimination. Damn, girl, you were a law to yourself. A force to be reckoned with. No matter what Stibley did, he couldn't break you.'

Imelda cogitated the name he had spoken, not that it was familiar to her.

She felt her chest tightening as she urged those memories crawling to the surface, to recede.

He caught him glancing down to where she felt a tightness in her chest. He let a single digit brush a nipple and had her gasping.

'Kiss me,' she implored softly and trembling with anticipation.

Instead, the hand moved to push her long lank hair around her shoulder to fall at her back and then he was stroking her cheek and underside of her chin. His tenderness was exquisite and had her closing her eyes and moving closer. She moulded herself to his frame.

She opened her eyes and they became dilated as her vision began to swim in and out of focus. She drew lazy circles on his chest, clawed his stomach, and as she leaned away slightly felt his hand supporting the nape of her neck. His other hand splayed one thigh, fingers trailing away, their intent obvious to her. The application of a kiss was to set off fireworks behind her lids as she closed her eyes and duelled with his inquisitive tongue.

She pressed closer and thrilled to the hardness of his torso rubbing her skin. He had her moan and couldn't help herself, raked his back with her nails, inflamed his scars.

He suddenly pulled away and when she opened her eyes to beseech him continue, believed he was blushing.

Why she stated her claim, she had no idea, yet asked him if he was a virgin. She caught his shy nod in answer to her query and liked that his face had softened. Imelda smiled and moved one of her hands to his chest, teasing a nipple before allowing its journey lower. She gave another involuntary moan to discover he was aroused and the unexpected physical contact had him grunting and breathing erratically.

'Me too,' she confessed, not that she believed she was a virgin, and not because she could remember losing her virginity. She only wanted to put him at ease.

Aidan had almost laughed aloud at her remark, as his own memory was not impaired. He knew her history. He'd watched her incessant teasing, not that he was one to judge. He was not about to say either as he didn't want to provoke her. Imelda could be sweet and light, effervescent and wantonly sexual. He was also aware of her dark side, in that she had a temper, and in that she could be spiteful when provoked.

He said nothing to the contrary, as the way she was conducting herself and giving pleasure to him, went beyond his wildest fantasies.

CHAPTER 26

Imelda was joyous and believed life could not be better. She lay on her back, the roof above blurred by a shimmer and film of tears. Her thigh muscles still trembled and her heart beat loud.

Her prince was beside her, himself recovering from their exertions, those she had brazenly instigated.

She was given to thinking and her smile was quick to dissipate as doors within her mind became unlocked and unbidden.

She didn't relish the prospect of her ghosts suddenly parading themselves for scrutiny. The past hour in the arms of her prince had been sublimely beautiful and did not want the feeling to go away.

Imelda sat up, knowing she had to compose herself and do something useful to occupy her mind.

She gazed down on Aidan's nudity. He had his eyes closed but didn't think he was sleeping. She hoped, he was savouring his elation.

'Are you hungry?' she asked him and leaning a cheek against her shoulder.

TALK TO THE ANIMALS

Aidan turned and rested his weight on an elbow, nodded, and trying not to look smug.

Imelda noticed how Dog had sidled up to him and was getting attention from Aidan in the form of pats and fur scrunching.

'He likes you,' Imelda said. 'I'm surprised if you must know. Like, when you carried me into the shelter and lay be down on the cot, I thought perhaps, he might have challenged you.'

Aidan wanted to explain this was not the first occasion he had acquainted himself with Dog. In the few days and nights, he had spent undercover of trees in the woods and on the occasions he went hunting and foraging for something to eat, he'd befriended the animal. Probably around the same time Imelda had.

He caught her looking around for Cat who had taken herself off earlier. She'd done a lot of grumbling having been disturbed from a contented slumber. Imelda hadn't noticed. She'd been in her own world for a time. Giving and receiving pleasure removed all substance of their environs at that moment.

Imelda went to rise and hesitated when a hand came up to grasp her upper thigh. She leaned low to kiss Aidan on the mouth and scampered away to where the bags of provisions were heaped against the wall.

There was not much by way of fresh produce remaining and did not think it wise to use the leftover sausages and bacon noticing they had discoloured and gave off a sweet and noisome aroma which had her wrinkling her nose. She thought it too risky, even for Dog.

TALK TO THE ANIMALS

'We only have biscuits and chocolate. There's also some boiled sweets,' she said, almost apologetically. She was devastated deep-down as she would have liked to have given her prince a hearty meal.

'It's okay,' he answered her. 'I'll go and forage for something, anything, later'

Imelda froze in a crouched position as her mind went suddenly blank.

'Could you dispose of the litter when you go?' she asked and snapping free of the inertia a particular thought had manifested. 'But not in the woods. I don't want us to be one of those inconsiderate types who ruin our countryside by leaving their litter behind.'

'Okay. So, what do you propose to do with yourself while I'm gone?'

Imelda didn't answer immediately as she unwrapped the last of the jumbones and tossed it to an eager dog.

She crawled to Aidan's position with two milk chocolate bars and a half packet of digestives, and what was left of the fruit juice. She hoped it was okay.

He sat up as she nestled her rump between his thighs and with a contented smile, passed him a share of their meagre rations. Despite feeling at ease there were still images vying for attention within her mind and they were given clarity. They seemed real and fresh and didn't think they were spawned from a fanciful imagination.

TALK TO THE ANIMALS

These were images to have ignited when she was rummaging around in the bags and clutching the packet of biscuits.

It had taken her back to a time when she was much younger and creeping around a dark kitchen. The spacious room had lost its familiarity however, seemed strange and alien in her mind. A voice reverberated around her thoughts letting her know she was being naughty and breaking rules.

The door to the kitchen was always locked and on this occasion she was able to enter as a key had been left in the lock. It had been a fortuitous oversight by someone, not that she could remember who it was made the rules.

In her mind she saw varying shapes cast in gloom and shadow, and she remembered knocking her hip on a small table as she crept around the kitchen. On one of the work surfaces she saw her hands smothering a large rectangular tin and when tremulous digits prised open the lid saw the packet of digestive biscuits. She remembered a feeling of elation, briefly, as suddenly her hair was yanked brutally by someone creeping up behind.

The vision ended there and it left Imelda wondering why she had to steal food. Where was she at that time? And who was it tugging her hair?

She couldn't and wouldn't admit her thoughts to her prince and how they made her feel. Just having Aidan with her and feeling him along her back helped quell her tremors and dismissed those thoughts and images from her mind.

Having finished the chocolate and biscuits they tentatively shared the juice.

TALK TO THE ANIMALS

It was all deliciously intimate; Imelda was thinking, especially as he allowed his free hand to occasionally massage a shoulder or play with her hair. She liked it even more when he swept an arm round across her stomach and pulled her tight to his frame and lightly tickled her.

She remained wary of the fact even good things in life could be tested and might invariably change. She supposed, not all in the real world could be trusted. She trusted the magical woods and its inhabitants, Dog and Cat, and even her Prince.

'I'm going to make you something to wear,' she quipped exuberantly, just to fragment the pall of silence in the shelter. 'My prince is deserving of the best.'

Aidan wasn't about to answer. He already believed he had the best of everything. It was all he ever dreamed of.

He had kissed and made love to her. They were like a couple.

He leaned back slightly to again run his fingers through her flaming red hair. With her head sliding down to nestle in his lap he stooped to kiss her. He felt her unravelling, became immersed in a tide of desire, and knew instinctively his foraging trip into the woods to find food would wait.

CHAPTER 27

Aidan had not returned as afternoon encroached, Imelda delighted Dog chose to go with him on his quest to find something to sustain them.

It was a summery day and pleasantly warm, and as Imelda had completed the task she had given herself in Aidan's absence which was fashioning a loincloth of interwoven leaves, Imelda decided to take a leisurely sojourn into the woods.

She hoped it would permanently clear her mind of any lingering traces of those memories she had no understanding of.

In her mind, she believed it was her solemn duty as a princess, to parade herself around her magical domain and commune with nature and its inhabitants.

Dressed in her own two-piece leafy ensemble and clutching a deep vessel of aged bark she left her shelter to start her own adventure.

Her period seemed to have settled and she had declined using a tampon. The thought made her smile, as even in her delicate position, she had refused to let the unpleasantness of her monthlies spoil the intimate experience she'd had with her prince.

TALK TO THE ANIMALS

He had confessed to her he was a virgin, not that she could have surmised he was, as he had been a considerate and diligent lover to her. He was neither clumsy or in a rush and seemed to know exactly, what was required to satisfy his princess. He did not disappoint.

The memory of their frenetic coupling stamped a smile on her face and she wore it with pride as she forged a trail through the undergrowth.

She was overjoyed to meet with a squirrel during one of her frequent breaks. He was quite nonchalant and naturally inquisitive of her.

'Good afternoon,' she called to the cute little animal with its silvery grey fur coat, bushy tail, and large eyes. 'Are you having a good day?'

'I suppose,' said the squirrel whose inertia was broken as he skipped around willy-nilly, tail bobbing and flicking side to side and up and down as he dug in the mulch for food. *'I need to start storing enough food for the winter.'*

Imelda giggled.

'My prince has gone in search for tonight's meal,' she stated.

'Good luck with that. Food doesn't just fall off trees, you know. Actually, mine does.'

The squirrel seemed to echo her joy.

'It's a pleasure, to finally meet with the beautiful princess of the woods,' said the squirrel and continuing to forage. *'Word gets around.'*

TALK TO THE ANIMALS

'It's nice that you think I'm beautiful.'

'You better believe it, young lady. You have the magic flowing in your veins and can have whatever you want. Your beauty alone will bring you great rewards, as it always has. Stands to reason; you like the attention.'

'And what do you mean with your remark, Mister Squirrel?'

'You are wondering if I am the Wicked Witch of the Woods,' the squirrel responded.

'No. But tell me, have you met her?'

'Naturally, as has your prince.'

'Rubbish. My prince would have said, had he met with her. Do you know where I might find her? The witch?'

'Look no further than between your thighs for the truth,' said the squirrel in a surly voice.

Imelda was struck speechless by Mister Squirrel's unexpected insult and the way he dismissed her presence by turning his back on her.

TALK TO THE ANIMALS

CHAPTER 28

Imelda was glad to be on her way once more even as she wished Mister Squirrel had not taunted her and by doing so, offer her the key which could open another of the doors within her mind.

Despite the denseness of undergrowth, she strode through it purposefully, rather than pick her way cautiously. Bursting suddenly into a clearing where the brightness of the sun seared her retinas, she sought the shade beneath a very mature and stout oak tree.

She tried to focus on her surroundings and not feel inclined to rummage around the squalid vaults within her mind where memories were clamouring for release.

'You must first face your ghosts, in order to exorcise them,' and she believed the tree had spoken to her. She craned her head up to have a view of the welcoming arms of its powerful boughs.

'What could you possibly know?' she enquired.

'More than you can imagine, as I am an ancient oak of centuries standing. I have witnessed much and in my time, have learned the old ways and the new.'

141

TALK TO THE ANIMALS

Imelda shuffled position and lay her hands palms down on the rough bark of its immense torso.

'Why would I torment myself and summon my ghosts, as you suggest I do?'

'*Understanding,*' said the tree. '*You may be loath to face the truth, but sometimes child, it is better to confront our worst nightmares, in order to have empowerment over them.*'

'I may learn more than I wish to know,' she admitted thoughtfully, and imagined the torso in her grasp was metamorphosing into human form. It was impossible; she told herself. Aware there was magic in the woods, the idea of a tree becoming a person was horrifying to her. She closed her eyes so that was not witness to the change as fear coursed along her veins.

Her hands were still splayed across the trunk and felt the trees inimitable power at her fingertips. She was suddenly welcoming its threat. As it was, she concluded, she truly feared nothing.

Not even death.

'*What can you remember so far?*' the tree inside her head asked.

'None of your business.'

'*What is it you are feeling at this moment?*'

'What do you mean?'

'*Admit it, the magic you possess has changed me. You feel my ancient power, my hardness, and you are thinking I am your prince, come to save and protect you from your past.*'

TALK TO THE ANIMALS

'You are not my prince. I know that much, even with my eyes closed.'

'I am no longer a tree in your mind as you crave more. The Wicked Witch of the Woods has been awakened and is seeking sustenance.'

Imelda shoved away from the tree and its sinuous taunts and fell sprawling into the mulch. Her eyes were shocked open as a high-pitched squawk slammed through her head. She saw the reason as her hand had alighted on a warm-bodied creature and her weight was pressing it into the ground.

Horrified, she released the grouse who was still alive, yet stunned and could not get up onto its spindly legs.

'Sorry, bird, I didn't mean you any harm.'

'Didn't appear that way from my perspective,' the grouse grunted miserably and trying still to get its breath back. *'You were angry. Not at the tree, but angry at your own shame. You act like you're horrified, yet you are the one instigating your own problems. You invite trouble and always have done.'*

'I do not!' Imelda protested and feeling the need to defend herself.

'You can't help yourself,' the bird accused her. *'Because you crave attention. You can't deny it.'*

'The Wicked Witch has possessed your soul!'

'Ha! Is that what you believe? The Wicked Witch is between your legs. Ask the tree. The tree knows everything, for he is ancient and wise.'

TALK TO THE ANIMALS

'I don't have to stay and listen to your poisonous barbs,' and turning to the tree, exclaimed, 'Oh, so you no longer flaunt yourself as a man and wish to impose your cruel will on me! You are back to being a stupid old oak!'

'And how's the Wicked Witch?' the Tree seemed to sneer. *'Does she seek assurance and sustenance. Will it make you feel better if you had them?'*

'If I had an axe, I would hack and hack and keep chopping until I have you on your knees!'

'Such a kind heart.'

I have no wish to stay and mix with unfriendly types. I am leaving.'

TALK TO THE ANIMALS

CHAPTER 29

The tree's hurtful accusations and taunts were swiftly dismissed from her mind as she continued attacking the vegetation with singular purpose.

She was angry and acted as a ferocious knot in the pit of her stomach. She believed the Wicked Witch had cast a spell on the mighty oak and had it transformed into a man. The image stayed to haunt her and was to settle in her loins. She felt the seeds of panic take root, as they had done the day she had fled to the woods. She caught herself whimpering. Her cheeks were damp with tears.

In time, the woodland opened out onto an area of undulating pasture, and it was a sight to take her breath away.

The magic within the woods to have gripped her was momentarily dispelled, as Imelda realised there had to exist a barrier separating the real world from the magical influence she had embraced since fleeing to the woods and making it her home.

The real world beckoned, a world she had left behind as it was a festering canker. Not so with the woods as, despite its witchery, it was the safer option.

TALK TO THE ANIMALS

Imelda caught sight of a rabbit hopping around a clump of fern.

'You are a long way from the warren and your family,' she said.

'Like you, I am lost! Tragic! Tragic!' clamoured the rabbit as it danced in tight circles.

'I am not lost,' Imelda countered.

'You're not? Then why are you here?'

'I'm on an adventure, since you ask.'

'I see, an adventure, as you are seeking the truth.'

'As a matter of fact, I have no wish to find the truth.'

'You're so close! So close!'

'Why would you say that?'

'It's why you're here, isn't it? Just a few miles, over yonder, is where you will find your answers. Sometimes, you must go back, just to get to where you are.'

'How would you know? You're just a silly rabbit hopping around in circles, and lost,' Imelda remarked. 'Do you consort with the Wicked Witch?'

'The Wicked Witch?' and Imelda believed the rabbit was chuckling, goading her.

It made her angry.

It was the moment the rabbit stopped hopping around and froze.

TALK TO THE ANIMALS

'Do you feel her presence? She's everywhere! She's close!'

'How close?'

'You know the answer to your question. The old oak knows. All in the woods are aware of the Wicked Witch. You are the only one, it appears, who does not see with the vision you have been given.'

Imelda was confused and shaken. She had arrived at the woods in a fearful state, yet it was her home, and not even the Wicked Witch was going to take it from her.

The Wicked Witch no longer conceals herself,' said Rabbit. *'She has been released and her power grows. Do you feel it?'*

'Yes, and she is turning the woods against me.'

'You have to take back control, princess,' Rabbit remarked, hopped around some more with curiosity having him move closer.

'How am I supposed to take back control?' Imelda asked.

The Rabbit leaned its head to divulge advice in barely a whisper.

'Your power,' Rabbit said and paused, to add dramatic weight to his proclamation, *'Lies as it always has, between your thighs.'*

Imelda's eyes widened and darkened with shock. She had no words to convey.

CHAPTER 30

Once she arrived at the brook Imelda felt the relief flood into her veins knowing, if she followed the chuckling flow of water, she would eventually come to the atoll and home.

Removing her trainers and carrying them by looping fingers through the laces, Imelda waded upstream, thrilling to the coolness and currents of the water.

It seemed to take an eternity, her legs and arms aching, and she only stopped to gather a varied collection of mushrooms. Using the long blade of granite, she had brought with her, Imelda occasionally dug and prised-up a selection of succulent and edible roots to compliment the meal she meant to prepare for her prince, Dog, and Cat.

She ignored the darkening bloodstains along the length of the weapon she grasped. What became difficult to ignore was the deepening gloom hugging the shrubbery either side of the brook as the sun began to dip away.

It was late afternoon by the time she reached the shelter. The heavy pall of sadness to have blighted her day's adventure was dispelled the moment she saw the capering streaks of firelight in the mouth of the cave.

Dog greeted her as she scampered up the edifice. She balanced the wood vessel in one arm, while feeling her way along the narrow ledge.

TALK TO THE ANIMALS

Her prince was recumbent on the crib and came alert to her sudden arrival. It was apparent he was eager to greet her and leapt sprightly to his bare feet and went to her. Imelda placed the wood vessel and blade on the floor against the wall and flung her arms around his neck. She wanted neither to speak or to be spoken to, desired only to savour his kiss and feel his hands sculpting her body.

The kiss was passionate and as she had hoped for, his hands were explorative and demanding.

'I was worried,' he eventually said and was first to break contact.

Imelda was having none of it and instigated another kiss. She heard a manic taunting cackle reverberating in her head and supposed the Wicked Witch was close or watching them as a reflection in her boiling cauldron of poison broth.

A while later both parties reluctantly ended the embrace to regain their breath.

She laughed. She was joyous. Her prince made her feel special.

'Are you going to tell me how you got on today?' she enquired with rising anticipation as she bathed in his beauty and strength and dove headlong into the fathomless pools of his eyes. She was giddy and believed she might faint.

'We lucked-out,' he admitted, grim-faced. 'Had I a spear or bow and arrow, I could have bagged us two deer. Something to think about. I could probably fashion a weapon of sorts if I put my mind to it. A slingshot or catapult; that would work. Yeah, but I would need elastic or string to make it work effectively.

TALK TO THE ANIMALS

Now, if I had a proper knife. Should have thought about that when I ran away. Shit! Sucks!'

He was babbling nervously and getting annoyed so Imelda kissed him, on the mouth and on the chest.

'It's lucky for us I came good getting us a meal for tonight,' she remarked around a smile etched with mischief. The Witch was chuckling. Changing the conversation abruptly she enquired as to whether he had seen Cat.'

'She was on the cot asleep when we returned and scampered off soon after.'

Imelda nodded, satisfied, and then she was crouching and grabbing his hand to join her. She held up the selection she had gathered on her personal adventure and was witness to amazement on his face. She saw pride in the way he looked at her and it meant so much to her at the time. She was letting him know they were a team and was quite capable of providing essentials when it became of necessity to do so.

She raised the wooden bowl for careful inspection.

'Wow!' he exclaimed and puffed his cheeks.

Heaped in the depression of the basket was a squirrel and rabbit, having been smote with a single killing blow of her improvised dagger. A grouse had been horribly distorted from having its bones crushed and its neck broken. He saw an array of vegetable roots and a few varieties of mushroom. He recognised one species and raised an eyebrow.

'I'm impressed,' he said and was evidently in awe of her achievements. 'You do realise, the smaller mushrooms make you ill.'

TALK TO THE ANIMALS

'They also expand the mind. And get me horny. We should both try them later.'

He nodded without adding a comment which might express his disapproval and ruin a beautiful moment.

Casting her gaze to one side as she placed the bowl on the ground, she tittered.

'I'm impressed you were able to make a fire,' she said. 'Something you picked-up as a boy scout?'

'I remember watching a program on TV a while back. Something about being self-sufficient if the world went to Hell. Anyway, it was the sort of thing which became stuck in my head. I had these wild fantasies, you see, that I might one day, burn the orphanage down as payback for the torment I suffered.'

'Shit! Really?'

'I haven't. Not yet, anyway.'

Imelda took a moment to appraise him and wondered if he meant his words.

'Do you want to help me skin those bad boys and cook us up a royal feast?'

He nodded.

'Hey, Dog!' she called, 'We're going to eat in style tonight.'

Dog huffed a response.

'And we must save some food for Cat,' she added and swayed her body provocatively. 'I was forgetting, my prince, as I made you something earlier.'

She reluctantly released him and crossed to the foot of the crib knowing his eyes would be devouring her. It's what she wanted.

Imelda revealed the makeshift loincloth composed of succulent hardy leaves.

'What do you think?'

Aidan gave a chuckle as he examined the item of clothing she had fashioned for him.

'You want me to wear this?' he tittered.

'Yes, Tarzan. You can, at least, try it on and tell me what you think.'

'I'll tell you what I'm thinking; in that it's not going to cover much.'

She raised an eyebrow and he saw the mischief playing in the firelight reflected in her eyes.'

'That was my plan,' she teased. 'Now, out of those shorts, I want to see how this looks on my prince.'

His hesitation encouraged Imelda to take the initiative. She dropped to her knees and tugged his shorts down without bothering to unfasten them. Her eyes widened in amazement and anticipation, her mouth agape.

'Dinner can wait,' she said.

CHAPTER 31

Later, and with Cat having returned and demanding attention, Imelda and Aidan set about stripping and gutting the haul Imelda had accumulated on her travail into the woods. All the varieties of meat were carefully sliced into strips and fed to the hot plate covering the fire. Imelda crouched over it using her improvised chopsticks to frequently move and turn the meat so that they cooked evenly.

Cat and Dog were getting excited and could barely contain themselves and it was Aidan who held them back while the food was cooking. Cat was mewling while Dog was huffing and salivating.

The feast was everything they hoped it might be and when all was devoured with relish, they lay back and rested. Dog was noisy licking his muzzle and then going to a bowl to lap up water. Cat spent an eternity washing and grooming herself.

Imelda suddenly leapt to her feet and crossed to where she had left the mushrooms. She placed them on the hot plate and braised the eclectic and succulent mix in the meat juices. A couple of minutes was all it took and she then scooped them into a smaller vessel and carried them to their crib.

'Let's get a little high and crazy together,' she insisted lightly.

TALK TO THE ANIMALS

'Are you sure you want to do this?'

'Oh indeed, yes.'

'You do realise, the smaller ones are going to expand your mind. Are you ready to face your demons, should they assist in revealing your past?'

'I was told today by an ancient oak tree I should confront my ghosts so that I may exorcise them.'

Aidan gave her a querulous look. 'A tree told you this?'

'Yes,' she stated simply as if it was perfectly natural to hold a conversation with a tree.

She fed a small quantity of cooling mushrooms to his mouth, kissed him, and raising the bowl she intimated he was expected to do the same.

He did so and she grabbed his hand and held it, as if she meant to devour two of his fingers. She released him when she was witness to his uncertainty and growing discomfort. They took turns feeding one another until the bowl was empty.

Imelda slumped along the length of the crib as the poisonous effects swept along her veins and ignited bright colours in her head. The bowl tumbled away as Aidan grabbed her hand and eased down beside her.

Neither said anything as they became prisoners to the magical world of distorted imagery within their minds.

Aidan raised the hand he dare not let go of and kissed the back of it before grimly clutching it to his chest. His flesh was afire, despite the fact he was trembling. He opened his eyes briefly and believed the ceiling above them was oozing, having acquired fluidity, and was constantly changing form.

He closed his eyes again as he felt the walls and ceiling pouring along his body and wondered if he was to be crushed.

'Jesus!' he cried. 'Honey, are you feeling anything?'

'My prince,' and her voice tapered away only to return fuelled with desperation. 'Don't leave me! The Wicked Witch has me under her spell.'

'No, baby, there is no Wicked Witch, I would know.'

'Yes, and she wants to take me on a spiritual journey.'

'Just tell her to fuck off!' and he laughed manically.

'She is too powerful. But it's okay.'

'Where is she taking you?'

'I don't know where I am, but it's beautiful and colourful.'

'Yes, I'm with you baby. I'm right beside you.'

She gave a gasp and a sigh.

'It makes no sense. I don't understand.'

'What are you seeing?'

'One minute I was in a tent and now I have been taken to a small room,' she said, her tone fading. 'There is a single bed with a metal frame, a mattress, but no covers. The only light is from a fat candle sat on a shelf.'

TALK TO THE ANIMALS

'The punishment room,' he informed her grimly. 'I should know, as I was another taken there. For a period of chastisement, I was told. If you didn't toe the line and conform to their rules, you were punished. They didn't tolerate antisocial behaviour, from anyone, no matter their age or sex.'

'Where is this place you speak of?' Imelda asked. 'The room and the tent stirred memories, but not those to make me fearful.'

'It is because, you have blotted it from your memory. You've returned to the orphanage,' he said, while gripping her hand tightly, as he was the one re-living a dark passage of time.

'I lived at this orphanage you speak of?' she enquired wistfully and caressing her stomach to invoke other memories.

'We both did, for a time,' he mumbled. 'They tried to keep the girls segregated from the boys. It didn't always work. If you got caught mixing with the opposite sex, you got punished. The bed you're seeing, if you were seen as a bad influence on the others, they would tie you to the headboard, naked, and beat you. It wasn't only the beating, they committed other disgusting stuff on those they saw as troublesome.'

'I do remember getting into trouble, often,' she answered and gave a little whine. 'I remember the occasional spanking. There was more, I know there was more. I don't want to think about it. I don't want to be in this room.'

'We're a team,' he said with more bravado than he was feeling. 'They can't touch you now.'

'Who are 'they'? What I fail to understand is how they managed to get away with punishing people today.'

TALK TO THE ANIMALS

'The Stibley's are clever. They knew how to pull the wool over the eyes of social services. All their paperwork was up to date, and always came across as model caring foster parents. They ruled with fear meaning, no one at the orphanage would dare complain.'

'Why did I run away? And how long was I at the orphanage?'

'Fucking Stibley,' he seemed to sneer. 'The situation worsened over time, and when Stibley's wife found out you were pregnant she gave you a poison to make you abort your baby.'

The revelation slammed Imelda's senses so that she began to convulse. Aidan came alert and leaned across her, hoping to placate her, except it made matters worse.

She let cry a piercing scream which had Dog barking dementedly.

'What are you going to do to me?' she spat and Aidan realised she was not directly talking to him, but one of the ghosts she was trying to exorcise.

'It's Aidan,' he expressed, even as the poison flowing in his veins distorted reality for him. 'I'm not the enemy. I'm your prince.'

'I was pregnant?'

'It would have been an abomination anyway,' he sneered contemptuously as was able to remember, even if Imelda could not. 'Everyone knew it had to be Stibley. Which is a reason his wife terminated it. She was another who was evil. She blamed you. She called you a witch and claimed you had cast a spell on her husband. You ran away soon after. I feared, for a moment, they had broken your spirit. It was a reason I fled and came looking for you.'

He chuckled.

'Before you ran away though, you plotted revenge against our gaolers.'

'Oh my God, but what did I do?'

He held and rocked her gently and she seemed to meld with him, to flow into him, knowing she was safe in his arms.

'What you did, babe, was take a log from the woodpile and cracked Stibley over the head with it. I wasn't a witness but by all accounts, you didn't relent until you gave the bastard a thorough beating. Following which, you went right up to his wife as she came at you with a rolling pin and just like that, you punched her lights out. You didn't stop there, as you were seen kicking the bitch in the head a few times, just for good measure.'

Imelda had no answering words. She believed Aidan's story, despite being unable to recall events of her past as he did. Her thoughts merely metamorphosed into a shadowy collage, except the one, which gathered momentum and clarity as she dwelt on it.

She was pregnant, her baby taken from her before she could conceive.

Imelda reacted by shoving Aidan in the chest and came against an immovable force. She shoved again with determined vigour and Aidan released her,

Ignoring the look on his face, one of hurt and surprise, Imelda leapt to her feet and ran outside, the fresh air striking her skin as with a chastising slap. She did not stop and shuffled along the ledge to where it stepped away to the woodland floor.

She was already fleeing into the woods by the time Aidan crawled to the hazardous precipice. He was unable to rise or give chase as he felt unwell.

Dog approached and sniffed his arm and hair before returning to the cot.

Aidan strained to keep the trees and shrubs from moving with fluidity. He believed they had acquired menace and instantly feared for his princess. Undeterred by his own predicament, Aidan crawled along the ledge to the steep gradient, intent on following Imelda and rescuing her from the spell she was under.

Imelda was keening and could not understand why the undergrowth was trying to haul her back. Her panic and anguish was perpetuated as each slap of a shrubbery frond was like a blow from someone's hand.

Exasperated, defeated, Imelda slumped to her knees and continued a feeble fight against the invisible hands she felt pawing her flesh. She put her forehead to the mulch and wept just as she believed the stultifying darkness had acquired substance.

'So, child, you have come looking for me?' came a familiar voice from within her mind.'

Imelda raised her head and tried to focus between ribbons of her hair streaking her face.

TALK TO THE ANIMALS

'The Wicked Witch of the Woods!' Imelda proclaimed. 'Why do you skulk in the darkness? Why won't you reveal yourself to me. Or is it, that you fear me?'

'If you fear yourself you will have your answer.'

'I am not afraid.'

'Yet you weep and grovel at my feet. You seek, not answers, but attention and security.'

'Where are you? Show yourself! I dare you! I double-dare you!'

'I am within you, child. I am your spirit, the blood in your veins. I am your voice and each one of your thoughts. I am the wind in your hair, the warmth on your skin. I am the architect of tears, the persistent ache in your loins. I am your joy as I am your rage. We are one.'

'I am not a witch. I am a princess and a good person.'

'You are a princess and your heart can be kind. Yet you choose to walk the corridors of darkness. You invite pain as if torment alone will grant you absolution. You manifest the darkness as an ally, to get all you desire.'

'I desire peace in my home in the woods, to live a life of joy with my prince.'

'Ah, child, there can never be peace when the soul remains tormented. You continue to doubt yourself and constantly crave attention, and that is where the Wicked Witch assists you.'

'How do you propose she assists me? That's silly. You're not my friend.'

TALK TO THE ANIMALS

'You have only to open your legs, child, for there lies your power and ultimately, your downfall. With every action there is a reaction, and it is not always what we hope for.'

'You're not real! It's the mushrooms!' Imelda conceded with a flurry of nods. 'The mushrooms invoked your spirit, not me. Why would I?'

'As you're aware, the mushrooms expand the mind where doors are opened, for spirits to leave and enter at will. The mushrooms free you from the imaginary shackles which have bound you to dark oblivion and doing so, has given you choices to make.'

Imelda lay down on the dank mulch and lazily clawed at a bed of brittle leaves.

'I'm tired,' she confessed. 'Leave me now. We will talk again when I am feeling better and I am lucid in my thinking.'

Imelda closed her eyes and was unable to react as bugs crawled over her skin to feed on her perspiration.

She yelped a frightful cry as hands grabbed her arms and tried to left her. She instinctively fought the person she believed meant to assault her and it was then, she invoked the Wicked Witch to assist her. She rolled over and raised her buttocks, anticipation stealing her breath.

'You will pay, I swear,' she hissed through clenched teeth.

Whatever the experience she was expecting, it did not materialise, as she was secretly hoping. She became mollified as she was turned and comforted and looking up through a glaze of tears, saw that her prince was the one comforting her and dispelling the call of the Wicked Witch.

He kissed her and she seemed to flow within him. She loved that he was tender in the way he let a hand caress her skin as she clung to him.

'Take me home, baby,' she sighed, even as the Wicked Witch chuckled her malicious intent and was to goad her on their way through the thicket to the shelter.

CHAPTER 32

Imelda woke the next morning, becoming instantly enamoured by the bright ethereal glow within the shelter. Dog and Cat were nowhere to be seen, but her prince was hard at work, it appeared.

He was using her sharp bladed tool and whittling away a thin, but sturdy section of a tree's bough, and seemed to be fashioning a spear from it.

What thrilled her more was seeing him wearing the leafy loin cloth she'd put together for him. He was right assuming it would not cover his modesty, not that it concerned him. For that matter, she found the view exciting.

He stopped shaving the point to observe her appraising him.

'You have a beautiful smile,' he said.

'I do?' and she gushed at the unexpected compliment.

'Everything about you is beautiful.'

'Are we to go hunting?' she enquired and easing onto her side. She looked down on her nudity with his eyes.

TALK TO THE ANIMALS

'We need to find food. We can't live on roots and mushrooms indefinitely. Dog has already shifted his arse. As for Cat, she's off doing what cats do, I guess.'

'I wish to bathe first,' she said. 'Will you join me?'

'Try stopping me,' he countered quickly.

She guffawed, and it sounded distinctly weird, she was thinking.

'You can help wash my back, or not. It's entirely up to you.'

Aidan ignored her and quietly went about sharpening the tip.

'I'm teasing. I want you to help.'

'You're very good at teasing,' he remarked coolly, and trying to dismiss uneasy thoughts playing on his mind.

Aidan was thinking back to the previous night when he searched for in the woods. He had only to follow the mellow tones of her voice. Before arriving at the position where she lay on the ground, he'd believed for a moment she was in a conversation with someone, only to find she was alone, with no other person in the vicinity.

He was reminded of a time he'd caught her talking to Dog and was answering herself. She believed Dog understood and could respond vocally. He declined saying anything which may antagonise her as he didn't want her thinking she had a problem. She wasn't harming anyone, he deduced.

It was the mushrooms! As if it explained everything.

TALK TO THE ANIMALS

He didn't think she was emotionally equipped to deal with the horrors of her past and would serve her best if she were to keep them locked away. She was living in a fantasy world, where it was safe and it was a world which made her smile and kept her content. It was a side of her he loved. Her little fantasy world had made his dreams come true and he wanted it to stay that way.

He was her prince and she was his princess. No matter they did not live in a palace, life was wonderful.

Later that morning he took Imelda on an adventure; just the two of them as Dog had still to make an appearance.

Aidan had his spear and it was something he was mightily proud of as it gave him a sense of power. Imelda had her sharp bladed slice of granite she tied around her slim waist with leaf vine. She chose to wear her two-piece attire to compliment the loin cloth she had made for her prince. It was a hot, humid summer's day and encouraged swarms of insects. Aidan hoped it would also encourage animals out of their homes as he could only think about their next meal.

Imelda didn't want to think of the encroaching changing seasons when they could expect temperatures to fall away. The shelter was home to them when the weather was favourable. Aidan believed it could be a place of Hell once Winter turned a corner and it was something they needed to discuss before that time arrived.

Since fleeing into the woods in search of his princess Aidan was of the belief he had acquired a steely resolve and courage he never thought he possessed. It was not only proportionate to his own self-preservation. He had Imelda to care for. His abiding love for her was the source to his growing power. He would do anything to preserve it. Anything.

Should it come to it, he would kill for her.

Imelda seemed to instinctively know where they were headed as not once did she pause to get her bearings.

They eventually arrived at a wide area of gently undulating hillocks of lush verdant grass which was sporadically pitted with small rabbit burrows.

'This is home to some of my friends,' she said and skipped away, painting a scenario with arms waving as she twirled on cushions of air.

She chose an area where the sun beat down in all its bright and ferocious glory and lay down, beckoning her prince to join her. She kicked off her trainers as Aidan placed his spear to one side and stretched his long limbs beside her. She was instantly in his arms and kissing him. What followed was a graceful and tender aria as they undressed and consummated their love.

Aidan viewed her effusive sweetness and charm as a positive step in the right direction. There was no clawing, slapping, or biting. The wildness was no longer prevalent in her eyes and at no time did it peak as she enjoyed her orgasms.

After they were finished they lay together, bathing in the aftermath of a spiritual and soulful connection and with the sun burning their skin.

Imelda's attention drifted from each of his delightful caresses and teasing kisses to watch families of rabbits at play on the grass. A few of them became inquisitive and approached. Imelda reserved a generous smile for them.

'Are they to be food for tonight?' her prince enquired and Imelda was aghast at his suggestion.

'No!' she exclaimed fervently. 'I couldn't. I would rather starve.'

'Then, I will starve with you, if it comes to it.'

She gazed deeply into his adoring eyes and felt a well of love within her chest, overbrimming and have her thinking she was drowning in the euphoria they had created for themselves.

She kissed him in earnest and liked that he became quickly aroused.

Aidan was enjoying himself, even as he tried to make sense of her sudden change of heart, considering the animals she'd hunted the previous day.

It could have been guilt and shame which had mollified her; he couldn't be sure.

He gave a little yelp and almost protested as she raked his back and buttocks. She bit his chest and shoulder, sucked on his neck. He endured the pain and reciprocated, knowing it was what she craved.

The beast within had been awakened.

It was while returning to the shelter they became startled by a brace of pheasant who had been disturbed amongst the foliage. Aidan was quick to cover his surprise with laughter, even as Imelda was fuelled with angst. A darkness seemed to creep into her psyche.

'Fuck!' she protested angrily. 'You scared the shit out of me!'

'You should watch where you're going and not go stampeding like a herd of elephants,' came the reaction.

'We are on our way home,' Imelda explained.

'This is our home! Not yours!'

'And you're very rude!'

'You're rude! And not a nice person!'

Aidan was frozen, a bystander to the exchange and became deeply concerned. He was once again a witness to Imelda answering herself and in a tone embellished with barely controlled rage.

He wanted to appease her and primed his spear in readiness. He didn't ask for atonement and struck with determination and accuracy. He impaled the cock pheasant into the mulch as the hen bird flapped, paced in harried circles, and became disoriented.

Imelda fell on the frightened creature and stabbed repeatedly with the improvised dagger and would have continued had Aidan not taken her arm and pulled her to her knees gently. She was crying and he dropped to a crouch and gathered her into his arms.

'I'm sorry!' she bleated and her plea was plaintive and heart-rending.

'It's okay, darling,' Aidan answered her, believing it was prudent to play along with her diverse personalities. 'They were rude and disrespectful. They had no right to speak to you like that.'

'Yes,' she concurred and giving him a quizzical look.

'Like you said, we were on our way home and minding our own business. We weren't thrashing through the undergrowth like a herd of elephants.'

'Horrid birds!' she whimpered.

'They got what they deserved. Anyone who hurts my princess can expect the same. Come on baby, let's go home and get a fire started. I think we both know what's on the menu.'

He tittered as he assisted Imelda to her feet. She clung to him and stared at her hands and was mesmerised and appalled at sight of the blood congealing around her fingers and speckling her lower arms.

'When we reach the stream,' he added and kissed her neck, 'We'll stop to bathe and get cleaned-up. Does that sound good to you?'

Imelda simply nodded as she became lost along one of the dark drear tunnels within her tormented mind, believing it could lead her to another lost memory.

Aidan carried the brace of pheasant and spear and used his free hand to help guide Imelda through the shrubbery and thickest press of trees.

Imelda stayed silent as she became confused, thinking she was being led in the wrong direction.

It had to be witchery; she was thinking, knowing the sorceress was at play in the woods.

She tapped the bladed weapon at her hip and it gave her comfort.

Aidan could feel her tension and only when they finally arrived at the stream was Imelda able to relax. Being close to sanctuary had her mood lightening instantly and she was able to delight in the cool embrace of the water lapping around her calves.

She gave a squeal when her prince unexpectedly scooped water into his palms and let it drizzle over her shoulders. He teased droplets around her lips and gather on her tongue. She watched him wide-eyed and trembling with love as he drew lazy circles on her skin.

His tenderness had her aroused quickly as all in her fantastical world became one of resplendent joy once again.

Despite the unnerving proximity of the Wicked Witch whose darkest essence flowed in her veins and took residence in her loins.

She was not fearful, knowing her prince was a young man who was fearless and could protect her.

CHAPTER 33

Imelda had a troubled night even though it heartened her to have her prince and Dog to comfort her. Cat was curled-up by her feet and was another source of wonder. Despite which, Imelda could not dispel the precognitive feeling their magical world was under threat.

The air was heavy and humid and thunder rumbled a warning in the distance.

Aidan was snoring, as was Dog, yet she saw no annoyance in this. It was consoling even as she was envious of their peace and contentment.

Imelda was reluctant to close her eyes as her subconscious was spiteful and wished only to summon memories and have a venture into territory she had no wish to visit.

It seemed she had no choice as a spell cast by the Wicked Witch compelled her to search for truth. There was no escape, no respite. She had become inexorably drawn and entwined within a story slow to relinquish its intent.

The moment her eyes fluttered and closed and her breathing slowed, Imelda imagined herself creeping along a gloomy corridor devoid of natural or artificial light. Even though her lower limbs were leaden and trembled with the silky webbing of fear to have heralded her journey into the unknown.

She sensed, that wherever she was she was not supposed to be there. She was alone and supposed everyone else was committed to their chores, as she should have been.

She hesitated at sound of someone weeping forlornly and it had her momentarily spellbound.

Next, she was entering a room and in the darkness, perceived only a single bed, a bedside cabinet, some shelving, and a small chair in one corner. There might have been other furniture but she wasn't looking for it in her mind's-eye.

This was a room lacking warmth.

Having entered the bedroom brought memories flooding back. She remembered occasions when she was kept in a similar environ. Imelda was thinking back to a conversation with her prince. He spoke of a punishment room or cell, where those who broke the rules were kept isolated for a time.

Taking a few tentative steps had her seeing the subject she was drawn to in the darkness. Curled up on the bed was a young boy whose tearful face was covered by small hands which trembled fearfully. Imelda supposed the boy was in his middle teens, and as she continued to gaze on the stricken figure she was certain he was someone she knew from her past.

Imelda listened for signs of others in close proximity and contented herself they were the only ones in this part of the house.

TALK TO THE ANIMALS

She wanted to whisper assurance to the boy and let him know he had no reason to be afraid. She was a friend. Imelda hesitated and continued to stare, wishing to implore the bedraggled boy to take his hands away and reveal himself.

Imelda had not been aware of the person hiding behind the door, not until she dropped to her knees and raised a hand to lightly shake the boy's shoulder.

The door closed with a resounding clunk and startled Imelda and had her looking over her shoulder. The silhouette of a monster, darker than the gloom, approached and towered over her. She saw the monster's features, a crazed look in his eyes even as she was drawn to his contemptuous sneer.

'Father?' she hissed, and even in her dream she could taste the fear stealing moisture from her throat.

'You know the rules, child,' came a gruff, familiar voice. 'You, and that little shit, never learn. You're no children of mine! I swear! Under my roof, you will abide by my rules, or else. And you know what that means, every time you cross the line, the witch has to be chastised.'

She knew instinctively the punishment she could expect and her brother would be forced to witness her shame. She leapt to her feet and went to barge past and flee the room, only to have her long flaming hair grabbed mercilessly and stop her in her tracks. A slap rocked her head to the side. Worse was to follow. To feel a hand pawing her had Imelda clawing free of the nightmare she was in.

Imelda carefully and considerately eased herself from between Dog and her sleeping prince, staggered to the entrance and inhaled the sultry ionised air in the hope it would cleanse her mind.

The storm was approaching with lightning flashes illuminating vast banks of dark cloud and the treetops in the distance.

Gripped by panic suddenly, Imelda scurried along the ledge and hauled herself precariously down the steep gradient before fleeing into the cover of the woods.

She kept running, despite the knifing pain in her chest and abdomen.

The darkness was her enemy and her friend.

An owl called to her and was answered by another as something brushed past her shins, causing her to gasp her dismay.

The sturdy fronds of the undergrowth clawed and lashed her flesh, and she was again reminded of hands pawing and slapping her. Her leafy top was snagged and her fear was exacerbated, so that she was able to taste it.

Unseen hands were grabbing her and pulling her back and she fought them with desperate tenacity.

The moment she imagined her thong had been snatched from her hips she wondered if she was lost to those dark denizens of evil who had been a part of her past life and were once again chasing her.

A clap of thunder had her yelping just as she burst into a clearing. She stopped running and peered into the darkness in all directions. She saw no person chasing and threatening her person.

TALK TO THE ANIMALS

She however recognised the friendly ancient oak tree and crossed to it and without a moment's thought, was hugging its torso as if the tree was her saviour.

'Ah,' sighed the tree. *'Has our princess or the Wicked Witch come to visit this night? Hard to tell in the darkness, and there's a fearful storm approaching.'*

'It's me, Mister Tree, your princess,' she cried. 'Your friend and not the Wicked Witch of the Woods.'

'Ah, so it is. Are you lost child?'

'I am, Mister Tree. At least, I think I am lost.'

'What are you running from?'

'The Wicked Witch has been chasing me through the woods. She wishes to inflict her terrible poison on me and have me remember things I have no wish to remember.'

'That will never do. Curl up at my feet and I will protect you.'

The remark had her giggling, relaxing, so that all the things to make her fearful were quickly gone from her mind.

'Trees don't have feet,' she admonished the tree lightly.

'We do, however, have sturdy limbs.'

'Yes, I suppose you do. Silly of me.'

Imelda lowered herself into the depression where the tree's protuberant roots were a comforting niche for her.

An intense slash of lightning illuminated all around and there followed a monstrous evocative rumble and deafening clap of thunder which had Imelda squealing. The first heavy splotches of rain performed a symphony on the leaves in the boughs above her and there came a deluge to obliterate a view of her surroundings.

She trembled and hugged a firm root to her stomach and breasts, as if her life depended on it.

'You are quite safe with me,' said the Tree.

'Thank you,' Imelda answered, her voice drowned by the incessant clatter of raindrops beating down all around her.

'What has become of your prince?' whispered the Tree.

'I don't know!' and she became distraught once again. 'What was I thinking! He will wake up and find me gone and will be worried sick, especially with the storm and the rain.'

'I imagine, your prince will come looking for you.'

'But how can he hope to find me in this wilderness of trees? He will not wish to venture out of a warm shelter into the storm. I should return home as I know I have been selfish and foolish.'

'Don't be so hard on yourself, child. You woke up from a nightmare and wanted to flee, believing you were caught in a spell and one to have you remember things better left buried.'

'How could you possibly know this?'

'Magic, my dear. It is all around us and it finds a home within us. I know that you feel it, as I do.'

'That may be, but I wish the magic would stop trying to get me to think about my past and the reason I came to the woods in the first place. I don't wish to remember. These dreams I am having make me miserable and worthless and fill me with pain, both in my head and in my heart.'

The Tree grew silent as the rain slapped the mulch and Imelda was once again reminded of cruel beatings; and worse.

Her prince had told her, it was Stibley who was the architect of her misery, past and present.

She should be free but something told her; she was not and could never be.

Unless…

She was to confront her nemesis and maybe then, her tortured soul could be appeased, her mind healed.

Why she should consider augmenting a confrontation with a monstrous evil eluded her. Despite which, if she were to face her demons it might be beneficial to her health.

It's what she needed to do, she convinced herself.

Imelda had no wish to immure all her woes and embraced the thick root with determined vigour; even adoration.

Tree was her protector, from the storm and the dark entities roaming the woods.

'What should I do?' she beseeched the Tree, as rain found insidious avenues through the overhead branches to spatter her flesh.

'Do you have the strength, little princess, to face your demons head-on? And what do you hope to gain from a confrontation? Stibley and his wife are lost to the darkness and

are not morally obligated to see reason in any argument. What has been done, cannot be undone. You can learn to live with your personal ghosts or take a journey into their dark world.'

'I was a part of that world you speak of.'

'And has it not taught you anything?'

'It has taught me, all in this world is not beautiful. There is much which is ugly and cruel.'

'And by returning, what do you hope to gain?'

'I seek retribution!' she cried out.

She clung to the gnarly limb with greater intensity where it left its mark on her skin. It stirred other memories to experience this, not within her mind but within her loins.

She was unable to comprehend why she should be having these feels or why she had an unnatural affinity with the Tree.

The sky rumbled, staccato flashes stabbing at Imelda's irises, invoking fresh memories of a time she had endured great suffering.

She pulled herself into a tight ball, imagining a lumpy mattress in place of a bed of sodden mulch. She felt pressure on her arms, preventing her from moving. Being naked and vulnerable had her weeping and wondering what her punishment was to be this time.

She felt herself toppling, being turned over and if she dared open her eyes she would be face to face with her tormentor.

Imelda had wished for a confrontation but didn't think she was ready. There may never come a time when she would be ready.

She opened her eyes a fraction and the persistent rain distorted her view. Imelda believed she saw a face and the thin slash of a leering smile. In her mind she was able to inhale the stale aroma of alcohol.

The monster was speaking disgusting things to her, saying what he proposed to do to her.

Imelda received her revelation as the truth was given clarity.

The monster of her past enjoyed feeding on her terror.. It was his sustenance and food to a dark, narcissistic obsession. He cast a spell she was unable to resist as in turn, it was to feed something dark and insidious which had a home inside her.

The memory ignited and believed for a moment she had screamed. Even though she saw tears in her eyes, she was laughing and taunting her tormentor. By doing so, she knew he would lose the control he hoped to exert on his victim.

He was cruel, relentless, but the power was not his to wield. She had the power. The Wicked Witch was her ally, even back then, at a time she had wanted to forget. And the Wicked Witch had cast her spell on Imelda's tormentor.

CHAPTER 34

Imelda was delirious and confused, as one moment she saw herself skipping daintily with families of rabbits, only then to feel claustrophobic and confined to a tight space where moving and breathing was difficult.

Escape was impossible.

She clung to the magical image of rabbits hopping around their burrows and greeting her arrival with joy. Their chatter was incessant and she envied their peace and pace of life.

If she was to die and could be reincarnated, she hoped to come back to a life such as the rabbits were enjoying and to be one of them.

Or a bird, she was thinking. Imelda tried to imagine how it would feel to have wings spread and gliding along currents of air, with an opulent vista revealed to her wherever she looked.

Imelda gave a gasp and a grunt as she sought to repel the force binding her to reality. Her fear returned the moment she sensed another's body pressed-up against her.

TALK TO THE ANIMALS

It felt both familiar and alien and at the same time, repulsive and enjoyable. Darkness once again loomed on the periphery of her vision and clung as a leech to memories she wanted expunged.

A voice came to her from the depths of a long narrow tunnel within her mind, gentle, tender, and edged with concern.

It was a voice she recognised and it had her heart aching and singing.

The voice was of her beautiful guardian, her prince.

She relinquished her tenacious grip on the tree's exposed root and moved int a comforting embrace. She was instantly swept along on emotive currents of joy as she revelled in the softness of his caresses, the hardness of his naked torso and the wonderful kisses dropping like rain on each one of her tears.

Imelda yearned for more and lay back in the cradle the depression afforded her, legs spread as an invitation she hoped he might accept.

The Tree whispered in her mind. *'I see, the Wicked Witch has joined the party.'*

Imelda ignored Tree's obnoxious taunt as Aidan lifted her easily to settle astride his lap. Imelda's laughter soared as for a time she had believed she had lost the will to have fun.

Not for the first time her Prince was to carry her home, as if she weighed no more than a feather.

The rain continued to lash down and made passage through the undergrowth treacherous.

TALK TO THE ANIMALS

Her prince did not complain once and through a misty haze was witness to his grim expression and steely determination. His strength poured from him in glorious waves.

Her white knight without the need for armour.

He had no need of armour, she conceded, as she believed him to be omnipotent.

He had been given the magic which had been granted to her the moment she fled to the woods and used the magic to venture into the storm and find her huddled at the base of a tree. If not the magic, it was the measure of his love for her which drove him to find her.

Without the magic flowing in his veins, he could wander around throughout the night and not found her.

Imelda wept against his neck and enjoyed the feel of him against her skin.

Inside their leaking shelter and with Imelda placed lovingly on their cot, Aidan set about reviving the fire and when he was done, encouraged Imelda to hug its warmth. As she did so he comforted her in silence until he sensed she was ready to speak of her ordeal.

'You're naked,' he said, not as an accusation and punctuated his remark by lightly kissing her neck and shoulders. 'What happened to your top and thong?'

She eventually answered and her comment surprised and shocked him and him tensing.

'Stibley,' she had mumbled dejectedly.

TALK TO THE ANIMALS

Aidan took a moment to analyse her response as he didn't think Stibley, as obsessed as he was, was the type to search for them in the woods at night and during a storm and torrential downpour.

'Are you quite certain it was Stibley?' he pressed lightly. 'Did you get to see the person's face?'

'It's enough that I felt him. He ripped my clothes off and would have done a despicable thing had I not escaped.'

'I take, he didn't give chase when you got away from him?'

She turned her head sharply and he caught her expression of growing annoyance.

'Obviously, he did not! The storm would have confused him and would have no way of knowing in which direction I had taken, is my guess.'

'The fact remains, if Stibley knows you live in the woods, he will keep searching until he finds you and the shelter.'

'That's okay. Let the bastard come. We'll be ready for him. I'm telling you this much, Aidan, I am not going back. He can't make me!'

She saw the granite dagger on one side of it and made a grab for it and held it against her stomach with unsettling tenacity.

'The Wicked Witch is his ally, I can vouch for it,' she added. 'If he comes for me I will use this on him. I will! You mustn't stop me!'

'Okay, sweetheart,' said Aidan in a placating tone. 'In the morning, I'll take my spear and investigate the woods. I know them better than Stibley does. If he comes back I will know.'

'Silly; he may wait a few days before he returns. He might not be alone next time.'

'Okay, then I will go to the orphanage under cover of darkness and follow his plans from there.'

'You must not!' she blurted and grabbed his arm in anguish. 'What if you get caught? Aide, promise me you won't return to the orphanage. If you leave the woods, you leave the magic behind. Think your spear will be enough against Stibley and his posse?'

Aidan relented and placed an arm around her, noticing the way the dagger was put aside out of harm's way.

Dog had become attuned to Imelda's distraught condition and with a little whine, nudged her with his head to get attention. She responded instantly and wrestled Dog onto the crib where he became happily vocal and kicked with his legs.

Cat had been asleep against the back wall and came awake, hissing, and disgruntled she stomped off the bed to settle close to the fire Aidan was feeding wood to.

Glancing off to the side Aidan was witness to Imelda's effervescent joy as she played with Dog. He couldn't help but admire the way she had her buttocks raised in the air and in the way they moved side to side. He couldn't be sure if she was aware he was watching her and whether it was an invitation.

TALK TO THE ANIMALS

There had been a lengthy pause in the storm since they returned and now another was approaching, heralding its arrival with a sizzling flash followed by a strident clap of thunder which echoed off the rocky atoll and trees in the vicinity.

Aidan laughed to dispel his sudden shock and the fact the sound had made him flinch and jump. Imelda seemed not to notice as she had drifted into her own fantasy world for a time.

Stuttering flashes of lightning illuminated her nudity and had Aidan aroused. Removing his loin cloth in a hurry he moved closer to join his princess and Dog and their frolics.

With a hand splayed against the small of her back she stopped and looked back over a shoulder. Damp trails of her fiery red hair were stamped to the fullness of her mouth.

She reacted the way he hoped she might as she strutted and flounced her buttocks, sending out a clear message. It was a taunt much to his liking and he was not one to refuse an invitation when given.

The last few hours of anguish having awoken to find her gone from the shelter and with the first storm breaking were quickly dispelled from memory as he shuffled into position behind her.

He had her arching her back, even as she continued to give attention to a playful Dog. He had her moaning. She was then speaking in a voice he did not recognise.

'You know what I want! Give the Witch sustenance, you naughty boy. Is that all you got?'

TALK TO THE ANIMALS

Aidan was first to wake as dawn encroached and did so with a start. He was thankful an exhausted Imelda was asleep with her head and an arm resting on his chest.

He was unable to recall whether he'd cast himself from an unpleasant dream or if his subconscious was tugged by something in the real world. He steadied his breathing and listened for sounds beyond the entrance to the shelter

He needed to relieve himself, and extricating Imelda from her comfortable and peaceful position without disturbing her was no easy task.

He put a finger to his lips to warn Dog not to bark, or move, and was thankful Dog lazily complied and settled again.

Aidan staggered to the entrance and stretched, only then realising it had stopped raining. He went to pee over the ledge and felt completely exposed, feeling logically or illogically he was being watched from the cover of the trees below.

When he was finished he edged along to where the ledge sloped away to the woodland floor and became curious as to why all the wildlife in the woods was preternaturally quiet. It helped as Aidan was trying to determine sounds which did not belong.

You're losing it, he chided himself.

Unconcerned he should venture from the shelter naked he approached the perimeter wall of trees and trekked all the way to the edge of the atoll. Satisfied, he returned to the shelter and instead of snuggling up to Imelda's soft skin and inhaling her unique scent, he grabbed up his spear and vacated their home again not bothering to cover himself with his shorts or the loin cloth.

TALK TO THE ANIMALS

He was on a mission and it was one where he hoped he might get some answers to an array of troubling thoughts. He scaled the edifice, crossed the clearing, and sloped off into the bushes.

Tension continued to build within his mind, his heart beating a crescendo and was erratic, discordant. His hearing was keen though and he stopped every so often and listened to determine sounds and movement around him. He was concerned he had left Imelda at the shelter, and dismissed any worries, knowing she had Dog for protection should they have an uninvited visitor.

The spear hurt his hand where he gripped the shaft tightly and saw how the blood was leeched from his knuckles.

'Show yourself, you ugly fuck!' he suddenly and angrily hissed, his eyelids as slits as he believed it gave him greater focus.

Aidan didn't believe Stibley had come to the woods and attacked Imelda in the storm. The fat fuck liked his home comforts too much, he was thinking. Aidan had to make certain they were safe from outsiders, for his own peace of mind.

Stibley was someone who was obsessive and psychotic. It was not only Imelda who was prey to the monster. Others had suffered and continued to suffer. Aidan was another who was victim to the monster's penchant for cruelty and narcissistic control.

Stibley was lazy but he was clever. He could masquerade as a perfect role model when it suited. Aidan knew differently.

The more he thought about his enemy, Aidan almost convinced himself Stibley might be driven by obsession to search for Imelda. Not Aidan. He liked young, beautiful fresh meat. It was conceivable Stibley knew the woods intimately and may consider the woods to be a perfect hideaway for someone who wanted to escape his evil clutches.

Aidan gritted his teeth in anguish, as now he believed the enemy was close by.

Something heavy disturbed the undergrowth and ploughed a path through the sodden leafy mulch. A badger revealed itself and instinct had Aidan raising the spear, ready to defend himself should it be necessary to do so.

'Jesus! Where did you come from?' he rasped and giggled dementedly.

'In case you hadn't noticed, I'm a badger, and the woods are my home.'

Aidan's gaze flitted side to side, eyes bulging, as he wondered who was speaking to him.

'I almost stumbled over you,' Aidan snapped, with frustration and confusion taking control of his senses.

'You should watch where you're going,' and Aidan drilled his gaze lower, believing it was the badger answering him.

'For your information, I wasn't moving. You stumbled into me. Now that you're hear, maybe you could tell me if you have seen anyone else in the woods around these parts.'

'You want to know if there are any other humans in the vicinity?'

'Yes! Yes!'

TALK TO THE ANIMALS

'I know there is the princess. I have heard much said in regard to the beautiful young lady with the flaming red hair who is kind and talks to the animals. And the trees.'

'I am her prince and protector,' Aidan said and thinking he was possessed or under a spell. His eyes stabbed at the gloom. 'There is one who hunts the princess and he is cruel.'

'Human nature. It is rare to find one, such as the princess, who is friendly and considerate to all things living.'

Not always; Aidan wanted to add, as he recalled the devastating way she had attacked a pheasant with an improvised dagger.

'It has been a pleasure talking with you, Mister Badger, but I must continue on my way and ensure the woods are safe from predators. And know my princess is not in danger.'

The badger turned and waddled away in its cumbersome gait to be swallowed-up by the undergrowth and gloom.

Aidan resumed his solo quest and eventually arrived at the stream bed having been drawn to its chuckling sonata from afar.

The morning sun was making its presence felt and birdlife was a stir in the branches of the trees and in the shrubs.

Aidan took a moment to wash himself as it gave him an opportunity to assess his position and intentions and reflect on his meeting with a badger. He chuckled in response to the remark he could have expected to hear from his princess.

It is the magic of the woods!

TALK TO THE ANIMALS

Despite which, Aidan was still in a stupor and unable differentiate reality from imaginary.

He espied clusters of mushrooms scattered around the base of a tree and as he needed sustenance he went to them and munched a few. It occurred to him they were the variety to expand the mind.

Aidan needed to formulate a plan of action and he hoped the mushrooms would help. Imelda believed the mushrooms were anointed with magic cast by the Wicked Witch and to enter her dark realm you had to embrace her power. To do so, one can understand and is given clarity.

Aidan puffed out his cheeks and scoffed at Imelda's words. It made no sense, to swallow the Witch's poison just to enter her realm. It would make the person vulnerable and a chattel to the Witch.

Stupid! He was thinking. And a big mistake.

He laughed, realising it was too late. He had swallowed the Witch's poison and invited a confrontation with another of their enemies. He scrabbled around the mulch for the spear he'd discarded when he did his ablutions and felt a measure of comfort to have it in his grasp.

He would sit and wait for the Witch to come to him.

She had her sorcery, but Aidan had something more powerful, or so he hoped and believed.

He had his courage, but importantly, he had love for his princess.

CHAPTER 35

A short time elapsed and Aidan felt the poison ignite in his veins, driving him to his knees. He chuckled, rolled his eyes, and then he was leaning to the side, retching. His mind was in total disarray and knew he had to fight it and merge with the tide of magical influence flowing in his veins.

He was suddenly thinking about his princess and wondering if she had come awake and was fearful he had vacated the shelter.

This was quickly followed by another thought, as he imagined the beast who was Stibley, had come to the woods in search of his prey. It was conceivable Stibley might ignore Aidan and continue to the shelter.

Aidan wondered if the enemy had located the home amongst the rocks. The fat fuck would have found some way to approach the entrance even if he was unable to scale the edifice at front. He might have worked his passage around from behind where access to the top of the atoll was easier.

Aidan almost cried out in a moment's panic when he saw in his mind's eye, the lumbering beast bearing down on his sleeping, naked princess, a leer etched cruelly on his demented features as one he had seen all too often.

Dog would have leapt to Imelda's defence, in this he was certain and he gave in to a spate of giggling as he imagined Dog tearing a chunk out of the gross pig's leg. His laughter was exacerbated as he saw the man hopping around the shelter on his one good leg, pleading for mercy.

Aidan believed he had heard Stibley's frightful scream from afar as Dog attacked and ripped Stibley's flailing arm off, tossing it to the side and wanting only to get at the man's throat.

Aidan couldn't help himself as laughter became his mantra. Stibley was done for.

He scrambled on to his feet and hefting the spear launched himself through the press of undergrowth, the fronds of fern and succulent leaves caressing his skin. Soggy twigs and vegetation crackled and squelched beneath his feet.

A while later, Aidan came to realise he was heading in the wrong direction, with the shelter at his rear. He kept going as a voice in his head was pushing him to continue and not return.

His princess was safe. She had Dog as her protector.

Aidan eventually arrived at the edge of the woods and the glaring brightness of an unspoilt sun stamping its brilliance on the field stretched before him caused an eruption of colour within his mind. His senses reeled and had him hugging the trunk of a tree for support. He needed to clear his mind before continuing as his thoughts were a jumble and made no sense.

'The magic of the woods cannot go with you,' said the Tree as Aidan slumped to the ground in shock, landing painfully on his rump.

He thrust with his spear at the unseen perpetrator of the voice even though the words were spoken and echoed within his mind.

TALK TO THE ANIMALS

'Who's there?' he called out.

'What do you mean to do with only a pointy stick for protection?' the Tree taunted him. *'You are quite exposed in the daylight. Anyone can see you approaching from distance. You have obviously not thought this through logically. You are on a fool's mission, young man. Are you a fool?'*

'I'm not a fool!' Aidan protested sharply and stabbed the Tree's trunk with the tip of the spear.

'And you're not the mighty warrior you believe yourself to be.'

'I am!'

'You're scared. You've always been afraid of monsters and you will always remain in fear of them.'

'I will fight these demons and defeat them. It is my mission to free the princess from their tyrannical control and influence. And I will free myself at the same time.'

'Think you have what it takes to face your nemesis, boy?' and the taunt was malevolently dark. *'You could just sit here and wait for them to come to you. Supposing they mean to come. Or, you could return to your hovel and lay with your princess. Is that not preferable to facing your nemesis after all this time? Is not your love for the princess greater than your desire for revenge?'*

'I fight for love!'

'You could be holding your princess in your loving arms and receiving her kisses.'

'Yes.'

TALK TO THE ANIMALS

'She would be receptive to the love you mean to give, would she not?'

'Yes.'

'What are you waiting for?'

'I don't know anymore,' Aidan bleated despondently.

'Take your time. Rest a while. The Witch's poison still flows in your veins, confusing you. It will pass, it always does.'

'And when it does, I will return home to my princess.'

'Where she awaits, perhaps fearful her prince has abandoned her. She will be desperate, sad, and wishing only to have her prince's arms around her and satisfy her craving.'

'I'm sorry! I'm sorry! I shouldn't have left her!'

'No, you shouldn't have. What if Stibley was there while you grovel pathetically on the ground? Your princess will be helpless.'

'Dog will protect her!'

'And what if he can't? What if Dog has left the princess to come looking for you? She will be all alone in the shelter. Naked and vulnerable. Stibley would know this. The princess is no match compared to the cruel power Stibley wields. Your princess may call to the Wicked Witch to assist he and we both know what that means. She will use the Witch to feed his lust and make him weak. You're imagining this, I can tell.'

'Stop it! Stop, please, stop!'

'We are both as one, young man. You wish to imagine the princess and Stibley wrestling on the crib as it nourishes the

darker side of your own psyche. You like to watch from a distance, always wishing you were the one. You have watched them together numerous times and it excited you as much as it horrified you.'

'You're wrong!' Aidan protested

'You didn't try to save your princess on those occasions, because you were afraid.'

'No!'

'And curious.'

'No!'

'You watched your princess suffer at the hands of the beast and did nothing, because you liked to watch them. It excited you.'

'Bastard! Stop!'

'You're missing all the fun being here. Imagine the two of them together at this moment. You are, as you have become aroused at the memory.'

'Please, stop torturing me. My princess would not let the bastard touch her.'

'She is under the Witch's spell, and we both know what that means. She will not be fighting him. It was not always the way. There were occasions when the princess invited attention, as you know. You really think Stibley is the controlling influence? I believe, as you do, the princess is not dissimilar to the person you detest. You have failed her, young man. You deserted her in her hour of need. And Stibley has returned to fill the void you have left. Think long and hard, as we both know,

TALK TO THE ANIMALS

Stibley was not trying to exert his will on your princess. He was called upon to control the Wicked Witch, as he has been called to do at this time.'

Aidan wailed miserably and ran headlong into the thicket, hoping these formidable denizens would pummel him awake and remove his confusion. The Tree's taunts remained as he continued frantically to be away from the perimeter of the woods and it was more luck than judgement he should find the streambed and follow it.

No words came even as his mind called out; *I'm coming to rescue you, princess!*

In his hurry to return he often stumbled and cried his despair as he believed the woods were conspiring to hold him back.

He fell exhausted to the mulch at the base of a tree and wept, feeling as if his powers had deserted him. Through a coruscating haze of tears, he saw a group of mushrooms alongside him and they too were taunting him. Aidan swept a hand across the small insignificant caps and tugged a few from the ground. He stared at them for a moment and then he was gorging on them.

Aidan believed they were the source of the power he needed if he was to face his foe in combat and save his princess.

He continued at a more leisurely pace and covered a short distance only before collapsing and coughing up water he had rinsed his mouth with. He dragged himself wearily to the side of the stream and collapsed onto the mulch, unable to quell a relentless montage of images filling the void of his mind.

TALK TO THE ANIMALS

He rolled onto his back and screamed and lost consciousness.

When he eventually recovered the gloom in the woods was more substantial with grey cloud above and threatening rain.

He couldn't be sure if he was dreaming or not as he observed his naked princess abluting herself in the stream.

She looked up as if she sensed she was being watched.

'Sleepy head,' she beamed at him. 'Where did you take yourself off to?'

Aidan rolled his head to remove the sticky webbing of confusion.

'Have you seen Stibley?' he asked.

'Why do you ask?' she countered calmly and the manner she delivered her response had Aidan believe she was keeping a secret from him. 'Have you seen him?'

'No. I thought, he might have discovered the shelter and you were in danger.'

'Silly. I feel good and wonderful. Everything is simply magical.'

Aidan studied the intricate patterns her hands made on her body as she continued to wash herself and became mesmerised by her fluid expressions and was in awe of her mystical calm.

'I spoke with a badger, and with a tree,' he admitted, even as wondered why he felt the need to share.

She will think him mad.

'I hope, they both gave good advice,' she said.

'Not really,' he bemoaned. 'The Tree told me you were in trouble. The Tree was adamant Stibley had found our home and entered while you were sleeping.'

'The Tree couldn't have known.'

'The magic would have shown the Tree you were to receive a visitor.'

'Dog was with me, even if you were not. Think Dog would let that pig anywhere near me? As you know, I always keep the dagger close to me and I'm not afraid to defend myself if it came to it.'

Aidan threw himself down on the mulch, exasperated, and cursed the pain pounding in his head.

He reacted the moment he felt a hand on his chest, another sweeping low across his stomach. He opened eyes brimming with tears and saw his smiling princess leaning over him and settling her weight on his thighs.

'Think Stibley can give me what I need?' a voice spoke within Aidan's head; tantalising, a consummate tease. He didn't think Imelda had spoken. *'You are my love, my world, my prince.'*

'And you are my love, my world, my princess.'

The Wicked Witch gave a chuckle.

CHAPTER 36

Imelda led him back and was evidently enjoying his predicament as he continually complained of a pounding head and the soreness she had inflicted on his body.

'We have nothing to eat,' he protested, disgruntled, as he clung to the rock edifice before he was encouraged to climb.

'Ah, but we do. And you can thank Dog,' she responded light-heartedly. 'We have three grouse to prepare. I will do the honours as I need you to rest and get your strength back. I will have you complain some more before this night is over.'

She chortled and the sound reverberated all around the atoll.

Aidan paused to study her side profile on the ledge and was a witness to her impish smile as a playful taunt on her lips.

'Your sorcery astounds me,' he uttered and in awe of the strength she exuded. Before continuing to the entrance, he eased her into an embrace. His own mouth trembled as if he was close to tears. 'I could not bear to lose you.'

'You will not lose me, silly. Our love is forever.'

TALK TO THE ANIMALS

He kissed her and let his hands roam, had her moaning and becoming demanding as he was aroused. She was the one ended the embrace and gave him a gentle nudge to get to the shelter.

Dog bounded off the bed to greet them and having thanked Dog for protecting his princess in his absence crossed to the bed and lay down. He was quickly asleep as he became wrapped in the suffocating folds of exhaustion, both physically and emotionally.

He was nudged awake when the meal was ready and he ate the portion given to him with relish, following which, he needed to lay down again and Imelda contented herself by seeking comfort in his arms.

Aidan came awake once again at the sound of a fox barking in the distance. It disturbed wildfowl and the cacophony of noise had him curious. Not for the first time he wondered if someone was in the woods and causing a nocturnal disturbance.

Aidan kept the spear close to him as he knew his princess was never too far from her dagger. Looking down, he saw red hair clinging to Imelda's soft features. Dog was against the wall, snuffling and snorting. Cat had reappeared and was curled next to the firepit and its dying embers.

Aidan pulled the coverlet higher to enshroud his princess and she gave a contented moan. Her warm breath tickled his stomach and before he could become aroused he eased his princess to the side and clambered off the bed.

He pulled on his shorts and took up his spear with both hands. He went to the entrance and peered out across a canopy of deepening gloom.

TALK TO THE ANIMALS

All was eerily quiet again in the woods.

He was fully awake and alert to caution. His antics during the previous day had him feeling ashamed and worthless. He'd deserted his princess to venture on, what the Tree had called, a fool's mission. Aidan had protested his innocence at the time even as he reflected on his time in the woods away from his princess where he promised to always protect her. He had failed her and failed himself.

He was a fool!

He meant to change that and prove his worth and would do whatever it takes to achieve his goal.

To make amends Aidan established a position at the entrance, the spear leaning at an angle from his foot, and with the intention of standing guard all night if it was necessary to do so.

Anyone approaching would see him from afar, even in the darkness and will think twice about engaging. Aidan hoped they would turn and leave, never to return.

That is, if the enemy were coming for his princess. Nothing was definite.

After only an hour he became tired and agitated and chose to sit with his legs swinging over the lip of the ledge. He lay the spear across his lap and peered out across the clearing. His senses were keen. Too keen, he was thinking, as he was hearing things he shouldn't.

The Witch's potion had him ensnared still and served to disorient him. He saw movement on the woodland floor which did not exist. People were talking, yet there was no one around.

TALK TO THE ANIMALS

He sighed and grunted and puffed his cheeks.

He was on a mission, as sentinel to his princess.

He had a point to prove.

Imelda came awake in the early hours and went to her prince at the entrance, knelt behind him and slotted her arms around and across his chest. She loved the way he was smiling at her and rubbing her hands as she lay a cheek to the scars on his back. She kissed his unforgotten pain.

'What is it, my love?' she asked.

'It is my sworn duty as your prince to watch over you until we establish you are safe from the enemy.

'There is no one in the woods. No one is coming for me, not after all this time. I missed you in my arms when I woke up.' She licked the salt off his skin. 'I thought, for one awful moment, you had fled into the woods again.'

He turned himself and studied her expression of naked need before kissing her.

'You know, I can't help thinking about those who stayed and are still at the orphanage,' he said in soft tones. 'Those poor souls remain as prisoners, are not free like us. I imagine, our desertion would have angered Stibley greatly. What if he channelled his cruel anger on the others, accusing them of helping us run away?'

'Are you thinking then, we should do something to help them?' she asked and not able to picture the orphanage, or those who lived there.

TALK TO THE ANIMALS

'I would like to,' said Aidan unconvincingly and began to fidget, his eyes roving side to side. He blinked several times as if he needed to dispel those images at the fore of his mind, those Imelda had no access to.

'They could come live with us in the woods,' Imelda cogitated.

'The shelter is too small.'

'We could build dens for them.'

'More mouths to feed,' he added and hated he was being negative and opposing Imelda's options. 'It would be nice though. We will be doing a good thing, freeing the children, and giving them a chance to live a better life. We can give them hope.'

'Beautiful man, I love you so much.'

'The problem is; Stibley and his wife. If we free those at the orphanage they will inform the authorities. Do we want that?'

'You are forgetting, there is magic in the woods. It is our protection. Since arriving here, we have seen no other person. No one taking their dogs for a walk, no children on a playful adventure, no ramblers or courting couples.'

'What of the Wicked Witch? She controls the magic. She could, as easily, remove it and we would become exposed to outsiders.'

'It is my belief, the Wicked Witch serves what she feels is best for her. There are times when she uses her spells to guide us and there are occasions when she challenges our perception. We are a part of her world as she is part of ours.'

Aidan was content, on the surface. He stroked her cheek with a tenderness to pour fire on her heart.'

'The Wicked Witch will use Stibley and grant him powers,' he persisted.

'We are enough and more,' she insisted.

He was witness to the steely strength in her eyes and believed her.

'Jesus, Aide, take me to bed, now!'

He chuckled.

'I would be a fool to say no, and I'm not a fool. This, I said to the Tree at the edge of the woods. He doubted me and I mean to prove him wrong.'

He rose carefully to his feet and taking her hand, led his princess to bed.

Imelda threw herself down, desperate for his embrace, as the Wicked Witch was awake and calling to her.

'Hurry!' she pleaded as she watched him casually setting the spear aside and taking his time to settle with her. 'Your mind is not on me, I can tell. You want to defeat Stibley?' She put her mouth to his ear and rasped, clawing at his flesh to get him to focus. 'You must think like him. You must become him. It is the only way.'

'I can't be like that pig!' he grunted. 'No way!'

'You can! You must!'

'I don't know how to be a bad person,' he groaned.

'We can all be bad, my prince, if we choose to be or are forced.'

'Baby, you're hurting me!'

'Yes, and I need you to do the same.'

'Not to you.'

'Yes, you can. It's the only way. You remember what Stibley did, all the atrocities he committed, and you were powerless to stop him. It is different now as you are blessed by the magical powers of the woods. Embrace the magic and learn how to use it.'

'I want to, yes.'

'Hit me.'

'No, I can't hit you.'

She dug her nails into his buttocks and drew blood and him gasping. She bit his shoulder and neck.

'Hit me!' she hissed.

'No!'

She clawed his back, intent on giving him fresh scars, as a reminder.

'Fucking do it!' she snarled. 'Prove you love me.'

'The Wicked Witch has possessed you.'

'And I will have the Witch chastised. I would have you master of the Witch, not her slave.'

TALK TO THE ANIMALS

With a surge of strength and catching Aidan by surprise, she pushed him onto his back and straddled him. Both Cat and Dog vacated their places, each grumbling and protesting.

Aidan stared up into a face shrouded in the gloom so that her features were heavily distorted, almost appearing grotesque. He barely recognised her as his princess.

She became angry at him and thumped his chest, and then she was slapping his face dementedly.

She stopped when he refused to respond and scrambled off him. Frustrated and deeply agitated he should have failed her by not satisfying her demands she paced the shelter in small erratic circles. She let out a scream and startled the animals, terrified Aidan, as she bent over and clawed her scalp, tugged her hair.

Aidan was instantly beside her, pinning her arms at her sides to stop her inflicting serious harm to her person. She relaxed and wept, mumbling incoherently as her prince pulled her gently into an embrace.

She stiffened when his tenderness became unbearable.

'I wish to sleep,' she said coldly and shoved away from him.

She went to the cot and threw herself down, calling to Dog to lay with her. She kept her back to Aidan as he joined her. He was distraught, knowing in his heart he had failed his princess. She refused to turn over and face him, to make amends for their unexpected spat, and used Dog as an emotional barrier.

'Sorry,' he said in soft tones.

TALK TO THE ANIMALS

'Admit it,' she admonished him. 'You're not ready for a confrontation with Stibley.'

'I'm more than ready,' he responded, his pride hurt.

'If you believe that, you're a fool,' she goaded him.

'I'm not a fool!'

'Go to sleep.'

It was an end to their conversation with her barbs leaving their sting. Aidan was to concede, the magic to have brought them together had deserted them.

He was no fool! Came the mantra in his head.

He glowered at the imaginary marks on her back, those he believed had been inflicted on his princess by the brute Stibley and wife, Lenska.

He had an irrational urge to lash out as Aidan replayed her suggestive taunts in his mind, refusing to believe she meant them.

It was the poison, he admitted to himself, used as a spell by the Wicked Witch to destroy their happiness.

He had to find a way to make amends.

He would find a solution.

At any cost!

CHAPTER 37

He opened his eyes to an array of sunbeams stabbing at the floor of the shelter through the myriad chinks in the ceiling and walls, saw dust motes and insects caught in the rays of brilliant light.

Imelda's slight frame was pressed along his body, finger tips tracing his frown, her imploring eyes gazing down on his face.

'We should get married,' she entreated. She became momentarily pensive as she awaited his response.

'I would like that,' he whispered and close to tears, as the night's events seemed to have been forgotten. 'How can we do this? Where shall we get married?'

'We have no need of a church nor minister,' she confided. 'The magical woods will provide its blessing. I want this so badly, Aide. It's all of which I can think.'

'For me to be your prince and husband?'

'Yes.'

'For you to be my wife and princess?'

'Yes. Can we?'

He pulled her down and kissed her, had her moaning and chuckling quickly. She was the first to break the magical circle of love as her mind became a deluge of all the things she needed to prepare for, in readiness for the ceremony which would define and consummate their combined love.

'I will make garlands for our hair,' she enthused, with rapture glinting in her eyes. 'And cloaks of leaves, flowers, and berries. I will fashion rings from twine to bind us for eternity.'

'I can help.'

'You, my darling, are to go out and provide food for the banquet.'

'Yes, I can do that. I wish that we had something to play music on, so that we can dance together following the ceremony.'

'The music is all around us,' she mused. 'You only have to listen to hear nature's symphony.'

'Wow! You're right.'

'Dog and Cat can give us away.'

Aidan smiled, knowing Cat did what Cat wanted to do, and didn't play by another's rules.

'We don't have cake,' and his remark had his princess laughing. To see her joyously happy was, to his mind, the most special thing he could have hoped for. 'Not only do I not have cake,' he persisted. 'I have nothing to give you as a gift as a token of my love.'

TALK TO THE ANIMALS

'I would have you as my token,' and she paused to kiss him. 'The gift I would ask, is for you to give me a baby.'

The suggestion stole his breath even as he was witness to her sincerity. He didn't think she was remembering why she had fled to the woods. He hoped she was not.

'Grant me a daughter or a son and I will be forever content.'

He held her tight, her hair splayed across her smile and covered his solemn frown.

Deep down Aidan was jubilant.

The magic had returned.

CHAPTER 38

Summer had returned and Imelda was quickly into an obsessive regime preparing for her forthcoming marriage to her prince. Having bathed in the pool, Imelda's initial task was to gather leaves and wildflower buds to make ceremonial garments.

Aidan had taken his spear, and Dog for company, and set-off mid-morning on a hunting expedition to provide food to sustain them. He had made up his mind, if there was no roadkill to be recovered he would have to hunt the wildlife. Neither of them wanted to, but their situation was desperate and it was an avenue they had to take to survive.

Aidan had thought about raiding farms and nearby houses, and quickly dismissed the idea as foolhardy, as he had no wish to have the authorities called to investigate.

Life was fairly good, he would say to himself, no matter their ghosts intruded occasionally to spoil the idyllic existence they had made for themselves. They were free of tyranny, rules, and regulations. They were able to enjoy a life without fear.

Aidan could not dismiss the fact Stibley and his wife, Lenska, still posed a problem. He would often think of the others and the torment they were facing.

TALK TO THE ANIMALS

He was on an adventure and he had a purpose. He had no wish to labour over recriminations against the enemy, only to savour the forthcoming marriage to his one true love; his fairy tale princess. He pondered her words, in that the greatest gift he could give her was a baby.

He didn't want to think beyond the concept of making a baby.

It was whilst trudging along the side of the road with Dog the idea was given potency.

What did he know about pregnancy and the birthing element? He supposed, close to the time, they could find the nearest hospital for assistance. Not that he had an idea where the nearest hospital was situated and whether they could make it on foot.

The fact remained, they had plenty of time to discuss what was best for Imelda and for the baby.

They would have to give false names, and not mention the orphanage. He had no wish to have Stibley and Lenska informed as life could get difficult. Awk ward. Dangerous.

Having these thoughts had him realise he'd been gripping the spear tightly and his hand throbbed.

Aidan and Dog went to the end of the woods without having luck finding fresh roadkill to take back. They crossed the road and worked their way back.

On a few occasions they had to duck out of sight and use the undergrowth and trees as cover to avoid being seen by passing motorists and a lone cyclist.

TALK TO THE ANIMALS

The young man on his racing bicycle caused Aidan a moment's apprehension as he wondered if Dog meant to give chase or draw attention to their position by barking.

Dog thankfully behaved himself, perhaps realising the importance of their primary mission and to remain anonymous to outsiders.

'Why spoil a good thing?' he'd chuckled to Dog. 'Who needs to know we even exist? We're not harming anyone. What do you say?'

Dog chuffed as he bounded along the grassy bank on the side of the road. Aidan followed, alert to the groans of an engine in the distance either direction, and watchful for cyclists and ramblers.

They stumbled along almost to the far reaches of the woods without any joy finding food.

Giving up, they crossed the road with the intention of returning. Aidan had made up his mind to fashion a fishing rod and try his luck angling in the nearby river. His concern was having no food to show for their efforts and wondering how his princess would take the news.

Dog was first to stop in his tracks and emitted a low growl. Aidan then saw a deer loping in out of the trees further ahead. He grabbed Dog by the neck to keep him from charging and squatted beside him to observe the stricken doe.

It appeared to be injured and was favouring one of its hind legs.

Aidan glowered at his spear and asked himself if he had the courage to act on his thoughts.

TALK TO THE ANIMALS

The full-grown deer was in a lot of distress and was unable to flee, instead froze, having picked up the scent of intruders.

Aidan saw this as an opportunity to prove himself worthy to his princess and silently thanked the magical woods for the gift of provision.

TALK TO THE ANIMALS

CHAPTER 39

It was a difficult proposition dragging the heavy carcase almost a half mile to the atoll and by the time he reached home perspiration poured off his flesh. His arms and legs screamed in agony but he was proud of his achievements.

Leaving the corpse at the base of the atoll Dog went ahead while Aidan took his time climbing the gradient to reach the ledge. He paused to rest, sat down, and drew air into his lungs where it burned and had him gagging.

With the arrival of Dog Imelda appeared at the entrance to the shelter and she was smiling joyously to have her prince return. She seemed not to notice the blood smearing his arms and chest and legs. Imelda cautiously edged along the precarious shelf to be beside him.

Managing a triumphant smile, he indicated he had a surprise for her by pointing down to the woodland floor. Imelda's eyes lit up and she gave a yelp of surprise.

'My brave and strong warrior,' she gushed and throwing her arms about him, kissing him passionately. 'How did you manage to get it back? Jesus, Aide, you must be in a lot of pain.'

He nodded.

TALK TO THE ANIMALS

''Come inside,' she insisted. 'I'm going to give you a massage, after which, we will go down together and cut the deer into manageable portions.

He nodded again as he was too exhausted to answer.

'I'm so proud of you, my beautiful man.'

She somehow assisted him to his feet and navigated him to the shelter without mishap. She guided him to the cot and had him lie down on his back.

'Close your eyes,' she cajoled him in soft tones.

He chuckled to feel her weight and warmth settle on his thighs and was able to imagine he was drifting on currents of air as she applied her hands to his chest and worked unbelievable magic to his aches and pains.

'I have also been busy in your absence,' she confessed. 'I've already made our crowns and I think you will love the pendant talismans I have fashioned using animal bones and feathers. I'll show you when you're all done.'

To stop him from drifting to sleep she kept talking to him.

'I've been doing a lot of thinking, regarding what we discussed yesterday,' she added. 'I think we should help the others at the orphanage, or at least try. I've been remembering a few names even recalling their faces. When an image pops into my head it's like I'm sharing their pain and sadness. I can sense their hopelessness and an acceptance of the situation they shouldn't be in.'

Aidan opened his eyes and was witness to a strange, otherworldly light flickering in her irises, and it was quickly gone so that he was wondering if he'd imagined the daunting anomaly. He'd seen something else, that which moulded her features briefly. He'd seen another's presence and had him thinking his princess was possessed by the Wicked Witch.

Imelda lowered her head and kissed his chest where the teasing began in earnest.

The moment she elevated him from the abyss of his tiredness and had him aroused, she gave his stomach a playful pat and leapt to her feet.

'If you're up to it, we have some work to do,' she said and flounced around effetely. 'We will have to eat what we can and drag what's left into the bushes for the flies and wildlife to feast on. The meat will not keep in this heat and we don't want to risk getting food poisoning.'

Aidan almost quipped; it was okay to eat the poisonous mushrooms and thought better of it. He sat up and let his gaze roam suggestively from her smile to her feet as she removed her dress.

'This is going to be messy,' she winked at him. 'We'll hang a few steaks up and then I suggest we go and clean up before making a fire.'

'Or, you could come here and join me, and allow me to light your fire.'

'As tempting as you are, my adorable prince, I need you to keep your strength and help carve up the deer before moving what we can't eat into the woods.'

'If you say so, princess.'

'I do.'

TALK TO THE ANIMALS

She laughed and swayed her body flirtatiously and when he made a playful lunge for her, she easily avoided being taken hostage. She went for the granite blade and feeling its power in her grasp, flounced to the entrance and became silhouetted by a waning sun.

Aidan removed his shorts while unable to take his eyes off the eerie anomaly, of his princess without any discernible features on this occasion. Only the muted light on the fringes of her curves hinted there remained substance to her form.

He had no wish to succour the notion he might be having a premonition as he was unable to comprehend its meaning if he was. It was enough that her image made him anxious.

He quickly dispelled gloomy thoughts and raced after her the moment she dodged out of sight with Dog on her heels. Imelda was already along the ledge and gingerly navigating passage down the gradient to the woodland floor.

Her peals of laughter were enough to elevate his mood and it was not long before he too was feeling the magical joy his princess was exhibiting.

As expected, it was a grisly task dissecting the deer into manageable portions and dragging the remains of the carcase into the woods. It was when they went to the stream bed to bathe, the familiar anxiety returned, as Aidan was unable to see beyond the blood and gore congealing on her skin. Her face was speckled crimson as she turned to him, her smile fading when she saw the way he was looking at her.

'Want to help me?' she asked coquettishly in the hope it would break the spell.

He stepped closer; speechless and desperately wanting thee wrench to his heart to dissipate..

She slipped her arms around his neck.

'Life is perfect,' she whispered to him.

He nodded glumly, knowing he was close to tears.

Weeping for love and joy was not a weakness, he told himself.

Imelda had a unique way of tapping into his emotions. His love for her was a burgeoning entity, with no discernible boundaries. She was the one who had cast a spell and he was ensnared.

It had always been the way, even before his first kiss. Even before he was given an opportunity to hold her lovingly and protectively in his arms. From distance, he had nurtured love for her.

'Let's pick some mushrooms for later,' she implored in softly erotic tones, those which caressed his troubled thoughts suggestively and had him wondering where the encroaching night would lead them.

CHAPTER 40

Probably, as Imelda was in high spirits and had been since his return from a fortuitous hunting expedition, partaking of the spurious mushrooms they had collected did not veer towards dark and nefarious content. They expanded her inimitable joy and became infectious.

She danced naked by firelight, drawing intricate patterns with her sinuous arms while humming while humming a tune, which was itself, magical.

Aidan crawled off their crib to join her, Cat grumbling and Dog mooching to where the scent of venison lingered on the stone floor.

Lovers danced as one in a beautiful melding of souls, even though their combined movements became clumsy and comical caused by the euphoric tide of poison in their system.

Imelda stopped suddenly and used her prince's willowy frame for support as she held his face to get attention.

Aidan giggled as in the licking flames of firelight her cherubic face seemed to perpetually distort.

'We should think of names for our baby,' she said.

TALK TO THE ANIMALS

'We have plenty of time,' he answered, barely able to stand upright as he felt the ground beneath his feet give a lurch and for the wall at her back to move towards them.

'I would like all the animals of the woods to attend our wedding,' she moaned as she felt him aroused against her belly. 'I would like to invite Mister Tree.'

'What of the Wicked Witch?' he teased as he nibbled her shoulder and sucked the salty flesh. 'Should we not invite her so that we can make a pact and receive her blessing?'

'We could, I suppose,' she responded unconvincingly.

She leaned away and tilted her head back, long trails of coppery red hair gracing the floor as a waterfall of fire.

'Tomorrow,' she said and without straightening her back, 'I will finish our ceremonial gowns provided by Mother Nature and discuss our vows of commitment to one another. I will send a message to all our woodland friends.

She moved her hips suggestively.

'I want you to take me to our bed,' she rasped, raising herself and kissing him fervently. She jumped and hugged his hips and gave a yelp.

Aidan was witness to the carnal light in her eyes and felt her fetid breath on his skin as she exhaled and moaned deeply.

'Let's make a baby together this night,' she sighed.

CHAPTER 41

The following day was blessed by peak temperatures and an undiluted sun as Imelda contented herself putting the finishing touches to the leafy and floral robes prior to the big day of their marital union.

Her mind was besotted with the idea she might already be pregnant and tittered, reminiscing on the hedonistic night of lust she had enjoyed with her prince. She always dreamt of conceiving of a son or daughter and as quickly, dismissed the thought that she had been pregnant before.

It was ridiculous notion, she chided herself, as it would have meant she had fled to the woods and abandoned her baby.

She concentrated on her prince, marvelling at his beauty and virility, his unwavering love for her.

Aidan was on an adventure and had taken along his spear and a bark vessel, not for the purpose of hunting he'd informed her. His primary aim was to complete a reconnaissance of the woods and ensure their idyllic existence had not been compromised.

Imelda wished to focus getting his mind to think positively, as in recent days he had become significantly despondent, defensive, and negative. He was someone who did not believe all could be harmonious and wonderful indefinitely and expected something to come along and spoil everything.

Life situations had taught him to doubt and not to trust. His natural instincts were honed towards those elements they were unable to control.

Imelda was of the belief, this expedition he had embarked on, would go a long way to appeasing his troubled conscience should he be satisfied the Magical Woods was not home to outsiders and their safety was ensured.

Imelda was in her own happy place and wanted it to remain so.

Aidan's travail had not been carefully planned at the beginning. He moved in the direction of the road as a starting point and meant to criss-cross the heart of the woodland and cover as much of the area as he was able in the day.

He had to rely on his own instincts and cunning, not make too much noise and proceed slowly and cautiously while listening for sounds not made by the wildlife. He did not have Dog as a companion on this occasion as he believed it was best he should remain at the shelter and protect his princess.

Away from them at this time served to make him even more despondent. The solitude played on his mind and despite having the spear grasped in one hand, he did not feel the security for which he had hoped.

TALK TO THE ANIMALS

Those few animals he met as he traipsed through the woods, he asked if they had seen other humans in recent times, and received a mixed response.

A vixen had replied she had. A squirrel pondered its answer before stating he had not seen another human. A grouse stuttered and fled without giving a response, clearly startled and was afraid.

Aidan spoke with the trees and it was as if he had stirred them out of a slumber to get them to speak. One bemoaned the fact a ragamuffin had uncouthly urinated up its trunk. The Tree's remark had Aidan instantly wondering if the ragamuffin Tree spoke of had been a casual visitor to the woods or was still residing there as he and his princess were.

When Aidan continued he slowed his pace so as to make minimal noise as he advanced, occasionally stabbing at the denser clusters of undergrowth as a warning to anyone who was using the shrubs to conceal them.

He eventually arrived at the rabbit warren which invoked wonderful memories he had shared in recent times with his princess. He became instantly in awe of its simple tranquillity and beauty and quickly soothed his troubled conscience so that the last threads of lingering doubt were removed.

He chose an area ablaze with sunlight and sat, placing the spear and vessel to the side as he stretched his long limbs. He watched families of rabbits at play without drawing them into a conversation and before long he lay back and closed his eyes.

Aidan used the interlude to put his life into perspective. He tried, as Imelda was constantly encouraging him, to keep his thoughts positive. It was no easy task though. Not when he had his memories to reflect on.

Despite now having everything he had ever dreamed of, his painful past would not allow him respite for too long.

It had him constantly wondering why freedom and a union of love was not enough to grant him peace.

He hoped, in time, it would change so that he did not have to wake each day fearful and feeling anguish.

Aidan could feel a smile stretching his jaw as he was imagining becoming married to his princess. They were to have a baby. It was a topic which should have been the motivational tool he was seeking to progress and leave the past behind.

Nothing in life was easy.

'How will you know if the baby is yours or not?' came a strident voice and had Aidan sitting up sharply, his gaze meeting with that of an inquisitive buck.

'What the…?' Aidan blustered as he sought to desperately align his train of thoughts. 'How could you possibly know my princess is to have a baby?'

'There is magic in the woods, but you already know that,' said the Rabbit as it nonchalantly hopped in tight circles on the sun-bleached grass.

'Why would you even think the baby could be someone else's?' Aidan protested.

'The Wicked Witch of the woods will decide.'

'Have you met the Wicked Witch? Does she even exist?'

TALK TO THE ANIMALS

'Yes, and yes,' the Rabbit chuntered, became nervous, and agitated as it sensed Aidan's emerging hostility.

'I would love to meet the Witch,' Aidan sneered, his voice having grown brittle.

'You already have,' said Rabbit, its bright starry eyes twinkling in the glare from the sun. *'I'm surprised you didn't recognise her. The Witch is clever. She is spiteful. She can be seductive and very persuasive when she chooses to be, and they are the moments you let your guard down and become caught in her spell.'*

'Since you are here, are you coming to the wedding?' Aidan suddenly asked to steer the conversation onto safer territory. 'The princess and I would love to have the animals and birds, even the trees attend our ceremony and for all to give their blessing.'

'You have our blessing. No need to leave our homes and travel as it would not be safe for the little ones to venture too far from the warren.'

'It will be a special and magical occasion,' Aidan added thoughtfully. 'It is to be my dream come true, if I'm honest.'

The rabbit hopped away.

A colourful Jay swooped and landed on the grass, studiously pecking at the ground, and seemed unconcerned a human was observing her nearby.

'Are you coming to the wedding?' Aidan asked hopefully.

'Wedding? Know nothing about a wedding.'

'I'm to marry my princess.'

'Good for you, young man.'

'I'm more than that. I am a prince and fearless warrior.'

'Yet you are afraid.'

'I am not!'

'You worry, that you are not enough for your princess. You can't stop thinking about the past and how it once was. Your princess is always one to seek attention. She is flirtatious and her behaviour sometimes gets her into trouble.'

'That was the past. It's different now.'

'If you say so.'

'She loves me. I love my princess more than anything in the world. We're going to make a baby.'

'Think, you can raise a baby in the woods without medical supplies and professional guidance? What are you going to do for necessities, as with nappies, baby food? It's not right, I tell you! It will not be as easy as you think. That is my point, you are not thinking straight young man.'

'I'm a prince!'

The Jay leapt, stretched its wings, and flew away.

'Stupid bird,' Aidan muttered. 'You're all stupid!'

CHAPTER 42

Aidan returned to the shelter as afternoon dipped towards twilight and believed for a moment he had entered the realms of an enchanted world.

His princess was oblivious of his arrival as she sang, laughed, and danced with an excitable Dog.

Aidan's love for his princess soared as there was never a more beautiful image, than seeing her free-spirited and parading around gloriously naked.

He paused and the magic swiftly dissipated as, on this occasion, her gaiety and nudity in the company of an aroused Dog he saw as unnatural.

Laying the spear and vessel on the ground he made a sudden lunge and possessively grabbed her waist and lashed out at dog with a foot. Dog yelped.

Imelda went from happy to crazy-angry in an instant, rounding on Aidan and shoving him back, slapping his chest.

Don't you dare fucking take out your problems on Dog!' she screamed at him. 'What's got into you anyway? Jesus, Aide, you can be such a fucking arsehole!'

TALK TO THE ANIMALS

'I wasn't seeing Dog for a moment,' he lied, 'Thought…'

'You thought, what? That I had someone else to entertain me while you were gone?'

'Sorry.'

He tried to reach out and she stepped away, firelight distorting her features unnaturally, so that she no longer resembled the princess he loved and was devoted to.

She barged past him and ran to the ledge, hesitating, before turning an angry scowl at her prince.

'Don't follow me!' she warned. 'I wish to be on my own.'

She ducked to the side as Aidan was rooted, both undecisive and helpless.

Dog gave him a wide berth and scooted past his position, intent on being with his mistress and as with Imelda, had no wish to stay in the angry, foolish young man's company.

Aidan eventually reacted by throwing himself onto the cot and wept, disturbing a slumbering Cat who had not witnessed the volatile exchange and was unable to voice an opinion either way.

Cat yawned and stretched, gave a sobbing Aidan a rueful look and settled again.

Imelda threw herself assertively through the fragrant undergrowth with Dog hugging her heels. She kept her lips pursed in a grimace of anguish as the dry, humid conditions encouraged swarms of insects to dance around her head and cling to the perspiration on her skin.

If it was witchery, she was thinking, the insects would devour her and put an end to the misery she was immersed in.

When eventually she arrived at the chuckling brook she dropped to her knees and began scrabbling around the base of a tree, and then another, as she needed sustenance. That, which she craved more than anything.

The light was so poor she was barely able to define anything specifically as everywhere was in silhouette.

She continued to probe around the exposed roots and mulch and gave a squeal of delight when fingers brushed against a small cluster of tiny mushrooms. She eagerly tugged them free and munched on them without thinking to wash then first.

Within her trouble mind she sought an urgent need to encourage a confrontation with the Wicked Witch, in the vain hope she could make a pact with her. If a compromise could be reached to satisfy all parties, Imelda believed her fantasy world would again become magical and beautiful.

She smiled to catch Dog mooching around, snuffling the mulch, and seemingly not distressed following Aidan's unexpected assault.

Imelda rolled her head and eyes thinking, her prince could be an insufferable fool at times.

What was he thinking? Her mind screamed a rebuke.

She had seen a side to her prince she did not like. It had her wondering if her prince was just like all the others, those who could so easily masquerade in the guise of kindness, even love.

TALK TO THE ANIMALS

When, in truth, there resided a monster just beneath the surface, waiting for the right moment to reveal itself.

She berated herself, as she was the one who wanted her prince to be just like Stibley, not that she was able to recall why.

She had no idea who Stibley was. If the monster Aidan often referred to had been a part of her life and was the reason she'd fled to the woods, she was still unable to remember.

Dwelling on Aidan's sudden and unexpected attack on Dog, she supposed it's what Stibley would have done, not that it made it right.

Her prince had accused Dog of being unnaturally aroused, if at all he saw Dog and not Stibley dancing with her. Imelda did not think as Aidan did, and believed Dog was merely expressing happiness and excitement, and she had been.

Imelda puffed her cheeks and noticed her companion was nowhere around, surmising he was following an interesting scent.

An owl hooted in the distance and the eerie haunting sound had her smiling.

Eruptions of light ignited in her head, consumed her vision, so that the trees and undergrowth were magically transformed and became animated entities around her.

The owl called again, the ethereal sound reverberating, as if to herald something momentous was to occur.

In her miasmic state of perplexity Imelda suddenly clutched her chest and staggered to her feet, believing she had seen a strange light moving in and out of the shrubbery opposite.

TALK TO THE ANIMALS

A fairy light sprang to mind and then she was thinking the Wicked Witch had answered her call. She had no choice but to wait and prepare for a confrontation.

The light anomaly approached, wavering, and stuttering and becoming larger.

A tall, shadowy form, blacker than the gloom, became silhouetted behind the bright glare of a heavy torch the figure was holding.

Imelda froze, all substance seeping out of her limbs as the wide arc of light illuminated her nakedness.

'Are you the Wicked Witch?' she asked in a tremulous voice.

The light beam swept up from her legs to her face, momentarily blinding her. She winced against the sudden stab of pain to her eyes, yet brazenly stood her ground as strength returned to her gelid limbs.

'Are you in trouble?' a male voice enquired and the tone was kindly, in no way oozing with menace.

As she'd expected.

'Who are you and why are you creeping around the woods?' she asked and trying to see beyond the light through the sits of her eyes.

'It's what I do from time to time,' came the person's mild retort.

Imelda was a little relieved when the full beam moved from her face, before realising the intruder was using it to highlight her nudity. Her aroused breasts seemed to glow.

TALK TO THE ANIMALS

'I am on a hunting trip, if you must know, and came to bag myself some fresh kill,' he added, and hoped his comment did not conjure up an alternative meaning. 'What's your story if you don't mind me asking? I mean, what are you doing in the woods without clothes? Were you attacked? Are you running from someone and became lost?'

'No. I am the princess of the woods. This is my home,' she informed him and feeling the powerful magic coursing through her veins to give her courage.

She didn't say as much, yet she quite liked the way the stranger was observing her and the way he caressed her flesh with the beam of light from the torch.

'Do you consider me beautiful?' she asked, and the sudden obvious question startled her.

She even believed for a moment, she had heard the Wicked Witch chuckling and goading her.

'I guess,' came the stranger's response.

Imelda was trying to see around the light beam as it had now travelled lower, in the hope the stranger's features had acquired definition.

He could have been a faceless monster, she deduced, even as she marvelled at her own fearlessness.

He was wearing a dark combat coat with bulging pockets and matching trousers. A belt was cinched around his waist. She clearly saw the knife concealed in a long sheath.

The magical euphoric tide from the poison in her blood had her reeling again. Her gaze flitted side to side to determine where Dog was. A terrifying thought sprung to mind and had her clutching her chest.

'Have you harmed my dog?' she asked firmly.

'No, I have not. Your dog, I think, took himself off, that way,' and he indicated the direction by raising his free arm and pointing.

'What do you propose to do now?' she enquired, as strength ebbed away in her tone.

The stranger responded by sweeping the torch beam down to stab at the ground and reflect off his boots.

'I suppose, I could move on,' he said without conviction. 'As long as you can convince me you're okay and are not in trouble.'

'I must ask, that you do not speak to anyone of my presence here in the woods,' she pleaded.

She maintained her position, despite swaying, as the stranger stepped closer, his large frame swallowing the gloom between them. Imelda tensed, feeling a moment of contrition, as she imagined she was caught between two opposing magical forces.

She watched the stranger stoop to place the torch on the ground and gasped as he straightened and placed his hands on her hips. She didn't protest or fight him as he pulled her close and quietly accepted her fate as the stranger – the Wicked Witch – kissed her on the mouth in earnest.

Imelda let herself flow with him, a part of her hoping Dog would return and rescue her, while the darker side of her psyche had no wish to be rescued.

TALK TO THE ANIMALS

Colour, as a tangible roiling tide, pushed around her thoughts and behind her eyes. The poison, the Witch's potion, had claimed her soul and set her spirit free.

She moaned as her own unequivocal desire matched the stranger's.

He lay her down on the mulch and his big frame swallowed and absorbed her, the Wicked Witch cackling in her mind.

CHAPTER 43

Imelda eventually summoned the strength to crawl off the faceless, nameless entity, leaned away and retched. She was unable to fully cleanse her mind or was able to embrace the elation she had expected to feel.

She took a moment to steady her breathing, swallowing deeply and clutching her breast and stomach. Her flesh was afire, her muscles complaining as she wiped her mouth and gave a throaty growl.

Her gaze swept the gloom and managed a smile.

She'd triumphed against the Wicked Witch!; her mind clamoured.

She shuffled closer to the figure stretched alongside her and prodded his bare chest. Her efforts, unsurprisingly, gained no response as she clasped the hilt of the hunting knife, twisted, and eased it from his sternum. She wiped the blade on his open shirt and proceeded to remove his belt, placing the weapon securely in its sheath when she had done so.

Remaining pensive she rummaged through the pockets of his coat and combat trousers which were gathered around his feet.

TALK TO THE ANIMALS

There was no money to be found. All he had about his person was a sleeve of gum and she popped one into her mouth to freshen her breath. There was a utility knife with an array of blades and a corkscrew. There was an unopened pack of tissues and a tobacco tin. This she discarded by launching it into the shrub.

The bag he'd dropped revealed two rabbits and three grouse and she was delighted. There was also a metal flask and the contents seemed quite potent when she sniffed and recoiled.

The knives, belt, and flask went into the bag and she strapped this over her shoulders and under her arms.

She called to dog and waited before moving away upstream. Dog eventually caught up with her as she stopped to bathe and remove traces of blood from her skin. She greeted her companion with a hug and kisses.

'We're free, Dog,' she rasped. 'I have defeated the Witch and put an end to her sorcery.'

Dog thrashed his tail excitably.

'Have you nothing to say?' she asked exuberantly. 'Come on, let's be heading home.'

They entered the shelter, the walls and ceiling illuminated by flickering orange images from the dying flames of a fire.

Aidan was on the cot with Cat, his back to the entrance, the residual capering light exploring the shadowy scars on his back and bare buttocks.

TALK TO THE ANIMALS

As she put the bag down and with Dog choosing to lie at the opening to the shelter, Imelda felt a measure of remorse seeing Aidan's scars which served as a reminder of a torrid past and was a reason he had fled to join her.

Inwardly, she felt the stirrings of anger, knowing her prince had suffered as she had.

She lay down and moulded her body to her prince, absorbing his heat and sensing he had come awake.

'Sorry,' he whimpered.

'I'm sorry,' she answered, kissing his bicep, and allowing her fingertips to trace each of his painful reminders.

The poison still flowed in her veins, distorting perspective on her thoughts. She wondered whether to confess she had been embroiled in a battle with the Wicked Witch and had to use seductive guile to defeat their nemesis.

Aidan rolled over and pulled her tight to his slender frame.

Imelda gave a chortle as once again, bright whorls of colour ignited behind closed lids as her body instantly responded to her prince's sweet caresses, powerful kisses, and urgency. He crawled between her thighs and she sought not to think of her desperate battle with the Witch in the woods as he made her cry aloud.

She felt her essence flowing into him and there came a sultry peal of laughter from within her mind. There was something disconcerting in the manner of the cackling and did not believe it was her own.

TALK TO THE ANIMALS

She cried out, and reserved another cry for within, as she believed the Wicked Witch had taken up residence inside her.

CHAPTER 44

Aidan awoke, befuddled and sore, dry-mouthed, and hungry.

He caught his princess laying out their ceremonial garments she had lovingly prepared for their special occasion.

Dog and Cat were nowhere to be seen.

'Baby!' he called to get her attention.

It was the moment he noticed the bulging backpack against the wall yet said nothing.

Imelda turned to face him, her vivacious smile lighting up her face and revealing her consummate joy.

'I suggest,' she said, 'We go and bathe and prepare ourselves. Afterwards, I would like you to try on your ceremonial regalia.'

'Are we to get married today?' he asked, breathless.

'It is my wish, yes. I cannot wait a moment longer if you must know. I want to be your wife, princess, and mother to our baby.'

TALK TO THE ANIMALS

Aidan was unable to answer as he had hoped to, was completely at a loss for words, as he clambered unsteadily to his feet and went to her. She took his hand and led him from the shelter. On their way out he noticed several bark shells filled with an assortment of berries and an array of wild blossoms. A smaller vessel contained mushrooms, and they were of a variety he recognised instantly.

Imelda had been busy; he was thinking. She had everything meticulously planned and he was expected to go with the flow and share her joy.

He wanted to; he supposed. Marrying his princess and settling down with her, had been his dream since the day he met her.

There were times when she was like a beautiful angel, an ethereal spirit, a magical presence who was able to weave enchantment with a smile.

There was her alter persona, that which lurked in the shadowy recesses of her mind, an entity which unnerved him if he was honest. It was a side of her which frightened him.

They bathed in the rockpool and revelled in the sultry heat of a morning's summer sun. The day was starting like a dream.

Back at the shelter, Aidan quietly succumbed to Imelda's enthusiastic attention as she adorned him in an exquisite robe, an interwoven tapestry of leaves, flower blossoms and large berries. She took time adjusting the loin cloth as he was to become aroused quickly and she delighted in his predicament. She was constantly slapping his hand away as he tried to get her to commit to more.

TALK TO THE ANIMALS

Lastly, she was to place the crown of entwined sinewy twigs, leaves and blossoms atop his unruly mop of blond curls.

She stepped back to admire him and saw that he was mesmerised. Her smile, as always, had cast a spell.

Imelda showed him the delicate rings she had fashioned, along with a braid of vine she proposed to bind their wrists as they spoke their vows of eternal commitment.

Having confessed he loved the attire and stated just how proud he was of her achievements, Imelda proceeded to undress him and set everything aside in readiness for the big occasion.

Having had his advances rebuffed all Aidan could think about was food.

'I'm going to collect water,' she said softly. 'Would you be a dear and prepare the fire? We have plenty of wood.'

Considering it was hot, humid, and stuffy, a smoky fire would be distinctly unpleasant, he reasoned.

Aidan did not protest as he had no wish to spoil the moment. Everything was perfect in their little personal world.

Lost in thought, Aidan was unaware his princess had vacated the shelter as he was intent on getting a tuft of dry grass to light. Only when he glanced over his shoulder did he realise he was alone. That was the moment attention drifted to the mysterious backpack against the wall and it had him wondering how his princess had come to have it in her possession. It concerned him she had not mentioned it.

Frustrated at his failed attempts to start a fire he crawled across to investigate the bag and its contents.

TALK TO THE ANIMALS

He flinched as he saw the stiffened carcases of a rabbit and a clutch of three grouse. He was more intrigued by the other objects; a knife secure in its sheath and looped to a belt intrigued him more than the other contents, despite the fact his stomach was growling as a reminder he was hungry.

Lifting the belt, he popped the fastening stud and removed the heavy weight knife with a ribbed bone handle. He turned it first one way and then the other, the blade glinting as he observed the way it had been honed to razor sharpness.

The feel of it in his palm and the power it gave him, had him smiling. He replaced it carefully and cast attention back to the bag. Next to gain his interest was the Swiss army knife and he spent time inspecting each blade and utilitarian appendage,

The flask beckoned and he ruefully unscrewed the plated cap and sniffed the contents, instinctively recoiling as the heady aroma of brandy burned his nostrils.

Imelda returned as he was replacing it and moved to hover over his crouched position, letting her fingers toy with his loose blond curls.

'Where did you get this?' he asked her and waited anxiously for a response, aware of her proximity and relaxed poise.

'I found it abandoned in the woods,' she answered him.

'Why would someone leave this behind? It makes no sense.'

'I have no idea. Fortuitous, is how I see it. We needed food for the wedding banquet, and we have knives. Perfect, for cutting into carcases quickly and easily.'

TALK TO THE ANIMALS

'Whoever left this will probably return to reclaim it.'

She crouched down and draped an arm across his shoulders.

'It's my belief, the woods provided for us. Whoever left this behind may have become frightened by something and fled. Chances are, they won't return, supposing they could even find the exact location of the bag they left behind. I think, the magic worked in our favour. What if, this person confronted the Wicked Witch. She might have turned him into a toad.'

Astonished, Aidan shuffled round, and her softening beauty and unwavering smile melted his resolve. She had him believing anything was possible.

'What now?' he asked hopefully.

'Getting the fire started would help.'

'What are you going to be doing?'

'I mean to go in to the woods and speak with the animals and trees, and the birds. I wish to let them know, this is to be a special day, a magical day, and would have them all give their blessing.'

'Take the knife,' he insisted calmly. 'For protection. Just in case.'

She kissed him and then she was tugging the belt and knife from the backpack, enjoying his avid attention as widening eyes explored her nudity. She cinched and fastened the belt around her slender waist and posed for him.

TALK TO THE ANIMALS

She kissed him again and despite his obvious excitement and urgency, laughed and flounced away, blowing him a final kiss as she slipped away along the ledge.

CHAPTER 45

Aidan focussed attention on the task he'd been set, aggrieved there had been no matches or a lighter in the mysterious backpack. He tried not dwelling on the argument of the previous night which resulted in his princess taking off in anger.

He had been left with unrelenting guilt and shame and it seemed like an eternity in Hell before she returned to the shelter. He was forgiven, his attack on Dog forgotten. The marriage was going ahead, as planned.

Life was perfect again, despite the thought feeling vacuous.

He would make it his mission to keep it perfect if he chose his words carefully and did not allow his personal misgivings to intrude and mar her happiness.

The fire ignited as he blew on the tinder and let the grass burn. He added more to the infant flames before placing a few substantial small branches to the trough. The billowing smoke eventually dissipated and Aidan sat back, pleased with his efforts.

TALK TO THE ANIMALS

His next task was to prepare the rabbit and grouse and set aside the meat for later.

The Swiss army knife was an assertive addition to their array of meagre tools. The hunting knife would have been better. He was happy, knowing Imelda had it for protection.

Aidan reflected on the moment she had fastened the belt around her waist where the leather sheath hugged a hip and thigh, looking more like a Valkyrie warrior than a fairy tale princess. He'd been consumed with pride, and not for the first time.

Once the cuts of meat were prepared and left suspended in a bark shell with leaves covering their meal to keep flies from laying their eggs on the offering, Aidan took himself off to the rockpool.

Imelda returned soon after he had finished bathing, appearing as a Goddess, her skin gleaming, her hair as a waterfall of fire.

'My handsome prince!' she exclaimed happily. 'This day is wonderful, and knowing there is more to come fills me with hope our future is blessed.'

Aidan rose from the cot and went to her, wrapping her in his arms possessively as his love for her poured as an unyielding tide. They kissed, caressed, and each became aroused to fervour.

As the obvious power to their throne, Imelda intimated they should get the ceremony started.

Giggling infectiously, she dressed him and when all was finished to her satisfaction, she instructed her prince he was to do likewise.

TALK TO THE ANIMALS

Both dressed in their naturalistic finery they faced one another, sharing joy in a smile and with their combined love becoming a tangible and magical force outside of their bodies and mind, as within.

Never had his princess looked more beautiful, Aidan was thinking, as he struggled to repel the tears threatening to spill down his cheeks.

He caught her looking around for Dog and Cat, as if she had only just realised they were not present. Aidan prayed, their conspicuous absence would not spark dismay and ruin a glorious moment.

When she faced him again her smile radiated happiness, not sadness or disappointment as he had expected her to feel. Nothing could steal the lustre from her eyes or replace a smile with a frown.

CHAPTER 46

She stooped to where she had placed the interwoven binding she'd created and looped the taut plaited vine around his right wrist twice. She then encouraged him to do the same with her left wrist so that they were eternally bonded, she explained.

With fingers linked in a tremulous grasp, Imelda lifted her eyes from where their hands were joined, to his face, and liked that he was smiling effusively and was eager for the ceremony to take place.

'I'll begin,' she said breathlessly. 'When I have finished narrating the first passage of our vows I will nod, as a sign for you to proceed. Ready?'

'Ready,' he answered, his voice barely above a whisper.

'By the powers invested in me from the magical woods, Imelda and Aidan are to receive the blessing of all trees, the animals, and birds, cementing a marital union of two souls.'

She paused, inhaled deeply.

'Right!' she proclaimed. 'I, Imelda, take Aidan as my wedded prince for eternity. Your turn.'

TALK TO THE ANIMALS

'I, Aidan, take Imelda as my wedded princess for eternity,' he answered in quiet mumbling tones, as a measure of just how nervous he was feeling.

'I will love, honour, and stand at Aidan's side for eternity, till death do us part.'

Aidan repeated the vows Imelda had formulated for the occasion, outside of a Holy Church.

'We stand as equals in all things,' she proclaimed. 'We will be as one. I will cherish my soulmate, in good times and in bad. I will nurse him when he ails. I will battle his enemies. We stand as one, always.'

Aidan needed a little prompting to get his words to flow easily before Imelda continued with the next passage of their vows.

'The magic of the woods to flow in our veins has given its blessing, and will protect us always, and protect our son who grows even now within my belly. Aidan, I place your hand now over the heart which beats with joy in y womb.'

She raised his other hand to splay her stomach and kept it pressed there for a short time, before encouraging it to lay against her own heart,

'The beat you feel here, is of a heart adorned with love, for you Aidan.'

Aidan placed her hand on his chest.

'The heart you feel, beats with the love, for you Imelda, my princess.'

She chuckled.

TALK TO THE ANIMALS

'My body is not your possession,' she added, and Aidan experienced a moment of confusion, his smile replaced by the shadowy elements of a frown. 'But it is mine to give freely to you, my prince.'

'As I give mine to you,' he blustered.

Imelda turned and stooped to retrieve the hip flask, unscrewed the cap, and placed it to his lips.

'Anoint yourself of the spirit and feel the fire, as it represents the forces and power of adversity we may have to endure. And we do so, together, as one.'

Aidan swallowed and spluttered, Imelda doing likewise as the burn in her throat and nose encouraged a cluster of tears to her eyes.

She sealed the flask and put it down, stooping next to take a few mushrooms from one of the wooden vessels. She placed a small amount on his tongue and had him do the same. She began to chew and Aidan mimicked her actions, despite his reservations. They both swallowed and grimaced and spat. It had them giggling.

'The woods provide us with its magic,' she said, 'And we partake of its influence willingly.'

She placed her hands lightly on his hips beneath the cloak of leaves and florets.

'You may kiss the bride,' she intimated.

Aidan pulled her close and kissed her deeply.

When they eventually eased apart, Imelda declared, 'We are now, man and wife, prince, and princess. The woods are our realm and kingdom and we will honour its magic with love. Have you anything to add?'

'Only, that I promise to love you always. I love you so much, Immy, and I make it my sworn vow to have you live a life of happiness. No matter what obstacles we must face together. We live, as one.'

'And we will die, as one.'

She stepped closer and kissed him with passionate fervour as the poison coursing along her veins ignited bursts of brilliant colour in her mind.

'We should go into the woods,' she said and feeling him aroused despite which, she was determined to delay the moment they should consummate their special and magical day on the marital bed. 'We will parade our joy together and let the trees and animals see, that it is done. We are prince and princess and it is my wish they all witness our eternal union of two souls and to embrace the love we feel and share.'

Aidan only wanted to lay her down and rip her clothes off, even as caution beckoned him to rein in his desire and go with her into the woods.

He gave a groan and slapped his forehead as the magic burned a passage all the way to his toes and opened his mind to another world.

Still adorned in their ceremonial finery they ventured into the woods together and the wildlife and trees would be alert to their parade as Imelda's laughter and singing echoed high and wide and travelled a great distance.

TALK TO THE ANIMALS

Aidan could only think; what if someone else was in the woods and heard his princess? What if they were not friendly? What if they were the enemy?

Imelda was swept along on currents of magical wonder as spoke, waved, and sang to the trees. She called to the birds and cried her joy to the animals they were to meet along the way.

They eventually arrived at the rabbit warren where the rolling sea of verdant grass was dotted with scampering parents and their offspring.

Aidan became caught up in the mystical world his princess had woven for them and joined her by speaking to the free-spirited rabbits gambolling around their burrows, even to answer himself as he was also of the belief, the animals could communicate.

Happily, tearful, Imelda danced and pirouetted on her heels, the cloak of leaves spread, so as to give the impression she possessed the resplendent wings of a bird of prey.

Aidan imagined himself floating across to her where he grabbed her from behind and raised her up at the hips. She squawked her initial surprise and was then laughing manically, arms to the side, face tilted to the sun, and with her long trails of fiery red hair billowing down to smother his prince's face.

He lowered her gently and she turned in his arms, inviting a kiss and more as she slowly undressed him. Aidan removed her cloak and thong and wearing only their crowns, lay down on the warm bed of grass.

Their lovemaking was gentle, to begin with, and a deep mutual yearning was soon to change the tide of their mood.

TALK TO THE ANIMALS

Aidan saw the light in her eyes dissipate, her pale irises darkening, as a prelude to the beast residing within her emerging.

When they were spent, an energetic Imelda was again her carefree, spirited self as she skipped away from their position to continue singing and dancing.

She became lost in a world within her mind.

Aidan's confusion had him weeping and was ashamed of his overt display of weakness. He complained, not vociferously, but to himself. He was in a lot of pain and sore from the score marks her nails had raked along his flesh and from where she had bitten him.

At no time had he protested as a tide of emotion had driven him and had him endure the assault on his body. He had become ensnared within a spell he could not escape from.

He lay back, needing a moment to recover, his mind in disarray as he silently observed the spectacle played out before him – of Imelda dancing with the rabbits.

Imelda talking.

Singing.

Laughing.

Aidan sat up with a start as his ghosts came to their reception, unbidden by him, unwanted.

He blinked furiously, disbelieving all he was seeing, as he couldn't be certain if, what he was witnessing, was real or a figment of a cursed imagination.

TALK TO THE ANIMALS

Stibley was there; dancing up close to his naked princess. Others had joined to make up the party of revellers and Aidan recognised them as those who had stayed at the orphanage. There was Stewart, Ricardo, Blue and Ethan. Off to one side was Clara and Rachel and Aloise.

Aidan shook his head and searched each of the faces swimming in and out of focus. There was no Lenska, and he supposed it was a blessing.

Aidan was unable to comprehend how Stibley and the others could have known about his marriage to his princess and how it was they had found their way to the rabbit warren and the reception.

Aidan tugged his jaw and slapped his cheek to get his thoughts in perspective.

All around was gaiety, singing and laughter. All were dancing to music Aidan could not hear.

He didn't think it was right they should come uninvited to the reception and discard their clothes.

He supposed it was because his princess was naked they should feel obliged to do likewise. He was naked.

Aidan couldn't move and was unable to call out, or even to speak.

The shadowy melee merely swam in and out of focus against a backdrop of exploding colour.

Not surprising, Aidan's attention was mostly on Stibley as he didn't trust the gross pig. He hated that Stibley, with the pot belly and arrogant swagger, was jigging around in an aroused condition.

TALK TO THE ANIMALS

The others kept cutting across his vision and smothered a clear view of his princess and the evil tyrant.

Imelda might have been oblivious to the guests around her as she twirled, laughed, sang, and drew exotic patterns in the air with her sinewy arms and tapering fingers.

Even as he thought this, Imelda suddenly flashed a smile in Stibley's direction and even encouraged him to close the space. His princess seemed unconcerned he should approach and was overtly aroused.

She even beckoned Stewart and Ricardo to join them following which, she waved her arm in Rachel's direction and would have her join what was to become a tight intimate group.

Aidan saw the rabbits laughing at him and wished he had his spear.

Aloise and Clara were dancing together and it was a sensual aria which became physical as each embraced with an intimacy Aidan found shocking. Not that he hadn't witnessed such shenanigans before this day. The real world threatened to blend into the magical fantasy woven for him and only served to confuse him further.

Stewart and Blue were nearby, applauding and encouraging the girls.

Aidan's attention flitted to the larger group with his princess in the centre of the cheering, gyrating revellers. He was unable to react seeing Stibley pressing himself up behind his princess and wife, hands moving around her hips and stomach.

They all danced in unison, with Imelda keeping her balance only by hanging onto Ricardo's shoulder. She pulled him closer so that she became sandwiched between the two. She was laughing, grinding, and swaying, and only ceased to dance when she had two sets of hands exploring her intimately. She had one hand behind her rump, the other pushed down by her stomach.

Her lips parted and Aidan heard her sigh and growl and cry out; *Yes! Yes!*

Stibley had come to the party prepared, it seemed, and at no time had he relinquished his controlling ways. He snapped his fingers and Stewart and Blue approached, seemed to know what was required as they wrestled a laughing Imelda to the grass. Stibley dropped to his knees between her parted thighs.

Aidan was certain he had heard the Wicked Witch cackling.

In his mind, Aidan was screaming and tugging at his hair, wanting only for his ghosts and demons to disappear.

The rabbits continued to mock him, giving a running commentary as to what Stibley and the others were doing to his princess. Even Rachel was involved, and it was not the first time she'd expressed sexual interest in his princess.

All became horribly graphic, Aidan rolling onto his side and retching. Nothing came. Probably, as he'd not eaten for hours. The effort hurt his chest and stomach and he welcomed the pain.

Imelda's voice floated in the calm of a warm day to lay siege at the defiant walls he'd erected around his thoughts.

'Baby! Baby! Are you okay, my prince?'

TALK TO THE ANIMALS

She was carefully manoeuvring him to lie on his back, fingertips caressing his face and through a hazy prism of tears, he saw that she was smiling.

Looking beyond where she was straddling him he saw no sign of his demons. The guests had been dismissed from the party; his mind gleefully proclaimed.

All, save one; the Wicked Witch had stayed and meant to steal the ambient joyful glow from the eyes of his princess.

He could fight her or submit.

Aidan succumbed to the Witch's cunning wiles and power and cried aloud. He was to cry aloud several times before the Witch was finished with him.

CHAPTER 47

Back at the shelter, Dog was waiting and Imelda was eager to regale the boisterous companion with a rendition of the marriage ceremony and of the vows they had made, of their procession through the woods. She confessed, she was expecting a baby and it was sure to be a boy.

Aidan wanted only to crawl onto the cot and have all the unpleasant imagery disperse from his fevered brain.

His princess had refrained mentioning the guests to have attended their reception, as did Aidan. It was enough he had witnessed Stibley and the others taking full advantage, without any concern to the marital vows he and his princess had pledged.

Aidan couldn't stop weeping, it seemed.

When he eventually awoke it was late evening, and the pungent aroma of cooked meat in a wild berry coulis assailed his nostrils and had him salivating.

Cat had returned home; a family together again.

Aidan ate his meal in silence, wary of the mushrooms dotted around the meat and cooked into the sauce. He was ravenous and ate everything he was given. The feast was awesome.

Imelda conversed for both and even spoke for the animals.

Aidan didn't mind as he had more important things on his mind.

He needed to lay his ghosts firmly to rest.

Following the meal, Aidan could only throw himself back on the cot as his mind exploded with colour, expanding, and contracting, with fire burning in his veins.

A sense of déjà vu returned as behind closed lids he heard Imelda laughing and singing. He was instantly transported back to the reception at the rabbit warren in the afternoon. He knew his princess was dancing with Dog and serenading him, but all he could see in his mind's eye was a naked Stibley and the others, and the unnatural and disrespectful intimacy they had shown to Imelda. She encouraged them, he was thinking, couldn't help herself because she liked the attention. She liked they were happy and excited. She didn't mind being wrestled to the grass or protest when Stibley knelt between her thighs.

He tormented himself further, thinking their uninvited guests had followed them to the shelter. It was possible.

All he really wanted to think about was getting revenge.

'We should go to the orphanage,' he mumbled even as his words sounded incoherent to him. He raised his voice so that all would hear him. 'Yes, we should return to the orphanage!'

'Why?' Imelda enquired, having stopped singing and dancing and had possibly approached.

TALK TO THE ANIMALS

Aidan couldn't answer or open his eyes. He was unable to move, almost as if someone was holding him down. He sensed his princess kneeling beside him, the heat off her skin basking his nudity.

'We ran away, remember?' she stated in soft tones. 'We both had our reasons for doing so. The orphanage is a distant memory now. This is our home. The magical woods is our home. Here is our castle. You are my prince as I am your fairy tale princess.'

'Payback,' he groaned. 'Stibley and the others should be punished for what they did.'

'I don't remember what happened,' she answered quietly, thoughtfully, as she tried to soothe his temple with a hand. 'There is a reason I cannot recall events of my past, those which had me flee into the woods, and I prefer to keep it that way.'

'I don't feel well. I really don't.'

'Try to sleep, baby, you will feel better in the morning.'

Aidan rolled over placing his back to his princess and groaned, as griping pains sliced across his abdomen.

CHAPTER 48

With nightfall Imelda was unable to sleep or even to relax. The poison dictated the path of her thoughts and gave substance to each of them. Not all were of nefarious content, what they did, was keep her confused and to question so much she failed to understand.

Aidan had been wretchedly ill for a time following their wedding feast and she'd helped soothe his feverish ague with cool water. She hadn't minded removing vessels of his vomit and disposing of it. These were moments to be expected.

What surprised her, was the maturity she'd exhibited handling his situation and even wondered why she had not been afflicted as her prince had.

Lying awake exacerbated her frustrations and she desperately needed to formulate a strategy she hoped would appease her own conscience.

With a moon blinking in and out of a silhouette of cloud, Imelda crawled off the cot and put on the dress she'd worn when she had initially come to the woods. She put on her threadbare trainers and slipped the belt and knife around her waist.

TALK TO THE ANIMALS

She hesitated to massage her stomach and imagined it was already swollen with their growing baby.

From the backpack she retrieved the torch and was thankful the batteries still threw out an intense beam.

A memory ignited, of the time she was embroiled in a battle with the Wicked Witch and triumphed, bringing an end to the reign of the sorceress.

Imelda instructed a sleepy dog to remain and keep her prince company and quietly left the confines of their shelter.

It was a chill, late summer's night, not that it concerned Imelda as trudging through the trees and undergrowth kept her warm.

The torch light cut a jerky swath in the gloom, yet she found its source comforting and spiritually uplifting.

Where the shrub thinned tree trunks glared a garish silver as the beam cut across them.

Night creatures scurried away from her path and the strident, brittle snap of twigs and mulch beneath her determined tread. She stopped only to get her breath and placate the irregular beat of her heart.

Voluminous colour swatches exploded behind her irises as the mushroom's hallucinogenic poison boiled once again in her veins.

Imelda continued her relentless quest to reach the outskirts of the woods, at times wondering why she had left the shelter, or where she was headed. All became vague at times.

TALK TO THE ANIMALS

During a prolonged moment of lucidity, bolstered with courage and determination, Imelda continued ploughing a path through the trees and undergrowth. She eventually arrived at the edge of the woods and despite the open vista connecting fields to the dense body of trees in stark silhouette, Imelda felt its familiarity and it was eerily calling to her.

Almost, she believed, in seductive tones to lure her into a spell.

She was to leave the magical aura of the woods into a realm where the real world beckoned, a world and a time she had left behind, yet now sought to understand the reasons for doing so.

Imelda patted the knife hugging a hip and thigh and was comforted by its presence. Trying to keep a clear mind and not invite the whorls of confusing colour to ignite within her mind again she pushed away from a slender tree trunk and entered the field which had been recently harvested of its crop.

Despite the cloying cloak of darkness Imelda felt exposed in the open and away from the sanctity of the woods and its beautifully potent magic.

She kept going, having to clamber over the occasional fence separating one field from another. Even in the darkness with the torch light fading, Imelda seemed to instinctively determine where she was headed.

Her throat had dried and become acerbic of taste and she silently berated herself for not thinking of bringing water with her. She could have used the flask as a container.

Apprehension was like a blossoming flower and ensured her heart beat loud and fast.

TALK TO THE ANIMALS

She almost quit as the poison still coursing along her veins had her imagining she was being stalked by ghostly shadows either side of her.

Imelda slowed and stuttered to a halt when she saw the large, isolated farmhouse in the distance, its dark edifice resembling a grisly mask in the black of night, the moon illuminating the mossy tiles on its roof and reflected in the upper storey windows.

There was a marquee situated in the front garden and it sparked a memory, of other tents and smaller marquees which she presumed cluttered areas at the side and rear of the property and adjoining fields.

She smiled, as she was remembering a chicken coop with fondness and those times every morning collecting eggs.

There was even a small sectioned-off corral which was home to a few sheep, another for goats. They were memories to lift her spirits, not fill her with dread.

As within a spell the house pulled her towards the wide wooden gate and hedgerow at front of the property.

Imelda believed she was being controlled by external forces, her gelid legs enticed to take steady strides towards the mysterious house and its wealth of dark secrets.

She arrived at the gate and clung to the upper strut, shaking uncontrollably so that the solid structure rattled noisily in the stillness of the night air.

Too loud; she was thinking, and feared she might alert the tenants.

TALK TO THE ANIMALS

She snatched herself away and waited, anticipating a light going on, a presence at a window or doorway. Someone, she was reluctant to meet.

Satisfied, Imelda proceeded along to one side of the property, using the hedge for cover should she need to duck out of sight.

She approached a small gap in the privet and was able to squeeze through and froze. In the lambent light of the moon and the dying embers of numerous fires, she saw a village of tents stretching away to the rear of the property.

Imelda recalled at least fourteen in total and were homes to most of the residents outside of the Winter months. A few of the residents were ensconced in the farmhouse.

Aidan was adamant this was an orphanage, and ruled by cruel tyrants, even as Imelda was remembering differently.

She had seen the home, the estate and the residents as her haven, a peaceful and spiritual retreat. It was a commune for displaced individuals seeking spiritual solace having escaped a world where trauma existed.

It had never been a place of fear and dark deeds as she'd perceived in recent memories, and not in the way Aidan described life on the estate.

Unless; and it was a thought to keep her stalled, in that all was a cover for those dark secrets kept hidden from the outside world.

She'd come this far, and if she was to seek those answers to have eluded her since the time she had fled into the woods at a time of despair and panic, this was an opportunity to do so.

TALK TO THE ANIMALS

She felt the comforting hug of the knife as it rubbed her hip and one thigh, as she proceeded cautiously along the side of the imposing property that, which had once been her home.

Imelda's courage stayed with her as she approached the first of the tents, the flap sealed to prevent her seeing the occupants within, or for them to be alert to her presence.

She became distracted and enamoured with the glowing embers of each fire, as it evoked memories of her home in the woods, and of those she had once enjoyed.

None of this discovery made any sense to her. Instead of trepidation she felt the growing seeds of joy and bedevilment. As with the woods, there existed a heart of magical mystery in the community of tents and the home at her side.

On the fringes of her subconscious lay a tapestry of fond memories and it was her belief, she was meant to come here this night for answers to a conundrum to have haunted her for weeks.

CHAPTER 49

Imelda entered the wider arena at rear of the stone property where a huddle of tents lined either side and with the pens and small animal compounds tucked further along. These were swallowed by a cloak of darkness.

Picking her way carefully and quietly, Imelda found herself hesitating as she approached the third tent on the right. It was quite large, in comparison to most others on the site, and felt the need to exercise greater caution as it had its entrance flaps pinned to the side.

She hesitated and wondered if she navigate a path around the tent or whether she should brazenly introduce herself.

The decision was made for her as a figure stepped into the open. Imelda froze and gasped. She was quick to note the surprised look he gave her, knowing the person recognised her.

Imelda's memory stuttered and returned, as she in turn recognised the young man glaring at her, but in a friendly way. His was a face she recognised with fondness. She believed, and it was more than a gut-feeling, it went beyond a friendship at some point in her shadowy past.

TALK TO THE ANIMALS

He didn't speak and neither did the young man as he took her hand in an affectionate grasp and led her inside the tent which she surmised was his home. She held a breath as her gaze absorbed the interior furnishings. The walls of the tent were adorned with tapestries, as was the floor, each one depicting the stars, or having mystical connotations,

All was familiar to her, as with his collection of crystals, and spread across a small low table was an array of hand-crafted bracelets, necklaces, and hair braids. Occupying a corner was an inflatable bed with a side table alongside, and on this sputtered a large, scented candle which offered the interior its only source of illumination.

The erratic flame cast eerie shadows around the walls and ceiling, cavorting over the meagre possessions he owned.

The young man lowered himself to the bed as Imelda stepped across to examine the beautiful beaded and feathered jewellery.

With her hand still held in a warm grasp she was encouraged to sit beside him and she did so, in the knowledge she was safe and with no reason to be afraid.

The young man's smile radiated warmth and calm and he was first to speak.

'Forgive me,' he said in soft tones, 'It's both a shock and a pleasant surprise to see you again. 'When you left, we were all heart-broken, and wished there was something more we could have done. We banded together and formed search parties, in the hope we could find and encourage you to return.'

She traced his smile with a digit and he did the same.

'Ricardo,' she said wistfully as she began to remember certain aspects of her previous existence.

'Yes, Ricky, that's me. You've been gone a few months now and if I'm honest, it's not the same without you with us. Where did you go to? Where have you been living all this time?'

'Does it matter?' she answered him and pouted thoughtfully.

Her curt response had him turning to the front even as he was unable to mask his hurt and dismay. Imelda felt his confidence dwindling as she cast her gaze to where he held her hand. He seemed reluctant to let her go, as she was to relinquish her grasp.

'I should probably put a call through to Ian,' he muttered and appeared nervous the moment he turned back and she got him looking down at the knife in its sheath laying across her bare thighs where her dress was hitched-up.

She might have read him wrong and wanted to believe he was staring at her legs.

'Who is Ian?' she enquired.

'Immy? How much do you remember? The reason I ask is, I'm getting the impression you don't really know me, or that you were once a resident of the commune.'

Imelda's hand dropped from his face to her lap where she lightly clawed her skin with frustration and confusion.

'What commune? Who is Ian? And why can't I remember? Did something happen to me to make me forget? Something terrible and shocking?'

TALK TO THE ANIMALS

'I should call Ian, he can explain better than I can.'

She caught him unawares when she slapped his leg in exasperation as she became desperate to make sense of all which remained a confused morass within her mind and heart.

She didn't apologise for striking him and would not if she was obliged to slap him a second time.

'Ian is our saviour. Our mentor,' Ricardo answered. 'Our guide and teacher. Some would say, he's like a guru. Ian is our inspiration, our source of hope. If not for him, there's no telling where most of us would have ended up.'

'You haven't mentioned Stibley once,' said Imelda coolly. 'Who is Stibley?' she demanded to know.

'Stibley? I fail to understand. There is no one of that name lives on the commune. Let me put a call through to Ian and let him answer your questions and perhaps, help you to remember.'

Not knowing how she might react this time, Ricardo stroked away wispy fire trails of her hair from around her pout, swept it back over a shoulder and caressed her neck.

'It's almost as if your mind refused to accept what happened and shut down. Something like a safety valve. That's why I think you should speak with Ian. He can handle the situation better than anyone.'

Imelda studied his profile as he reached for the mobile phone on the bedside table. He lifted a bracelet and headband for Imelda's inspection.

TALK TO THE ANIMALS

'You helped make these,' he said. 'You were a natural when it came to making things. They're good. If you'll just give me a moment, I'll make the call.'

'Sorry,' she said, 'For slapping your leg,'

He favoured her a handsome smile as he dialled the pertinent number in his contacts folder and put the slim phone to his ear.

Imelda caught him looking glassy eyed at her thighs where they gleamed as patinaed bronze in the muted light of the candle. She had her knees parted and supposed he was seeing more than just her upper legs.

She didn't try to cover her modesty as she came to realise she didn't mind him looking at her.

She liked the attention, and supposed she always had.

Ricardo shifted concentration to the person he was communicating with.

'Sir? Sorry if I woke you. Yes, Ricardo. Immy's come home. She seems confused. I thought, you should know. Okay then, see you in ten.'

He put the phone down and leaned back, resting his weight on his hands.

'Ian's on his way. He's another who's really excited you came back.'

'What of Lenska? His wife?'

The question had him jolting forward again and this time he held both her hands and shuffled round to face her.

TALK TO THE ANIMALS

He was rolling his head side to side, as if needed a moment to choose his words carefully.

'Ian's not married,' he answered and feeling awkward. 'Hey, I bet you miss the animals.'

He added this, just to steer the conversation onto a palatable subject.

'The animals were your thing when you weren't making stuff to sell. You liked to talk to them and damn if they didn't understand. You have a natural affinity with them. I don't suppose no, I shouldn't say.'

'What did you want to ask?'

'Have you seen anything of Ade? He left the commune not long after you had departed. I was just wondering. When he realised you'd taken off and was upset, he went a little crazy for a time. He didn't join the group searches and when we returned, Ade was gone. Never came back.'

Imelda refrained giving an answer as a matter of self-preservation, as she saw it.

'Who else lives here?' she enquired, even as spectral names flitted around her mind. Not that she was able to put a clear face to each name.

'Well, there's my good pal Stewart. He lives in the next tent along. Hey, you must remember Rachel. The two of you hit it off from the moment she befriended you and introduced you to the commune. She was inconsolable after you left. I guess, we all were. Ian was the one who tried to keep everything positive and upbeat. He always said you'd find your way home, in time. Ian's everyone's rock and focal point. He was the one who stayed strong, despite knowing he was hurting inside. He felt, rightly or wrongly, he'd failed you.'

Imelda was visualising a face and paused for the memory to acquire substance.

'Do you remember Rachel?' he persevered gently.

Imelda nodded imperceptibly, finally recollecting her friend and soul sister. She saw an image of her clearly, with her sweet and beautiful elfin face and bob of dark wavy hair. It was another time, another place, she acquiesced.

Something else transpired from reaching into her subconscious for answers. She and Rachel had been more than just friends. At one time they had enjoyed a physical intimacy and Imelda believed the thought had her blushing.

She recalled a few of their episodes together and her mind was to highlight the outrageously provocative. They had been a couple of flirtatious minxes who would do anything to get attention, not that they were ever in competition. It was fun, it was love, and it was free-spirited.

What was to confound her was in the realisation she could not recall getting punished for being coquettish, even as she supposed she must have been. Aidan had said as much and made her plight believable.

Imelda became suddenly fearful as attention was on movement on the periphery of her vision. The silhouette of a man seemed to fill the void at the tent opening.

She was to confront the man called Ian who, in Ricardo's words, was the commune's mentor and guru. He stepped forward and crouched in front of her, wearing an expression exuding joy and warmth.

As with Ricardo, he wanted to possess her hands and claim them for his own.

'Imelda,' he intimated in a sweet soft voice. 'Welcome home, child.' And nodding his head at Ricardo, added, 'Our princess has returned to the fold.'

With more confidence than Ricardo exhibited greeting Imelda, Ian leaned forward and hugged her, the embrace lingering, to have Imelda relax and flow into his warmth and musky scent.

She supposed it was suggestive of her to part her thighs and mould herself to his hips and pelvis and realised instinctively, Ian was not the person to have haunted her or could have harmed her at any time.

The person clutching her gently to his chest was someone with the key to the door and corridors within her mind and used his persuasive power step over the threshold. She welcomed him into her thoughts and memories as she was not seeing this as an intrusion.

It was the familiarity which encapsulated her and was soothingly drawn into an aura of intimacy she had perhaps once shared with him.

Ian leant away and it was apparent her wanton pressing around his groin was disconcerting. He placed his large hands on her shoulders and kneaded the skin either side of her neck with exquisite tenderness. He took a moment to appraise her.

TALK TO THE ANIMALS

'Ricky, here, has probably mentioned the fact we were all deeply concerned when you took off,' he stated in soft, lilting tones, and having a rustic brogue to its timbre. 'You were very distraught and needed time to come to terms with everything to have happened. I must ask, princess, but where did you go? It's been a few months now.'

He gave a light shake of the head, as if to clarify he wasn't dreaming.

'Had you stayed,' he said, 'I could have helped you through the pain.'

Imelda became pensive and defensive at the same time.

'How am I to know you are not using words cheaply to cover the truth?' she enquired boldly, as she too took a moment to appraise the forty-something man who could ply his charm easily.

He was handsome, and nothing like the image she'd conjured to her mind in the time she lived in the woods.

'I asked |Ricardo, about Stibley and his wife Lenska,' she added. 'Not that he was able to offer much by way of an explanation. Why is that, do you suppose? It is apparent to me, you are not Stibley, the person I have been fearful of all this time.'

'I can never lie, not to you or anyone of our flock,' he said as Imelda registered the pain locked within eyes which smouldered in the lambent light. 'You remember Aidan,' he continued and his expression was grim, 'He left the compound the moment he realised you had fled, and without knowing if you meant to return. Lenska and Hank Stibley were once Aidan's foster parents. When Aidan arrived and became a part of our community, it was not easy at the beginning to get him to talk of his past. When he eventually confided in me, that was information I kept in strictest confidence. His past was deeply convoluted and tragic.'

'You have a punishment room in the house,' she threw at him.

'Sorry, I'm not following you.'

'There is a room where troublesome individuals are incarcerated for a time. Those who prove difficult are tied to a bed and unspeakable things are done to them, as punishment.'

'Dear God! Immy, this is not a place of chastisement. Never has been. You are probably confusing our spiritual haven for lost souls with a memory of your childhood, as you revealed to me at the beginning.

'I have the scars on my back as proof and they are recent, a result of regular beatings.'

'Princess, I have personally seen those scars you speak of, and they were not because of regular beatings as you believe them to be. You suffered second degree burns in a fire which claimed the lives of your parents when you were in your young teens. You do not remember our frequent talks when you confided to me your reasons for fleeing the suffocating care of an aunt. Our Rachel was the spirited soul who befriended you and brought you here to our retreat. Rachel was your lifeline, to hope and salvation. The moment you arrived you fell in love with the place and with all who reside here. It became your new home and it helped you rediscover your self-worth. You found freedom and happiness here on the commune.'

TALK TO THE ANIMALS

'If, what you say is true, then why did I run away in abject fear, believing I was being chased by a monster? I sense you are not telling me everything. What is it you're hiding?'

'Sweetheart,' said Ian, as she felt his grip tightening on her shoulders. The truth is, you're the one hiding those reasons, from yourself.'

Imelda shook her head in search of clarification.

'Tell me,' she hissed and barely recognised her own voice.

She was instantly reminded of her conversations with the Wicked Witch of the woods and had to wonder if the witch's black soul had stolen a path within her.

She almost swooned to feel his fingertips gently kneading her shoulders and caressing her neck.

'You suffered terribly,' he quietly explained, 'following your miscarriage. Despite having the best care in one of our members, Sarah, you were inconsolable and blamed yourself. I was told, by those who witnessed events, you were in an altercation with Aidan prior to the miscarriage, in that he became irrational and out of control. Before anyone could assist he pushed you against the wood store bunker and did so with force. It is believed this was the cause of the miscarriage as you started bleeding heavily following that moment. You were devastated, we all were. At times you became hysterical and would self-harm. Following which you would become uncommunicative. You spent time with the animals and would even sleep with them. It was my hope and belief the animals were the therapy required to get you past the trauma you experienced. And then you left, very suddenly, and no one was aware you had gone. It is with regret I say this, princess, but I wish I could have done more. We all do.'

Imelda seemed to take an eternity digesting Ian's explanation when she suddenly unravelled her legs and sprang to her feet. Ian's hands slumped to his lap, like forlorn birds who had lost the ability to fly.

'This is your home, Immy. You have friends here. There are the animals.'

'I have much to think about,' she answered him and cast her gaze to a dejected Ricardo who didn't know how to react.

Ian rose to his full height and approached her, towering over her slight frame, yet not in a menacing way.

'Will you return?' Ian asked her, pleaded with her.

'If I do, I will not be alone.'

'Everyone is welcome, princess.'

He caught her off guard when he scooped her into a fierce hug and kissed her cheek.

'We can all rest easy knowing you are safe,' he said.

Imelda managed a smile and then she was moving towards Ricardo and dropping a kiss to the corner of his mouth. On passing, she lightly touched Ian on the cheek and then swept out of the tent and was gone.

Her redolent scent remained as Ian and Ricardo exchanged solemn looks.

'She will return,' said Ricardo confidently. 'Just a feeling. You have helped her remember, and it's my belief she now has the strength and fortitude to confront her ghosts and lay them to rest. I think, you have let her know, just how happy she was for a time when she lived here on the commune and will once again want to make it her home.'

'It would be good to have her back,' said Ian wistfully. 'She was like a firefly, who could spread joy with her natural effervescence. In the meantime, all we can do is wait, hope, and pray.'

CHAPTER 50

On her return to the woodland sanctuary Imelda was overwhelmed with disparaging thoughts and emotions crowding her mind and was desperate to speak with Mister Tree for invaluable advice.

The batteries in the torch gave up as she was crossing the last field leading towards the eerie silhouetted canvas of trees in the distance and cast the useless object to the ground, using intuition over sight to find the path she needed to take.

The moment she arrived at the familiar glade where moonlight dappled areas of grass and shrub in the vicinity and tinged the leaves and boughs of the trees with silver.

Imelda approached the grand old oak and called to it.

'Princess, you woke me from my slumber,' the Tree quietly protested.

'My apologies, Mister Tree, but I come to you seeking advice and wisdom.'

'And how can I help you?'

Imelda gave an account of her visit to the compound and her reasons for going.

TALK TO THE ANIMALS

'What you were told contradicts all you were led to believe, until now,' the Tree answered. *'You must determine what the problem is and who has failed you. There are those who claim to be your friends, yet it's obvious, someone has been lying to you.'*

'I cannot think straight. I am so confused and upset.'

She lay a hand to the broad trunk while the other caressed one of the exposed roots.

'Supposing you have a clearer understanding of the problem, what do you propose to do about it?' the Tree contested, its voice responding to her own train of thoughts. It was seductive and an aria of pleasantry to soothe her and placate her trembling. *'I believe you understand now why you fled to make a home here in the woods,'* said Tree *'Your prince is not the honourable young man you believed him to be. He made his troubled past your own. He is an angry young man and cannot be trusted. He became a cruel person when he found out you were carrying a child and was not the father. You could not reason with him, and you did try, my child. He lashed out and hurt you. Hurt the baby in your womb. Murdered the baby.'*

Imelda gulped down lungful's of humid air, shaking her head vigorously, as if she needed to dispel the images in her mind.

Her agitation ceased when she saw a small cluster of tight capped mushrooms in a shallow depression at the base of the tree. Her eyes lit up as she cackled wildly and stooped to gather a few in one hand. She greedily munched on them, ignoring their bitter and pungent taste, and swallowed, almost gagging as a reflex action.

TALK TO THE ANIMALS

She placed her forehead to the gnarly bark of the tree, hugging its broad torso as she closed her eyes.

'I was happy for a time,' she confessed. 'My prince had me believe there existed a punishment room for naughty offenders. I now know they are Aidan's memories. I have my own, yes. As a child, my father used to spank me. There were worse things than a beating. When you're young you do not have the strength to fight. You simply accept your fate. Some things, traumatic events, can erase the goodness in a person, even one so young. I have scars across my back, not from a cane or a belt. These were inflicted on me by fire. Our home was set alight.'

Imelda giggled as expectant whorls of colour blossomed behind closed lids.

'I was the one started the fire,' she said, 'Payback, for all my father did to me, and having a mother who did not try to stop him, despite knowing he was doing terrible things to their daughter. You're the only one I have spoken of this to. Now that you know the truth, my side of the story, does it make me a bad person?'

'It makes you courageous, a survivor. You did what you believed was necessary, to be free of your father's tyranny. You almost died as a result.'

'I spent a few weeks in the burns unit at hospital following which, I was taken in by an aunt. Investigations to determine the cause of the fire concluded it was from a gas leak. Arson was not suspected. My aunt Miriam was very austere, sympathetic but strict. In time, it was inevitable I should rebel against the rigid rules she put in place. It was like, I was unable to breathe or to think. I escaped one corner of Hell only to end up in another. I ran away. The authorities would have searched

TALK TO THE ANIMALS

for me and it's possible they still are. I'm one of those missing persons you get to read about all too often, with friends and family wondering if the person missing is either dead or alive. I was dead when I was living. Now I'm alive, despite my heart feeling as if it no longer possesses a beat.'

Imelda paused and held the tree tighter, feeling an imprint of its bark stamping itself to a cheek.

'Oh my, but I remember now. I was in a coffee shop with money I had begged for food and was approached by an angel. She introduced herself as Rachel. She was friendly, a considerate listener, and a source of light in the darkness. She offered to take me under her week and invited me to visit the commune where she lived. It is a magical haven for lost souls to find their path again. Not an orphanage as my prince would have me believe. Naturally, I stayed and made the commune my home. My prince was a resident and arrived a few weeks before me. He seemed reserved, not necessarily shy, and had difficulty communicating. I discovered eventually, he was the one who fled a cruel home and was punished frequently.'

'Your prince would have you believe the commune was a place of cruelty and dark deeds. In his twisted imagination, he was the one believed the commune was run by his foster parents, Stibley and Lenska. There was no punishment room. As with the woods, the commune was blessed with magic. It was a place of wonder. It set you free, princess.'

'It is all so very confusing still,' she cried.

She moaned, swayed, and held tight to keep her balance. She felt familiar stirrings. She even heard an echoing taunt, of the Witch she had defeated in battle. Or perhaps, the sorceress could not be defeated in the mortal sense. The Witch's magical powers would have transformed her into something else besides a young huntsman.

'You have not spoken of the baby or his father,' said Tree in consoling tones.

Imelda was shocked back on her heels and she stumbled and fell, hitting the mulch on her rump which had her spluttering an oath.

'That is a topic which is no concern of yours,' she sneered. 'I have nothing more to say to you.'

'Embrace the Witch.'

'What?'

'Have the Witch decide your fortune.'

Imelda shook her head to dispel a jumble of confusing thoughts, not that she succeeded.

'The Witch is no more! I defeated her in battle!'

'You killed a young man who only wanted to help. The Witch cast a spell and he became ensnared. You are the Witch, princess, and always have been.'

'I'm leaving now,' Imelda snapped obstinately. 'I am sorry, I disturbed you from your precious slumber.'

The Tree was silent as Imelda scrambled ungainly to her feet and chuckled, her flesh afire. She was overcome with a desire to be home and it had her scampering away without another word spoken.

Her mind cried to her, perplexed.

TALK TO THE ANIMALS

Where was home exactly, she wanted to know.

She was missing Dog; not so much Cat, as Cat was one to have her own private agenda much of the time.

Dog was loyal and her greatest friend.

As she stumbled onto the chuckling brook Imelda's thoughts turned to her prince. She paused to get her breath back. And then she was remembering what the Tree said before she departed the glade in anger and disappointment.

Tree claimed she was the Witch and not the huntsman. She wanted to scream, as the fantasy world she had created for herself had become all too real.

The young man's corpse was close; she sensed.

Or had the body been discovered?

She would know. There would have been sirens on the road. The police would have searched the woods with their trained sniffer dogs.

Can a person go missing, just like that? She asked herself. She had at another time.

If the authorities came to the woods and discovered the body, they would know it was a homicide instantly.

What then?

Imelda doubted anyone would believe her story; of the Wicked Witch to have possessed the young man and the formidable battle to follow.

TALK TO THE ANIMALS

She had to get to the shelter, her mind clamoured, and she continued her quest with her vision swimming in and out of focus, her mind in hopeless disarray.

She thought it odd she should be thinking of Dog and how she missed his company. Her prince was on the periphery of her thoughts only and it seemed subjective not to be overly eager to return to him and him comfort her.

Imelda blamed the Witch, thinking the sorceress was pulling her heart strings and getting them tangled.

Her body trembled and her legs became increasingly leaden, as if she was having to traverse through a mire. Instead of strolling she staggered and had to use the trees for support.

She eventually reached the atoll and gave a sigh, not that was able to summon a smile. She felt no elation reaching home, supposing it was her home.

The steep gradient seemed to stretch for miles in front of her as she carefully picked her way up to get to the crest. She took a moment to hug the bruising edifice as it enabled her vision to stop swimming out of focus and then she was cautiously feeling her way along the ledge to the entrance.

She was met with the most appalling stench and in the darkness she shambled her way to the cot and a recumbent Aidan who was sleeping restlessly in a pool of his own vomit.

Dog was pleased to see her and swiped at a trailing hand with a warm wet tongue.

Imelda crouched and scrunched his thick collar of fur before leaning over to shake Aidan's shoulder to get him to wake up.

TALK TO THE ANIMALS

The Witch was silent.

Imelda was inclined to think the Witch had been put off by the awful smell, as she was.

Aidan gave a groan and struck out, delivering a blow to Imelda's skull, with enough force to have her rocking.

Despite which, she remained calm and he quietly protested as he complied with her efforts to soothe him.

He allowed his princess to lead him on unsteady legs to the opening.

'Let's get you cleaned up,' she said. 'You're such a mess.'

At the lip of the ledge, she would have liked to have kissed him.

Instead, she gave him a firm shove and backed away from a plaintive scream as he plummeted.

Imelda smiled and with Dog eagerly on her heels, she inched her away along the ledge and crawled down the gradient to be on the woodland floor. She stumbled, crawled, and shuffled towards Aidan's position, where he was draped backwards over a jagged boulder.

His face was a mask of blood which he had spewed out the moment he struck the large rock and severed his spine. His limbs were twitching and spasming in his final death throes.

Imelda brushed fingers through his mop of damp blond curls.

TALK TO THE ANIMALS

She leaned close to an ear and whispered her final words to him. 'That,' she said, 'Was for murdering my baby.'

She straightened without showing remorse and unfastened the belt at her waist. She removed the knife from its sheath and wiped all traces of her prints on the hilt with the frayed hem of her dress. Following which, she moulded Aidan's left hand around the haft, squeezed and released, discarding belt and knife at the base of the rock.

There was nothing she could do at the shelter. The cot composed of leaves would have copious strands of her hair buried within and traces of her sweat and bodily fluids.

Should the police arrive there would follow a thorough forensics examination. Her prints would be on the bark vessels, the bag, the flask. It was unavoidable.

Imelda could only hope the magic of the woods might work in her favour and blind the authorities to the possibility another person had lived in the shelter.

With a lavish smile she called Dog to heel.

'We're going home,' she said.

'Is this not our home?' Dog answered within her befuddled mind.

'No, Dog. The shelter was a temporary sanctuary only. We're to return to my real home.'

'The others at this place you speak of, will they like me?'

'They will love you, as I do my prince.'

'Will there be food at this home of yours?'

TALK TO THE ANIMALS

'Yes. And we will not have to go in search of roadkill ever again.'

Dog panted and seemed to nod, as the princess with the long fan of red hair in a floral dress, gave a sudden peal of laughter and led the way into the thick dark press of trees.

CHAPTER 51

Imelda called a halt when they reached the glade and the grand old oak. Imelda approached her friend, the earlier exchange already forgotten.

'Mister Tree!'

'Princess.'

'Dog and I are leaving the woods and returning home. Our real home.'

'Will you come back and visit?' Tree asked solemnly.

'Oh yes, indeed I will, as this is home also. And I have you and all my woodland friends here. I will always be the princess of the woods, Mister Tree.'

'Oh yes, you are a princess and let no one say different. But you are so much more child,' Tree answered and quietly fluttered its leaves.

An owl hooted from a branch at a midway point and called down to Imelda.

'It has been a pleasure meeting with you, princess.'

'Thank you, Owl.'

TALK TO THE ANIMALS

'Do come back soon and bring your friends.'

'I will. I promise.'

'Is that your prince alongside you?' Owl enquired and gave a soft hoot.

'Yes. This is Dog, my handsome, wonderful, and loyal prince charming.'

The owl hooted again and was answered by another's.

'My own prince is calling me, says he is hungry. Always hungry. He wants to know if I'm bringing food home.'

'Bless you, and the little ones,' said Imelda happily.

'Not so little now,' said Owl with a showy flutter of her wings. *'How is your baby doing, princess? You must be extremely excited.'*

Imelda's joy seeped away quickly.

'He is doing just fine,' she lied around her confusion. 'We must be going now.'

'Take care,' said Owl.

'Be safe, princess,' said Tree. *'Don't be a stranger.'*

'I won't.'

Imelda approached and hugged the tree, feeling its sturdy torso pressing around her breasts and thighs. Dropping a kiss to the bark she stepped away with sadness as a heavy weight on her shoulders and called dog to follow.

As they approached the outer fringes of the woods Imelda felt a great weight falling away so that she walked with a light temperate grace. She was humming a tune, not that she recall its title or the artist. It was a happy tune and seemed in perfect harmony with her mood.

With Dog at her side and searching for interesting scents they emerged from the cover of trees into the harvested field where a star-spangled night sky shimmered overhead, a sliver of a moon barely illuminating the path they needed to take.

Not that she needed directions.

She knew the way.

Home was calling her.

CHAPTER 52

The residents at the commune all welcomed Imelda's return with open arms and hearts swollen with love. There were kisses and genuine happiness. All greeted her companion Dog with the same affection and Imelda became effervescent, like a firefly. Ian had always likened her to a firefly.

Imelda was instantly touched by the support she received, and meeting with everyone on the commune opened the door to memories a little wider, so that she was able to remember occasions of happiness spent in their company. There were campfire singalongs, dancing, and spiritual discussions. There were meditation and yoga classes where many gathered to create artifacts they could sell at fairs and markets to sustain themselves.

Ian and Ricardo became spiritual guardians, granting her the freedom and time to settle into a routine she was comfortable with.

With autumn approaching quite a few of the girls and women vacated tents and moved inti forms in the large farmhouse, the boys, and menfolk content to dwell in tents and marquees.

TALK TO THE ANIMALS

It was established, when the winter bite set in and there was not enough adequate heating for those on the outside, they would have accommodation indoors.

There was no segregation of sexes as all were given the choice how to live. There were no absolute rules, none which were rigid to speak of, not that any of the residents showed an inclination to disrupt a perfect balance and harmony.

Whatever traumas the resident experienced before coming to the spiritual haven were left in the past. Ian made himself available always should anyone need to redress elements of a troubled past. He was trusted. He was truly their mentor and guide.

Imelda was deeply affected by the tranquil ambience and wonderful nature everyone possessed, as her own personal issues became exposed and had her remembering how it once had been before the trauma of miscarrying her baby.

Imelda became reacquainted with Rachel not surprisingly and was transported into a world as magical as the woods she had left behind.

Imelda preferred the outdoors than to be confined to the home and was shown the marquee she once inhabited. Her familiar effects remained even as the residents donated offerings as a homecoming tribute to make her feel accepted.

Dog was happy with their new home, the attention he was to receive often and even the regular meals.

At the beginning Imelda would stand in awe at the spectacle within her tent, wondering how she could have forgotten the tapestries and collection of crystals. There was a single bed and she had an inflatable bed provided to go alongside it to accommodate Dog.

When the weather was fair the residents gathered and cooked on campfires, and it would transport Imelda back to the regular fires she had started in her shelter in the woods.

At times, when the weather was inclement, food was prepared in the communal kitchen.

Imelda often visited the home to spend time with her friends even though her visits were brief. She could never understand why the home made her feel uneasy.

There was no punishment room. This was not the home Aidan described. It was not an orphanage. More importantly, a brutal tyrant did not govern it.

The outside was where she belonged and much of her time was spent tending the animals in their pens. Other times, she chose solitude and made things to sell. Every day she would take herself off with Dog and go for long rambles around the countryside.

She had been given a reason to smile and to laugh.

She was treated like visiting royalty.

She was a real princess.

There came occasions when Imelda believed the Wicked Witch had returned to the real world, not to seek vengeance but as an architect to further the misery she once embraced.

She was naturally coquettish and supposed she had always been. It invited attention and loved the attention. Rachel had once been a lover and was again someone to kindle the flames of desire when she had these urges.

It was not only Rachel who gave her satisfaction.

Imelda felt as if she belonged, finally, but as winter encroached so did a deeper yearning to be at one with the magical woods.

She would have visited earlier, except there had been a lot of police and media activity in the area in recent weeks.

Imelda overheard someone say they were searching for a man who had gone missing months ago but his disappearance had only recently been reported as suspicious.

The authorities and reporters approached the commune, with Ian giving everyone a statement, not that he had much to say or give, as the man they were searching for was unknown to him.

Imelda chose these moments to stay out of the way and remain inconspicuous.

She had Rachel cut her hair short and dye it black. Appraising herself in a mirror after Imelda confessed she liked the new look, she repented having lost her flowing mane of red hair. It was from necessity she should remove traces of her natural hair, knowing the police and forensics will gather evidence should they find the shelter. Imelda believed it was only a matter of time. They would discover Aidan's corpse at the base of their one-time home. Imelda could only hope the magic of the woods would assist in deflecting interest away from their princess.

TALK TO THE ANIMALS

Everyone was sweet and complimented her on her new appearance.

Ian especially liked Imelda's transformation and said it made her even more ethereal than before.

She was still his princess, he would add, and when Imelda witnessed a light in his eyes in the way he appraised her, she knew he was seeing her with more than just affection.

There came occasions when Imelda could not stop worrying with regards to police activity in the area. They would easily assemble evidence from the cot she had shared with Aidan, from the back pack and hip flask, but didn't think they could associate their findings with anyone at the commune.

Unless, they became suspicious and had reason to interrogate everyone.

At the forefront of her mind was knowing they might interrogate Mister Tree, the Fox, Squirrel, Badger, the Rabbits at the warren, and Miss Owl. Would they protect her identity to save themselves and the woods? Did they not love her enough to not cast aspersions on her character and damn her for eternity?

She hoped they might put direct blame on the Wicked Witch.

Imelda confessed to herself, it was a difficult time, yet knowing it would not last forever.

She became distracted at Dog's gruff bark and was witness to a shadow flitting across the side of the tent and approaching the entrance.

CHAPTER 53

Ian appeared, stooping under the overhead flap to reveal a smile. He stepped forward and closed the entrance panels and studied his princess for a quiet moment before stating his reason for visiting.

Imelda didn't mind Ian was to see her naked. It was not the first time. She waited patiently for him to speak, or not to speak, but gently step close and take her in his arms. It's what she wanted.

His eyes naturally appraising her soft beauty he stooped to give Dog initial attention.

Imelda heard the Wicked Witch chortling and this confounded her and encouraged her to speak first.

'I was just about to put some clothes on and tend to the chickens,' she said, her mouth becoming dry with anticipation as Ian straightened.

As she had hoped he closed the gap in one stride and cupped her face with exquisite tenderness, the balls of his thumbs caressing her cheeks.

'You look amazing,' he said. 'You always look amazing. I have some sad news to impart, princess, and thought it best it came from me before you heard it from anyone else.'

TALK TO THE ANIMALS

She looked deeply into his blue-grey eyes and was moved by the sadness she saw in them. She felt her own eyes widening and become bright where a flame flickered, and tensed before Ian was to continue.

'I have just recently had another visit from the police,' he said.

Again, he paused and he would have sensed her trembling.

Imelda assumed she wasn't a suspect in their enquiries, otherwise they would have accompanied Ian to her tent.

'Aidan has been found,' he added softly as he was unsure how Imelda would react to the news he was about to deliver. 'I had to identify him from the photo submitted. It's not good news babe.'

Imelda said nothing as Ian needed a moment to make an emotional adjustment and compose himself.

'Aidan's body was found in woodland a few miles from here. It appears, Aidan's problems got the better of him. He was living rough, by all accounts. It's not the only news to speak of, as the police uncovered a second corpse, that of the man they were initially searching for. The police were reticent to give details. What they were able to say is the missing person bore a stab wound and a knife in Aidan's possession is thought to be the murder weapon. Aidan was using a shelter in a small outcrop of rock deep in the woods. Forensics are collating evidence from the personal effects they have uncovered. It's only an assumption at this moment, but the police believe Aidan fell to his death, either accidentally or suicide.'

TALK TO THE ANIMALS

'I must ask,' Imelda interrupted and not reacting as Ian might have expected her to. 'Will the police require a statement from me? Or anyone else, for that matter.'

'I don't think so. They asked questions, naturally, as to the involvement of the residents on the commune. I made no mention of the fact you had left for a time and returned in recent weeks. As I see it, you've been through enough, and feel it's my duty to protect your interests and wellbeing and of everyone in my care.'

Imelda's elation blossomed in the form of a widening smile and suggestive subliminal messages she was to telegraph with her eyes.

Taking one of his hands she pulled him to the bed and gave one of her coquettish titters. She lay down and encouraged him to lay with her, relaying her need to be kissed with a pout.

Ian obliged and was instantly ensnared within the spell cast by the Wicked Witch.

Imelda's loyal companion she refused to give a name to, other than Dog, gave a quiet grumble and settled on the low bed beside his mistress. He was content knowing his princess was happy.

After a time, Imelda was given respite to get her breath back and she used the moment to trace the solemnity around his mouth.

'It recently came to my attention,' she said in whimsical tones, 'You would have been father to my baby. It's okay, and know I was selfish not to share our pain together. 'I would have you give me another.'

TALK TO THE ANIMALS

Ian was on the verge of tears.

CHAPTER 54

On Christmas Day, with snow falling heavily to make it a festive season to remember, all the residents gathered outside for snowball fights and frolics. Even Dog joined in the antics and fed on the happily positive atmosphere. He danced and gambolled and became vocal, as if he had never experienced the feel of snow on his paws and fur before this moment.

No one complained of the cold and while there were those who were zealously energetic, others created ice sculptures in the front garden area.

Later they were all to enjoy a communal Christmas dinner following which, there was an exchange of presents.

After, and it was the middle of the afternoon with snowfall refusing to abate, Imelda excused herself and let everyone know she was taking Dog for a walk. Almost everyone in the commune offered to accompany her but she was adamant she needed solitude for a time.

She dressed warmly against the swirling flurries, wearing denims, a sweater over a tee- shirt, boots and quilted jacket Rachel had loaned her.

TALK TO THE ANIMALS

It was not her plan yet she was not surprised they should take a direction which would eventually lead them to the woods and one-time home.

Police activity in the area had dwindled away in the early part of the month and Imelda hoped she might have the woods to herself. Even the reporters had vacated their vigil. At the beginning the police had difficulty keeping away local visitors whose ghoulish curiosity became a problem for a time.

This would be her first venture to the woods since her departure late summer.

She missed its magic and believed there were occasions it called to her from afar. She missed the animals and her conversations with them. She missed Mister Tree.

She gasped and a smile stretched her jaw as they entered the smooth white plain of the last field where the shadowy façade of trees blinked in and out of the erratic flurries of heavy falling snow.

The moment they reached the perimeter line of vegetation the naked branches and spindly fronds offered some protection from the elements.

Imelda paused and inhaled the atmosphere and pine scent.

'Do you feel it Dog?' she rasped and placed a hand to her heart. 'Do you feel its magic?'

'Yes,' said Dog at her side and gave a gruff bark. *'We have come home.'*

Imelda led the way with an eagerness she could not contain.

TALK TO THE ANIMALS

She burst into song and only stopped when she saw something to excite her. A cluster of small mushrooms sheltered from the snow beckoned her.

Imelda didn't think it was the season for them to be growing but was thankful all the same.

Without taking the time to consider if she should Imelda plucked a few and savoured their familiar bitter taste, chewing slowly before swallowing them. She grimaced and with a sense of elation continued their adventure.

She didn't think chance brought them eventually to the glade and home to her friend, the ancient oak tree who, she considered, was hibernating as with many of the woodland inhabitants.

She stopped Dog cocking his leg as she gave a hoot and peal of laughter borne of immense joy.

'Wake up, Mister Tree! Wake up!'

'Is it you, princess?'

'Yes! Yes!' And I have my prince with me!'

'Welcome! Welcome! It has been so long since you graced the woods with your presence. Too ling. The woods are too quiet, too staid, when you are not here.'

'I am back now, Mister Tree.'

'Will you be staying? I thought, this was your home princess.'

Imelda stepped up to the broad torso and hugged it.

'Oh tree, you are naked. Are you not feeling the cold?'

TALK TO THE ANIMALS

'I sleep in the Winter months and awake with the advent of Spring.'

I wish that I could sleep all Winter long and wake to sunshine and magic.'

Imelda stepped away and began to dance, swirling her arms and creating mystical patterns. She hummed a melodic tune and realised it was a tune someone once hummed to her to get her to sleep.

She had been a baby at that time.

An innocent spirit and soul.

Before it all turned bad and she became corrupted.

Dog yipped and chased his tail, enjoying a romp where the snow was deepest.

Imelda ceased her gaiety and confronted the grand old oak.

'You are beautiful!' she cried.

'As you are princess.'

'I have wonderful news I wish to share with you,' she said and giggled, with her thoughts beginning to spiral against clusters of vibrant colour.

CHAPTER 55

Imelda stepped up to the imposing tree trunk and lowered the zipper on her jacket, smiling vivaciously and hesitating purposely to prolong Tree's anticipation. Imelda raised her sweater and tee-short to expose her naked breasts and abdomen.

'I am with child,' she confessed happily, even as a forlorn frown stole the brightness of a smile.

'We both know,' said Tree solemnly, *You are not with child as it cannot be. Not ever. The choice was taken from you.'*

Imelda hugged the Tree and rasped an oath to feel the rough bark abrading her flesh.

'I must go now,' she whispered and kissed the trunk with undisguised yearning.

'Are you to return home?' asked Tree.

'I am home!' she conceded with a petulant whine.

She tugged her sweater and shirt down and called to Dog they were to continue.

TALK TO THE ANIMALS

She stumbled, trudged, and chuckled her way to the bleak open expanse of the rabbit warren she remembered with fondness.

Dog loped and gambolled in the virgin snow as Imelda swept her gaze this way and that to determine if any of her friends were outside and playing. She saw an array of dark holes against the whiteness of a winter's carpet, each one resembling a small yawning mouth.

Not one of the inhabitants came to greet her, even as she called to them. A voice, however, grumbled out of the nearest hole she was inclined to believe.

'Having to keep the little one's warm,' the voice echoed within her mind. *'Have you come home princess?'*

'Yes,' she answered herself.

She sloped away from the warren and Dog eventually gave chase, yipping his effervescent joy.

In a short time, Imelda broke from the cover of trees into the open vista leading to the atoll which had been her home and that of Dog.

Imelda paused at sight of trailing ribbons of police crime scene tape adorning an area of boulders on the ground and across the entrance to the shelter.

Dog rushed ahead to investigate; sniffing, panting, and cockling his leg.

Imelda had difficulty motivating herself as a tide of memories came flooding back. She approached the large boulder beneath the entrance to the shelter, which was crowned with snow, yet boldly relaying an image of a sprawled, broken Aidan.

TALK TO THE ANIMALS

Sweeping an arm back and forth removed much of the snow so that the stained surface of rock served as a dismal reminder of a time she had almost forgotten. She was able to visualise the moment she had crawled down the edifice to be with him and believed Aidan's spirit was speaking to her.

'I'm sorry princess, I never meant to hurt you,' the voice said within her mind.

'But you did. You hurt me worse than my father. You let me down, as my mother did. You lied to me, deceived me, had me believe my friends were the enemy.'

Imelda stepped away and looked up, as a fresh flurry of snow stung her eyes and cheeks, and the biting cold froze her tears.

Scaling the incline was awkward as it was hazardous and very slippery and progress was slow. She eventually hauled herself onto the ledge where she was able to shuffle along to the shelter's entrance.

Dog had returned below and was content to sniff around for any interesting scents, snapping occasionally at the falling flakes of snow settling on his fur.

Imelda was assailed by a dank unpleasant aroma and barely recognised the shelter as the home she once resided in. Her palace and castle as she would like to remember it.

She could make it her home again, she was to tell herself.

Ignoring the odious stench from within and the remnants of tape left by forensics, Imelda crossed to the broken dishevelled heap of decaying leaves and rotten wood which had once been the cot she'd shared with her false prince, and her true prince.

Her eyes alighted on a smaller heap of appeared to be debris but was, in fact, the sadly pathetic remains of her ceremonial cloak. The flowers had long since died, the berries shrivelled having lost their vibrant colour. Nearby was the remnants of her interwoven crown.

It had Imelda smiling at the memory as she was seeing her apparel as it once was and not in the forlorn state they were in at present.

Lifting the cloak, she gave it a brisk shake and saw decaying dust fritter away in soft sad plumes. A few brittle leaves settled on the ground and resembled a small offering of discarded coins.

She saw bugs crawling around and smiled effervescently, as they too were creatures of the woodland and had made a home for themselves. A she once had.

Imelda clutched her stomach as the poison drifted on lazy currents through her veins to have her flesh tingle and ignite once again.

She was suddenly laughing, which was more of a witch's cackle, she surmised.

Lowering her ceremonial apparel, she removed her winter jacket her sweater and shirt, kicked off her boots happily and fed her denims down over her feet along with her thick woollen socks.

She patiently draped the sorry looking cloak around her and managed to secure it loosely against her chest.

TALK TO THE ANIMALS

The cold tried to seep into her pores even as an inner fire sought to dispel her trembling. Having affixed the crown to her hair Imelda stumbled to the entrance and swayed precariously on the ledge overlooking white-capped tree tops and the woodland glade beneath.

Dog was still running around frantically leaving heavy prints in the snow. He seemed to sense his mistress was watching him and froze, looked up and barked twice.

'My prince!' she called, her voice reverberating in the stillness of the glade. 'Look at me! Your princess has come home!'

She chuckled effusively, the poison filling her mind, her face awash with tears. Not those of sadness but of joy.

'Want to see me fly?' she called down. 'I have been given wings.'

She spread her arms, fingers clinging to the cloak. She leaned forward and dropped as a stone, striking the boulder beneath her which split her abdomen, crushed her ribs, and dislocated her jaw. Blood exploded from between broken teeth as she gave a final defiant cry to the woods and her prince.

Dog was instantly agitated, darting forward, barking furiously. He stopped and made pathetic moaning pleas as he swiped a tongue across exposed flesh and ribbons of blood and nipped her hair.

With a huff he was then running back to the woods, away from his adoring princess and best friend in the world.

CHAPTER 56

Dog returned to the compound as twilight was falling his frantic barking alerting the residents to investigate.

Witnessing Dog running in agitated circles, barking, and whining incessantly and tugging at sleeves to get attention, it became apparent to everyone Imelda was in trouble and Dog was alerting them to her plight.

Everyone volunteered to go with Dog, without exception. Ian, Rachel, and Ricardo were fearing the worst and donning winter clothing were quickly out in the fields moving at a relentless pace in Dog's wake, despite the thickening carpet of snow.

Dog kept ahead of them, constantly barking a chain of commands to the bedraggled group following.

Rachel believed she understood better than most as she often had intimate conversations with Imelda, when her lover confided of her months spent living in the woods. Imelda had woven a magical tapestry of her experiences and embellished each episode with such beauty, Rachel could almost believe she had lived those moments with her best friend.

TALK TO THE ANIMALS

Imelda had enthused over conversations with the animals and seemed to have particular fondness for an oak tree. Rachel understood Imelda was having conversations with herself, as she was a witness to Imelda's penchant for talking and answering herself with the animals on the commune.

Rachel was never one to judge her friend's behaviour, knowing Imelda lived a fantasy existence, as it became a world she could reside in without ever having to be afraid. She was able to live a wonderful life of her own devising.

Imelda spoke of the mushrooms which led her into the magical world of the woods. Rachel understood, as there had been a few occasions when she'd taken them herself. That was at another time, before even she had arrived at the commune.

Rachel believed in Imelda's magic, even if others were ignorant if her other world.

In Rachel's eyes, Imelda was a spiritual goddess.

Watching the others in front and behind her and being affected deeply by Dog's erratic behaviour, Rachel was fearful of what the woods might reveal.

Every time Dog cast a desperate gaze back at the large following group, Rachel believed Dog was talking and she heard him conveying his plea in Imelda's voice.

'Hurry! Hurry! My princess is hurt! No time to lose!'

Rachel felt the tears welling in her lashes and spilling down and freezing to her cheeks. She had a terrible premonition that all was not good for her Imelda. Her ultimate fear reflected Dog's.

TALK TO THE ANIMALS

They arrived at the woods and most in the group were tired at this time. There was no telling how much further they needed to go before they found their princess.

Dog was even more determined and frantic, his incessant barking strident and echoing in the silence. Rachel was spurred on and waved her arms for them to proceed when others had stopped to loiter and even to wonder why they were there.

When Dog eventually led them into the glade Rachel hesitated as she sensed a moment's Déjà vu. Snow hugged the ground and the limbs of the trees around them. One tree stood out from the others as it was majestic and ancient. Rachel was certain she was confronting the grand old oak Imelda had spoken of with fondness time and again.

She stared and was almost enticed to approach the beautiful monument, sensing she had become ensnared with the magic of the woods, as described to her by her soul sister.

It defined her premonition as the magic seemed tinged with sadness she was unable to comprehend.

Dog was becoming even more agitated and Rachel wondered if they were close. He disappeared into the trees and vegetation opposite and invited the search party to pick up the pace.

Rachel was feeling a great ache in her heart as she struggled to keep pace with those ahead of her. She heard constant murmurs and chuntering and it echoed her personal discordance and anxiety.

Dog broke cover onto the glade and atoll, rushing across to where a semi-naked figure draped a large boulder.

TALK TO THE ANIMALS

Rachel almost dropped to her knees the moment she was able to focus through her tears on the shoulder length raven-black hair and where the natural red was beginning to grow through.

Shock gave her a brutal slap and she screamed and clung to Ricardo for support as Ian was the only one moving towards the lifeless figure hugging the boulder at the base of the atoll.

He must have known in his heart and mind they were too late to save their princess as he calmly retrieved a mobile phone from his coat pocket and dialled emergency services. Giving coordinates would be easy as the police obviously knew the location from their investigations into a murder and fatal accident.

Except for the soft strains of sobbing, all within the magical woods was a ghostly calm and quiet. It seemed the trees and wildlife were in mourning for their princess.

TALK TO THE ANIMALS

CHAPTER 57

In the months leading up to Spring with police investigations completed and for the media to depart the newsworthy scene of once again yet another suspicious death, it was for the residents of the commune to move on with their lives.

It was different from, following an emotional funeral in January, there existed a pall of gloom at the commune.

There were frequent campfire gatherings where residents were given an opportunity to reflect on Imelda's influence and unique personality. All agreed, their princess had been a ray of light and epitomised the importance of living life in the best way possible and never to regret anything. She preached love and everyone responded.

Rachel and Ian were the only two striving for positivity in an atmosphere of solemnity. Rachel would explain, even though their princess had left them in the physical sense her spirit and soul lived on in each and everyone.

Embrace the spirit of our glorious princess as never before, she would say, adding, *Imelda will always exist in our hearts, as even in death, she continues to declare her love for us. Her dearest friends.*

319

TALK TO THE ANIMALS

As with the previous shocking incidents the woodland became a focal point of curiosity with locals and outsiders whose ghoulish behaviour and desire to be close to where death had loomed for a time, was frowned upon by those who were respectful and overcoming personal grief.

As before, visitors tapered away and the woodland was no longer a place for people to feed their unnatural obsession with death.

There was also talk the woods should be felled and the land given to housing developers. There was also a suggestion there should be a retail park.

It was a proclamation which stirred people, conservationists, and petitions with thousands of signatures opposing the plans were submitted to the local council. It was hoped the emotive feelings of those residing in the county would eventually sway a decision to destroy a landmark beauty spot and home to wildlife.

Rachel visited the woods often when all quietened down as she believed her sister would call to her in her dreams. Whenever she visited she was instantly ensnared by the spell the magical woods cast and came to understand why Imelda had an affinity with it.

The magic Rachel felt on these occasions was to incite the possibility of legends, of mystery and fairy tales. She was no longer saddened by the loss of her friend and lover, as in the woods she felt close to her.

There came occasions when she would swear she heard someone singing and of peals of laughter.

TALK TO THE ANIMALS

There was a time when Rachel visited the grand old oak, sat with Mister Tree, and munched the small mushrooms she had gathered. Her conversations with Mister Tree were always uplifting, as each wanted to keep alive the memory of their princess.

Rachel never confided to anyone of her visits. She never spoke of the one time she saw a figure flitting in and out of the trees at distance, a graceful beauty with a mane of flowing red hair.

Dog was her constant companion and Rachel observed his behaviour, as he was another who used the magic of the woods to have dreams come to life.

Rachel visited the warren and regaled the rabbits there with memories of their princess, as they were only to eager to share their stories.

Rachel felt an affinity with the woods and would hear it call to her when she was abed at the commune.

Before long, it was Imelda calling to her, and then she visited. She would lay with Rachel on her bed, always resting a cheek to a breast, and always she was content to be reunited with her friend and lover.

They would make love and talk and laugh.

Imelda would say, *Come home baby,* and Rachel would wake up next to a sleeping Dog. Imelda was gone, even though her musky scent remained to taunt her.

CHAPTER 58

Rachel approached the atoll for the first time since Imelda's body was discovered and saw the yawning entrance to the shelter beckoning her. An excitable Dog had already set off ahead of her, sniffing around the base of the boulder for a time and looking up he was stirred to clamber up the incline to the ledge.

Rachel followed with more caution than an agile Dog had shown.

Someone, at some point, had come to the atoll and stripped down the crime scene tape.

Rachel clung to the rock edifice and shuffled slowly along the ledge until she reached the entrance.

She peered into the gloomy maw and rubbed her bare arms against a sudden chill. She had reason to feel sadness and ignoring the stale aroma of decay and mustiness, was even able to smile at the memory of her beautiful soul sister.

Dog finished sniffing and snorting the entire inner sanctum of what was once his home in another existence, before taking off with a huff and going out to explore the woodland floor once again.

TALK TO THE ANIMALS

Rachel inhaled deeply to feel the presence of her soul sister close by and believed for a moment a kiss had been dropped to her neck and her hand squeezed.

Welcome home, a soft lilting voice echoed within her mind.

Rachel took tentative steps into the deeper recesses, pausing to push her trainer through the heap of wood and brittle leaves strewn against the far wall.

In her mind Rachel was trying to piece together an enigma as she recalled Imelda saying that she lived in a shelter such as this one after fleeing the commune and leaving behind the memory of losing her baby.

Rachel knew this was the shelter Aidan had inhabited and was also the place Imelda had visited in her final moments. There had to be a connection.

Rachel had at no time posed the obvious question to Imelda regarding the possibility of her and Aidan living together in the woods. It made perfect sense to her now.

In life, it was conceivable Imelda could not confess everything for obvious reasons, like shame and guilt. For a time, Imelda had forgotten her past and confused her memories with those of Aidan's tragic and traumatic existence.

There were numerous dark passages to Imelda's existence in the time she fled the compound, yet Rachel had no wish to dwell on them, only wanted to remember the good times and all those happy occasions Imelda spread love and light to everyone in the community.

TALK TO THE ANIMALS

Feeling her sister's presence in the shelter had Rachel remembering the fantastical stories Imelda had narrated so that she was again immersed in Imelda's other world. And it was one of magical beauty, where all around was laughter, dancing and singing and the sweet melodic chatter of wildlife.

Had Imelda carried dark secrets it mattered not to Rachel, as her love and loyalty to her princess was unconditional.

'I am home, baby,' she whispered, and closed her eyes around a mantle of salt tears.

CHAPTER 59

Rachel returned regularly to the woods as Spring opened into Summer with Dog as her eager companion always. She never invited any of her friends to accompany her on her sojourns as she doubted anyone would understand or could experience all she was able to feel.

In recent weeks Rachel arrived at a decision even as she was inclined to think Imelda was the one instigating her spiritual path.

Rachel was on a mission to make the shelter a secondary home, as it was at the atoll she felt an affinity with her princess, more powerful than at any other place. Except, she conceded, when she would lay alone in bed. Not that she was ever alone. Imelda would always visit and keep her comforted. Her spirit would pour into her and flow in her veins. She would hear her soft voice teasing a path in her mind.

Imelda's spiritual happiness was a burgeoning entity and it was something Rachel was desperate to embrace.

She spoke of her dreams and of the princess to the woodland animals and birds and notably, Mister Tree, and all were happily encouraging Rachel to follow the path of their adoring princess.

She spent hours creating firstly, a cot to sleep on and when this was completed it had a smile transform her features. She lay down, stamping her feet gleefully, and letting cry her happiness for the spirit of Imelda to hear.

Dog joined her and seemed impressed by her diligent efforts, even as Rachel supposed it conjured memories of a time Dog and princess had enjoyed ritual cuddles and kisses.

With Dog vacating the shelter to go investigate new scents around the clearing below Rachel set about creating a cloak of leaves, berries, and small, hardy flower buds, as Imelda had once stated she had done.

As it made her feel more like a princess to wear a cloak and a crown, she had said.

It took several days to complete as she was making daily passage to and from the commune to the woods, gathering those essentials to make her secondary home special.

She hung tapestries on the walls and placed large, scented candles at strategic points on the floor and in niches. She had a collection of crystals to promote spiritual well-being on those occasions she was to stay. These were something she was disinclined to leave whenever she returned to the commune, as it was always feasible the notoriety the woods had gained in the past year might encourage the curious and playful to visit.

As with Imelda, Rachel believed the magic would work to her advantage and protect her. She also had Dog to watch over her.

TALK TO THE ANIMALS

With the cloak completed, along with a top and thong as it emulated the memory of her princess, Rachel was satisfied all had been done to serve the memory of Imelda.

On one return to the commune, she had a visit from Ian who was quick to pose questions regarding her regular private jaunts. It was brought to his attention there were nights when she stayed away and it was a natural concern to him.

Rachel stated, in solitude she could be free and continue to grieve their loss. With Dog for company, she believed Imelda walked alongside her, she had said.

Ian seemed to understand and would hug and kiss her, and let her know, should she ever need to speak in confidence about her feelings she could go to him.

Rachel acquiesced as she needed to placate Ian's own troubled conscience and assure him everything was good and wonderful, as Imelda would have wanted.

She would not confess to him she received her comfort and guidance from their princess and was all she needed to survive.

On a day which was hot and humid Rachel and Dog left the compound to visit the woods. The moment they arrived at the stream Rachel removed her dress and bathed, knowing Imelda had often done so. It was another memory installed in her she was to gain comfort from and feel close to her sister.

She was preparing herself for spiritual divination.

Having abluted she picked those mushrooms she knew would enhance her mind, as Imelda had taught her, and took them back to the shelter.

TALK TO THE ANIMALS

It was with heartfelt relief she should find everything at her home untouched by outsiders. It was as she had left it on a previous visit.

She prepared a fire, having a lighter and matches to assist her and with it crackling and glowing fiercely, she again stripped out of her dress and undies and removed her trainers before adjusting the leafy top she had made around her breasts and tying the skimp thong to her waist. Next she shook and swept the ceremonial cloak around her frame so that it fluttered and settled along her back, arms, and buttocks.

She munched on the mushrooms she had collected and danced around the small campfire, rejoicing in the fantastical images cavorting across the walls and ceiling.

With the magic flowing in her veins, she hummed a tune she had often caught Imelda reciting in happier times and then she was dancing, her movements frenetic yet graceful. Sinuously erotic.

She not only felt the magic inside her, but Imelda's spirit had also joined her. Rachel believed her hands were being held and was guiding her movements. Rachel tittered and it became a wild and free cackle.

Rachel remained fearless, even as she sensed the Wicked Witch had come to the party. She stopped to hear Imelda's voice as a feathery whisper against her ear.

'Baby,' she said. '*You have brought me home. We are home.*''

It was the moment Dog arrived from his ritual exploration of the woodland floor and gave a howl of delight, as he was a witness to his princess dancing with his adopted friend.

TALK TO THE ANIMALS

They were a family once again.

THE

END

TALK TO THE ANIMALS

TALK TO THE ANIMALS

Author's Biography:

Born October 1954, my passion for writing began aged seven. I was a shy individual who would often lock himself away in his room and write. It was a way of expressing my fantasies and allow them to tell a story.

TALK TO THE ANIMALS

There is something quite beautiful creating a cast of characters to narrate an atmosphere of light and dark, and to make fantasies seem real.

My passion is unwavering, my imagination alive with concepts to explore in the future.

A writer's journey is time consuming and hours are spent in solitude. I would not have it any other way.

I have always said, if you have a dream, and are passionate about your dream, chase it and never let go, until you have it in your grasp.

Take the journey as I have and be content.

Love and light!

May the universe bless each and every one, as I have been.

FUTURE PUBLICATIONS

ANGEL WARS
CONTINUUM
TRILOGY

THE AVENGING ANGEL

Printed in Great Britain
by Amazon